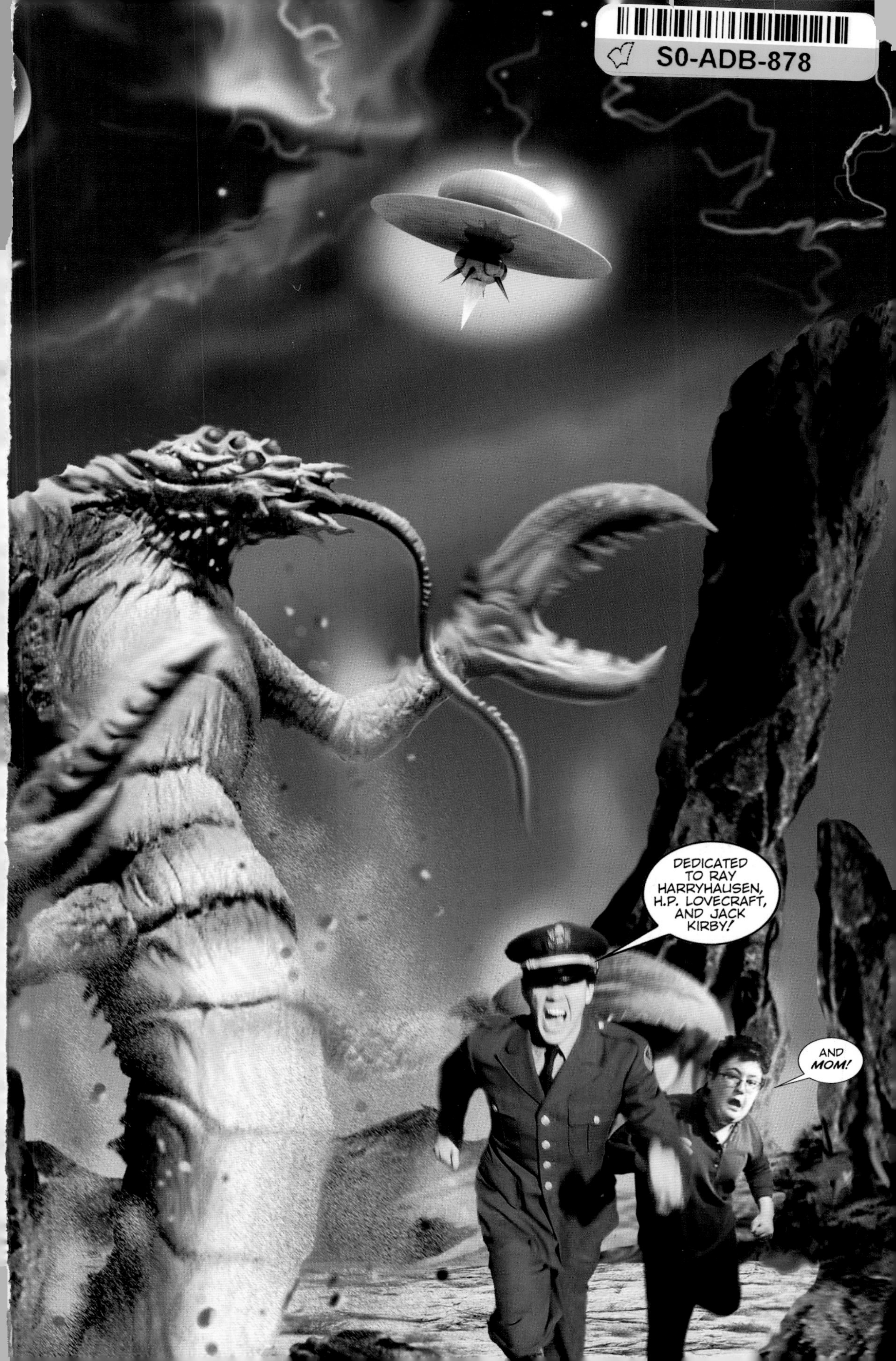
DEDICATED TO RAY HARRYHAUSEN, H.P. LOVECRAFT, AND JACK KIRBY!
AND MOM!
S0-ADB-878

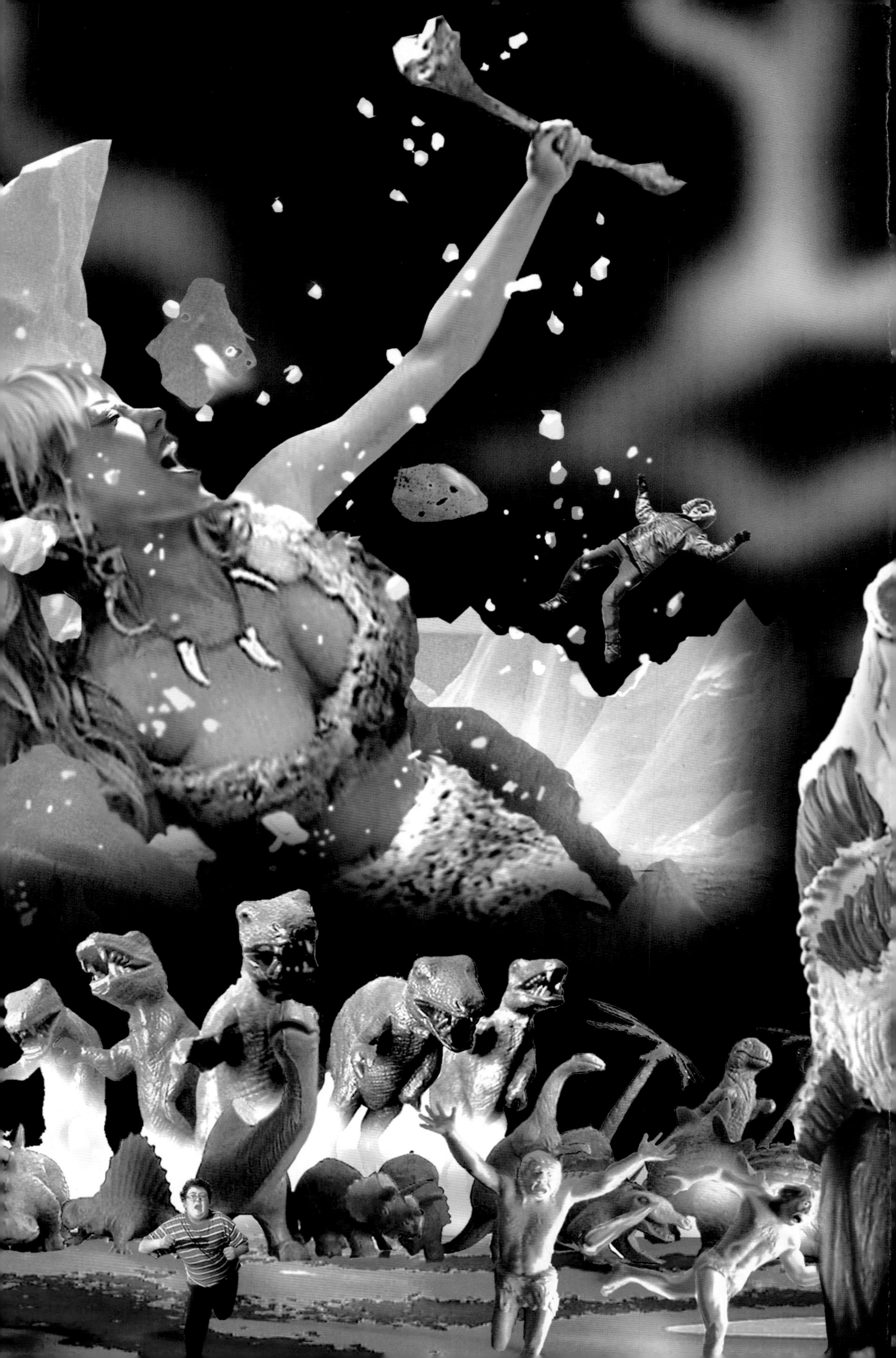

PETE VON SHOLLY'S

EXTREMELY WEIRD STORIES™

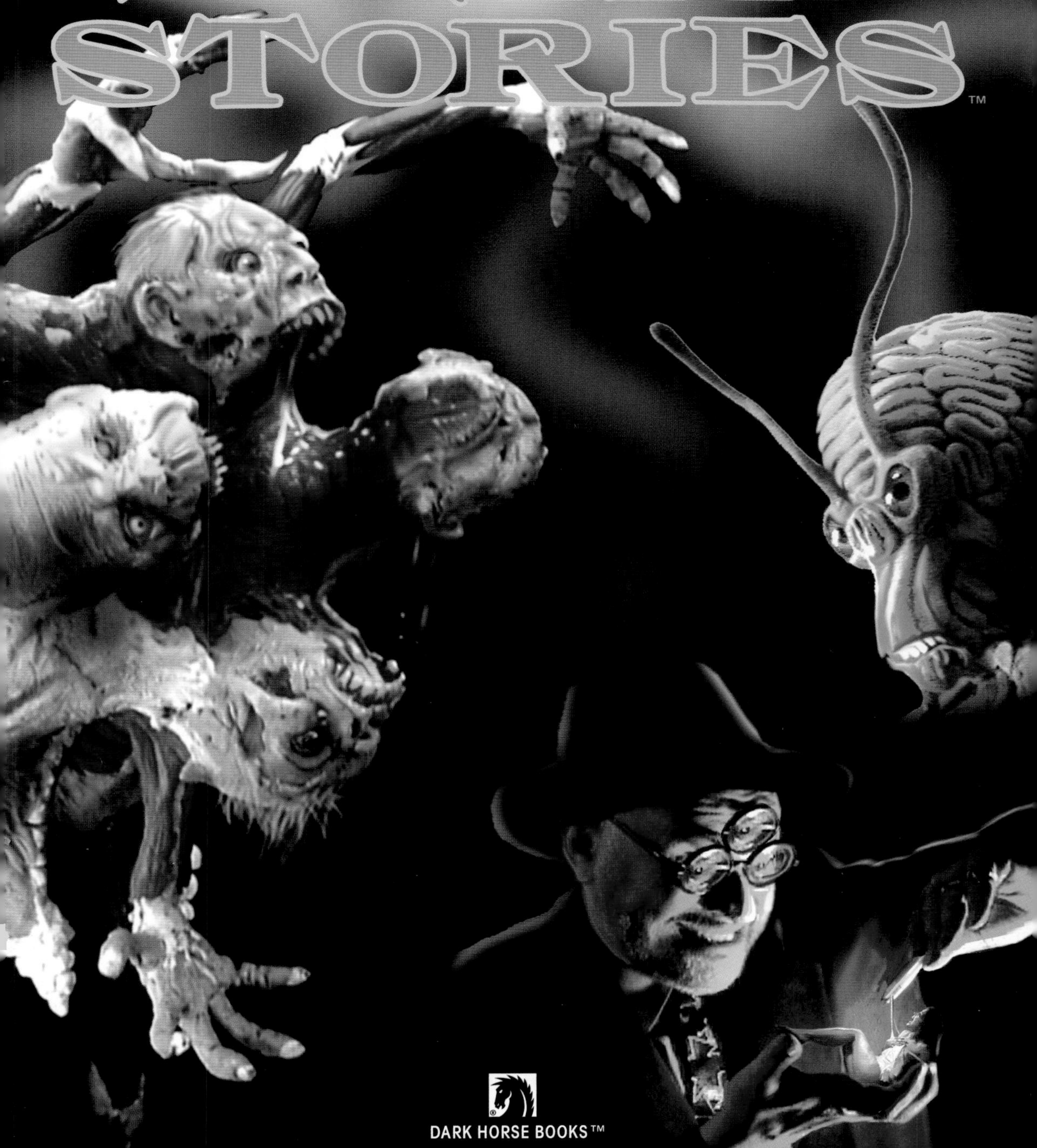

DARK HORSE BOOKS™

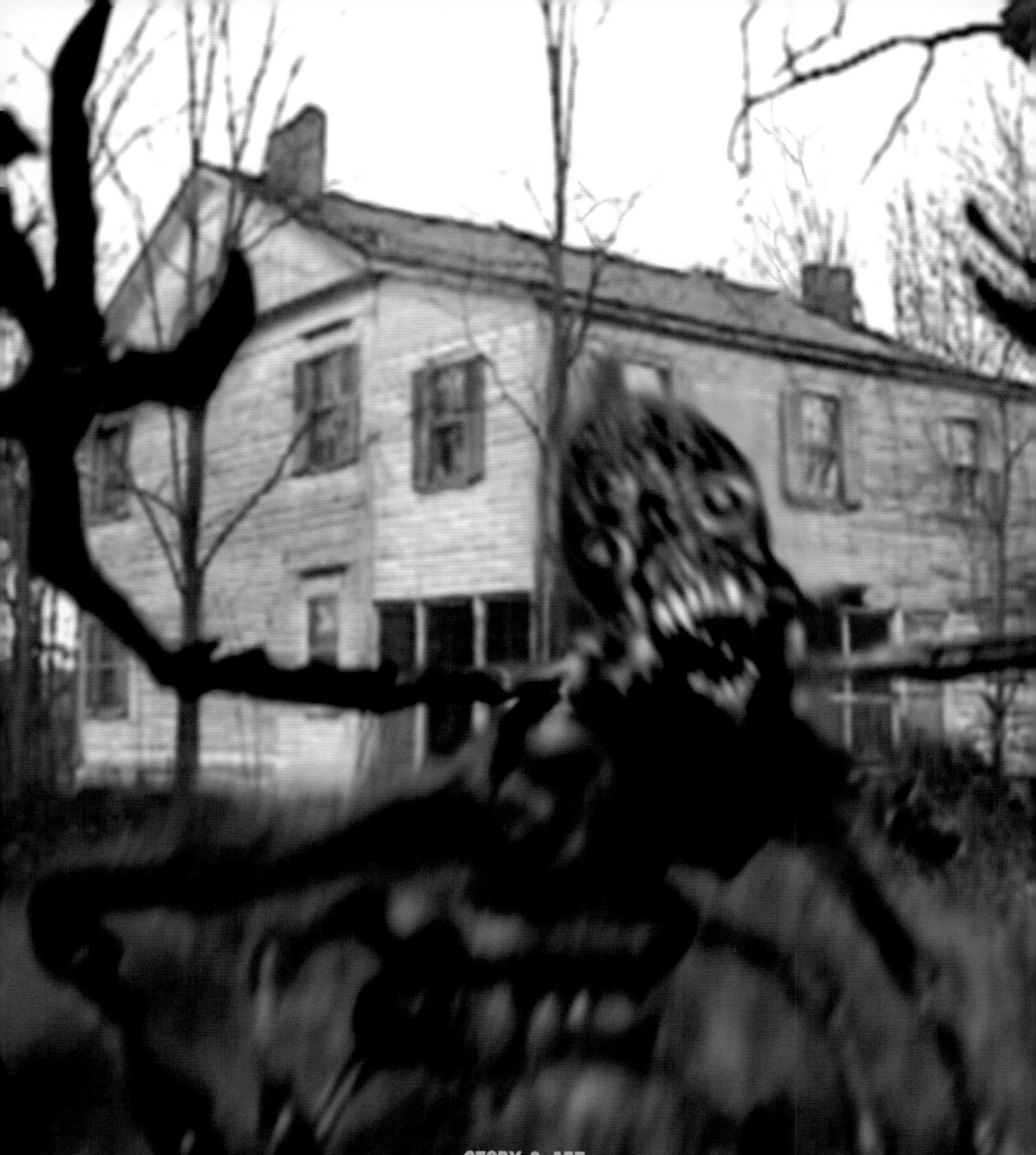

STORY & ART
PETE VON SHOLLY

COVER MODEL: CHRISTA SOS • FOREWORD MODEL: JENNIFER PARTEE

PUBLISHER **MIKE RICHARDSON** · EDITOR **DAVE LAND** · ASSISTANT EDITOR **KATIE MOODY** · DESIGNER **JASON STURGILL** · ART DIRECTOR **LIA RIBACCHI**

PETE VON SHOLLY'S EXTREMELY WEIRD STORIES

To find a comics shop in your area call the Comic Shop Locator Service toll-free at (888) 266-4226.

PRINTED IN CHINA

First edition: July 2006
ISBN: 1-59307-554-5

darkhorse.com

10 9 8 7 6 5 4 3 2 1

Published by
Dark Horse Comics, Inc.
10956 SE Main Street
Milwaukie, OR 97222

OPERATING TABLE OF CONTENTS

WELCOME to a parade of box-office blockbusters-on-paper, straddling the fifties to whatever you call now! We got horror, we got babes! We got laughs! We got monsters from beyond the grave and before the dawn of history! We got your sinister Scottish lakes, blasphemous black magic, and psychotic pseudo-scientists! Musty museums, virtual video-vermin, and foul fables! Things that creep and crawl from the pages of pulps and from under the covers of comics! All this and more await you within the pages of

EXTREMELY WEIRD STORIES

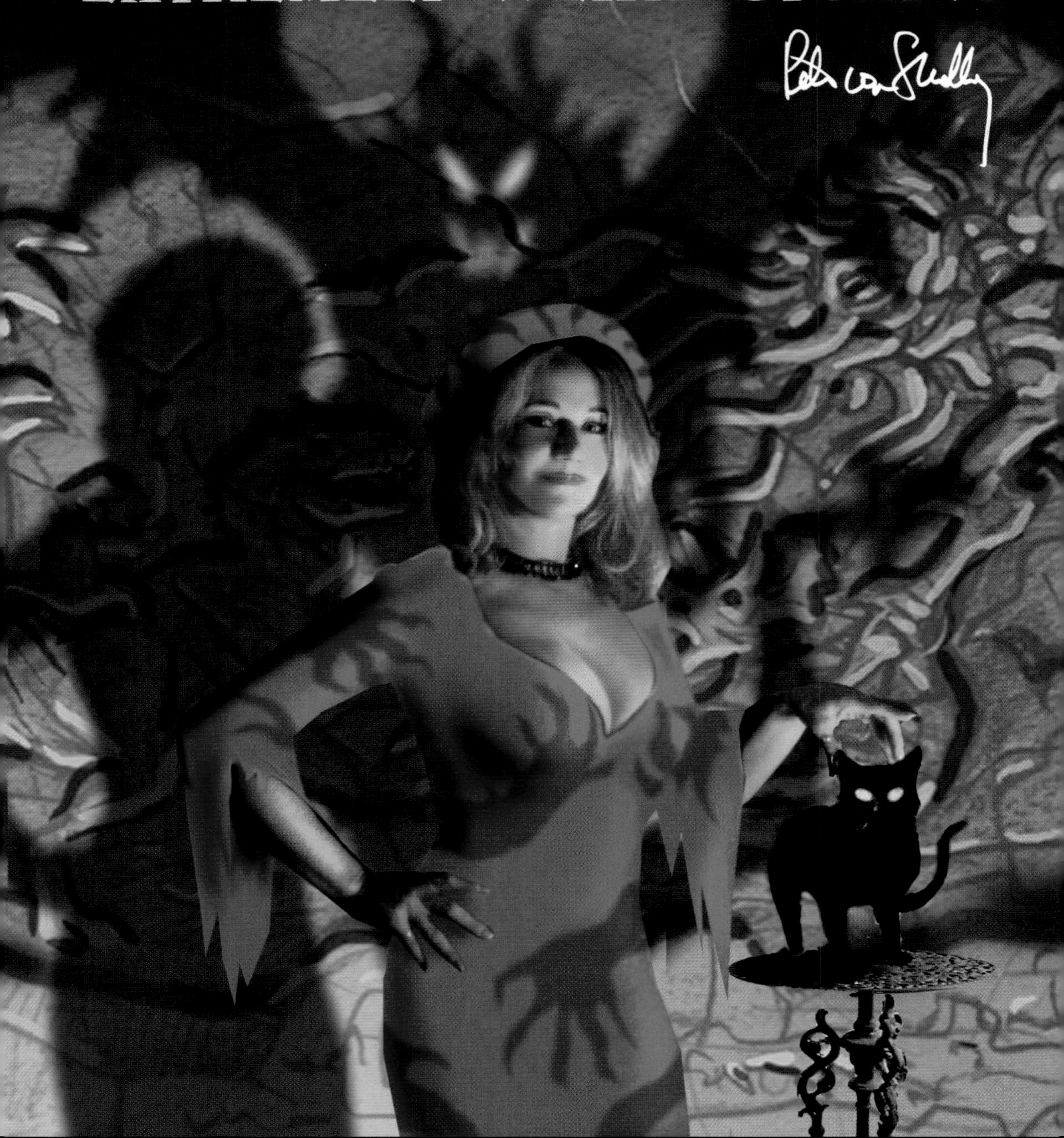

WARNING: DO NOT EXCEED RECOMMENDED DOSAGE! SIDE EFFECTS MAY INCLUDE SWEATING, NAUSEA, NIGHTMARES, AND AN INSATIABLE DESIRE FOR MORE! MAY NOT MIX WELL WITH NORMAL COMICS!

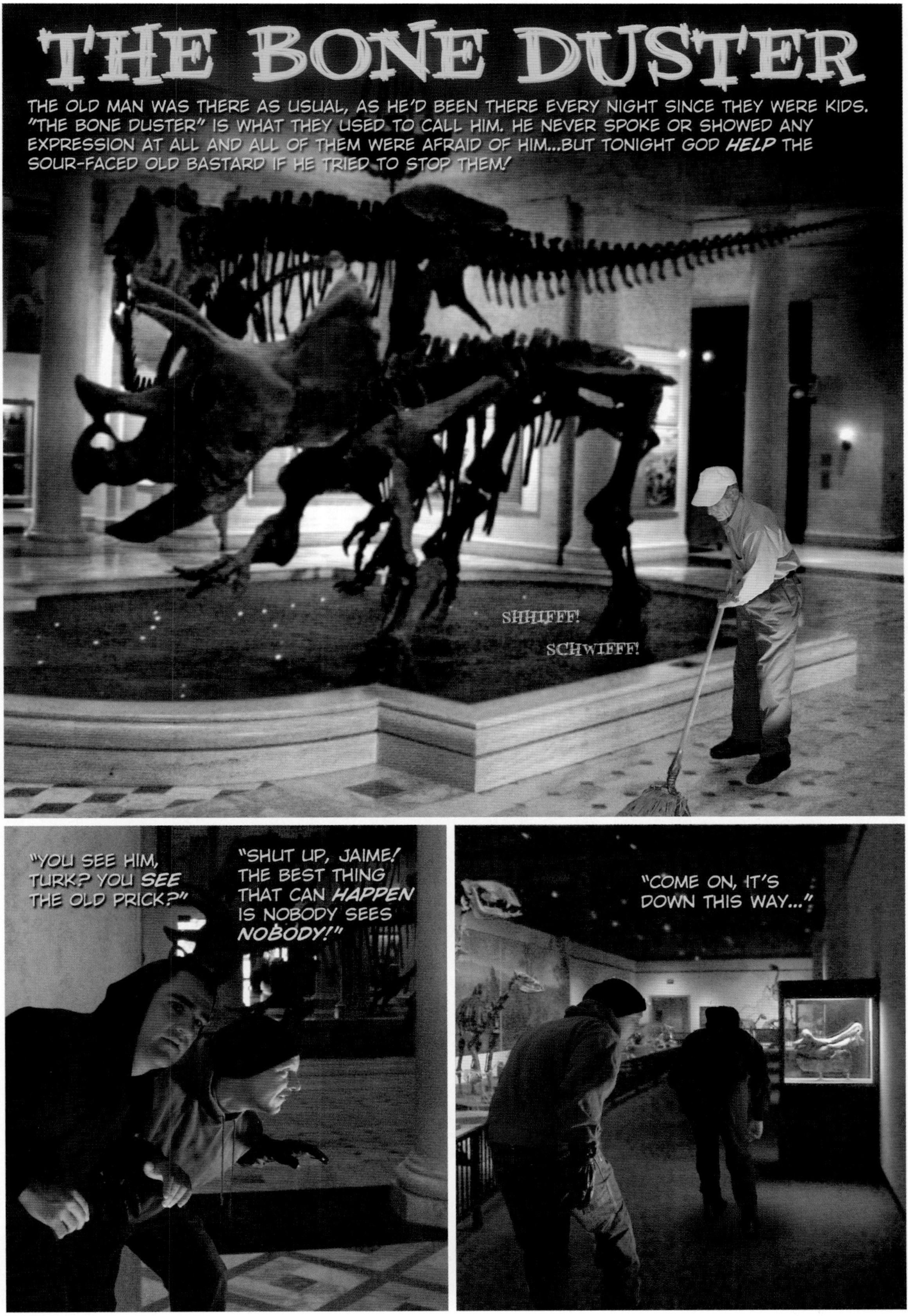
THE BONE DUSTER
THE OLD MAN WAS THERE AS USUAL, AS HE'D BEEN THERE EVERY NIGHT SINCE THEY WERE KIDS. "THE BONE DUSTER" IS WHAT THEY USED TO CALL HIM. HE NEVER SPOKE OR SHOWED ANY EXPRESSION AT ALL AND ALL OF THEM WERE AFRAID OF HIM...BUT TONIGHT GOD ***HELP*** THE SOUR-FACED OLD BASTARD IF HE TRIED TO STOP THEM!
SHHIFFF!
SCHWIFFF!
"YOU SEE HIM, TURK? YOU ***SEE*** THE OLD PRICK?"
"SHUT UP, JAIME! THE BEST THING THAT CAN ***HAPPEN*** IS NOBODY SEES ***NOBODY!***"
"COME ON, IT'S DOWN THIS WAY..."

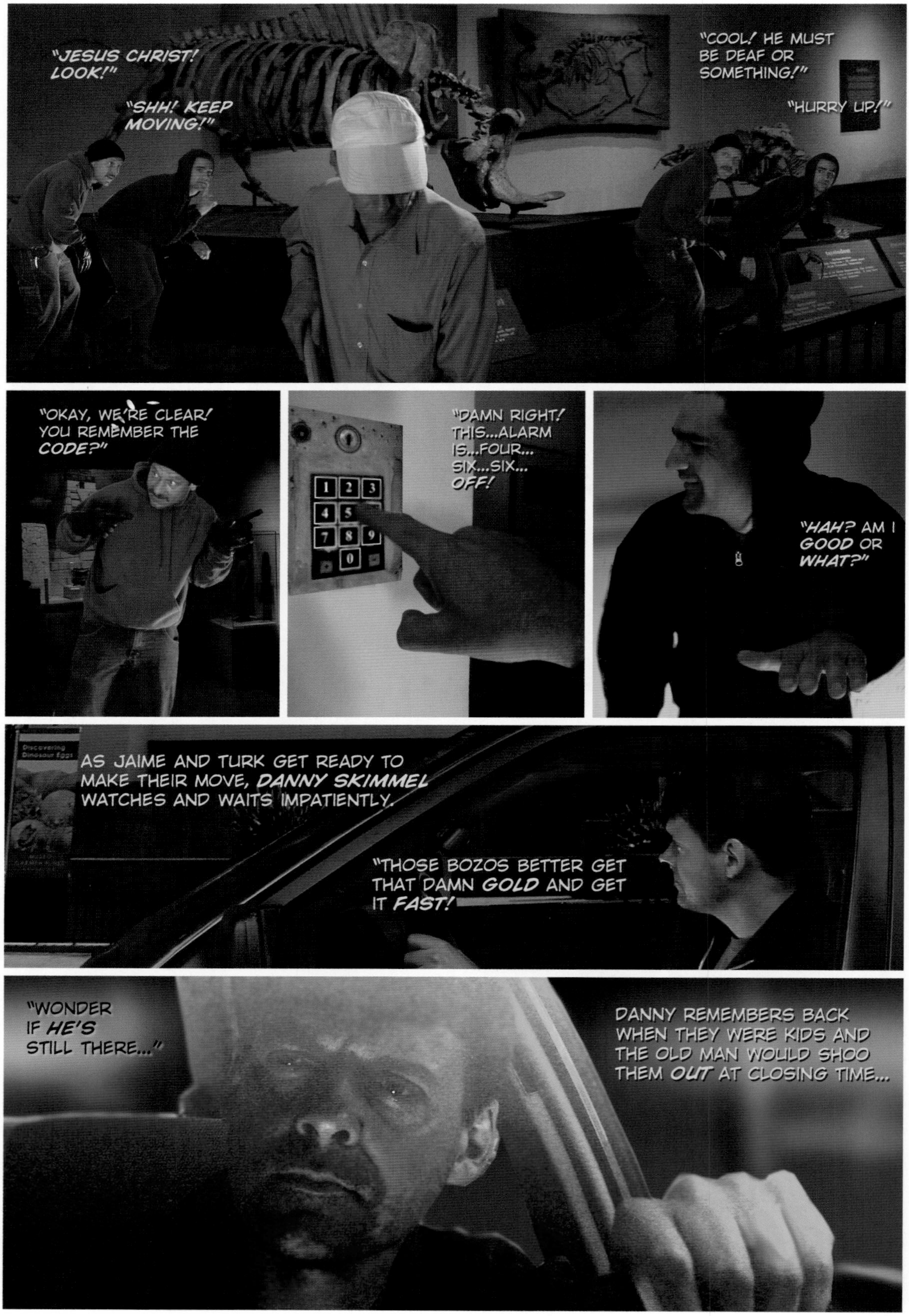
"JESUS CHRIST! LOOK!"
"SHH! KEEP MOVING!"
"COOL! HE MUST BE DEAF OR SOMETHING!"
"HURRY UP!"
"OKAY, WE'RE CLEAR! YOU REMEMBER THE CODE?"
"DAMN RIGHT! THIS...ALARM IS...FOUR... SIX...SIX... OFF!"
"HAH? AM I GOOD OR WHAT?"
AS JAIME AND TURK GET READY TO MAKE THEIR MOVE, DANNY SKIMMEL WATCHES AND WAITS IMPATIENTLY.
"THOSE BOZOS BETTER GET THAT DAMN GOLD AND GET IT FAST!"
"WONDER IF HE'S STILL THERE..."
DANNY REMEMBERS BACK WHEN THEY WERE KIDS AND THE OLD MAN WOULD SHOO THEM OUT AT CLOSING TIME...

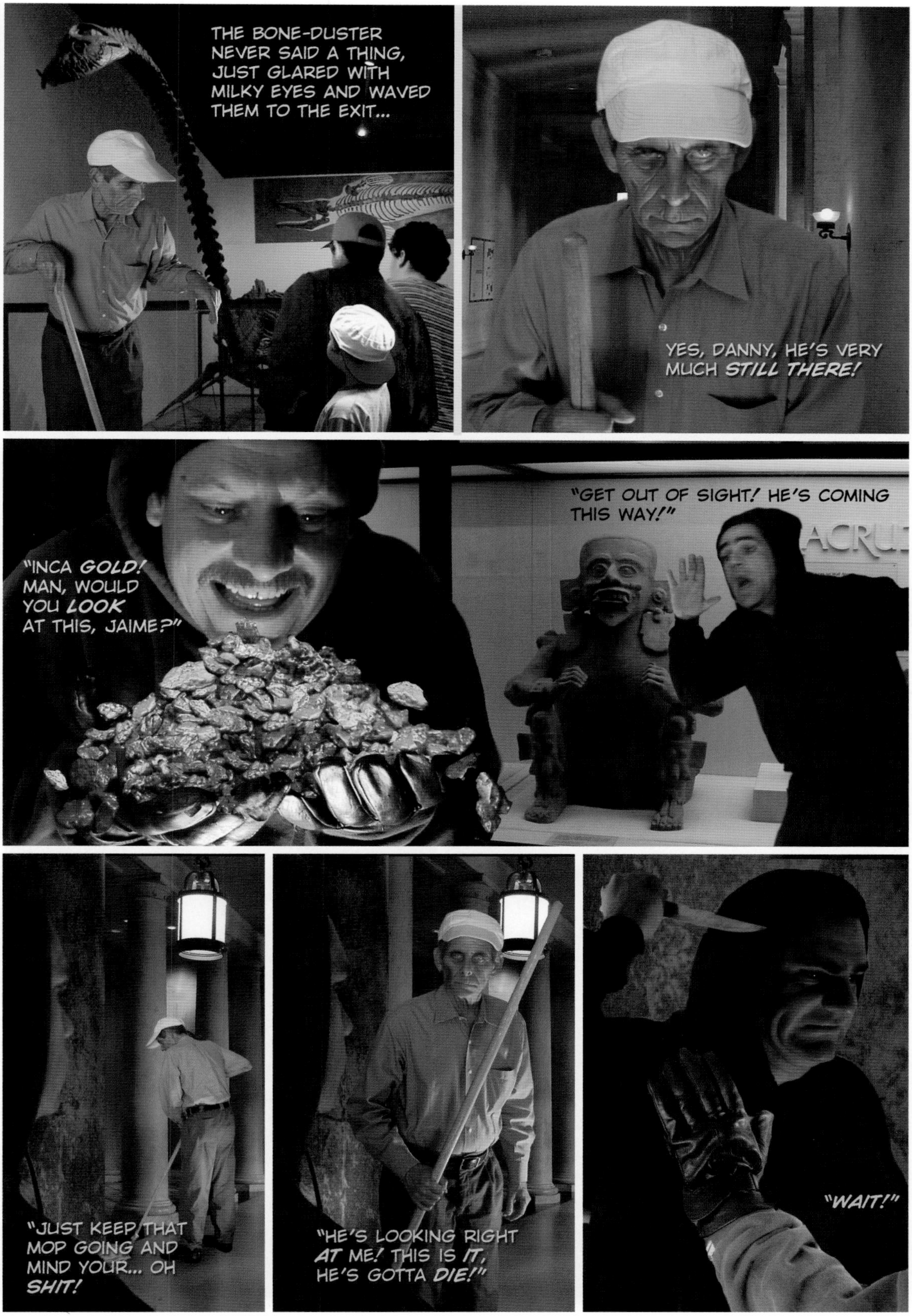
THE BONE-DUSTER NEVER SAID A THING, JUST GLARED WITH MILKY EYES AND WAVED THEM TO THE EXIT...
YES, DANNY, HE'S VERY MUCH STILL THERE!
"INCA GOLD! MAN, WOULD YOU LOOK AT THIS, JAIME?"
"GET OUT OF SIGHT! HE'S COMING THIS WAY!"
"JUST KEEP THAT MOP GOING AND MIND YOUR... OH SHIT!
"HE'S LOOKING RIGHT AT ME! THIS IS IT, HE'S GOTTA DIE!"
"WAIT!"

"BUT HE'S GONNA CALL THE *COPS!* WE GOTTA STOP HIM, MAN!"

"NO... HE DIDN'T SEE YOU. LOOK, HE'S GOING AWAY."

AND THE OLD MAN KEEPS WORKING IN HIS HALLS.

SCHWIFFFF!

WITH HIS SILENT FRIENDS.

WHERE THE ONLY SOUND IS THAT OF HIS ETERNAL PUSH-BROOM.

SCHWIFFFF!

SCHWIFFFF!

IF HE WEREN'T *MOVING* HE COULD ALMOST BE ONE OF THEM...

SCHWIFFFF!

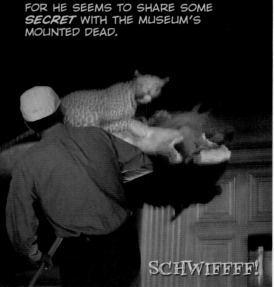

FOR HE SEEMS TO SHARE SOME *SECRET* WITH THE MUSEUM'S MOUNTED DEAD.

SCHWIFFFF!

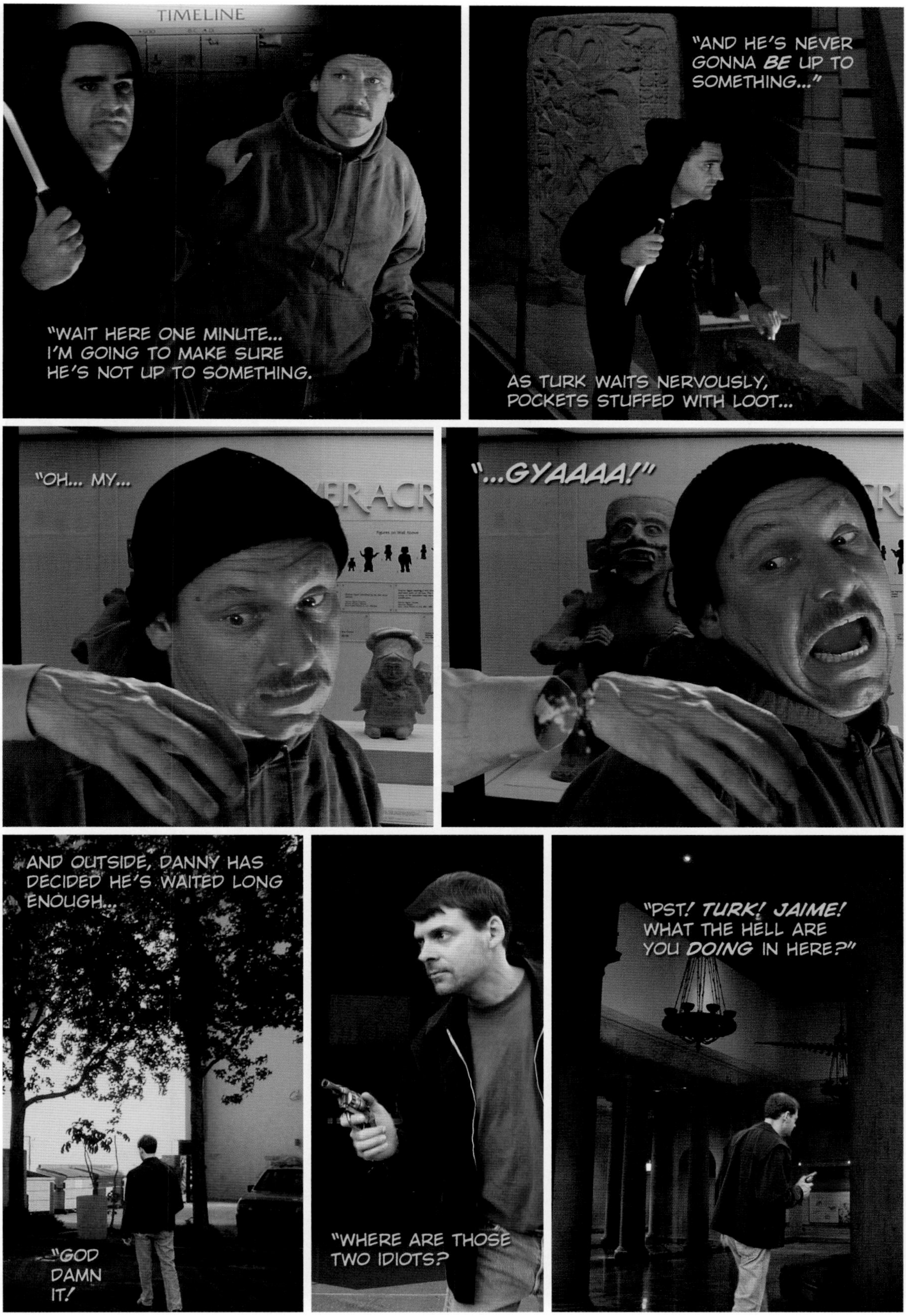
TIMELINE
"WAIT HERE ONE MINUTE... I'M GOING TO MAKE SURE HE'S NOT UP TO SOMETHING.
"AND HE'S NEVER GONNA *BE* UP TO SOMETHING..."
AS TURK WAITS NERVOUSLY, POCKETS STUFFED WITH LOOT...
"OH... MY...
"...GYAAAA!"
AND OUTSIDE, DANNY HAS DECIDED HE'S WAITED LONG ENOUGH...
"GOD DAMN IT!
"WHERE ARE THOSE TWO IDIOTS?
"PST! *TURK! JAIME!* WHAT THE HELL ARE YOU *DOING* IN HERE?"

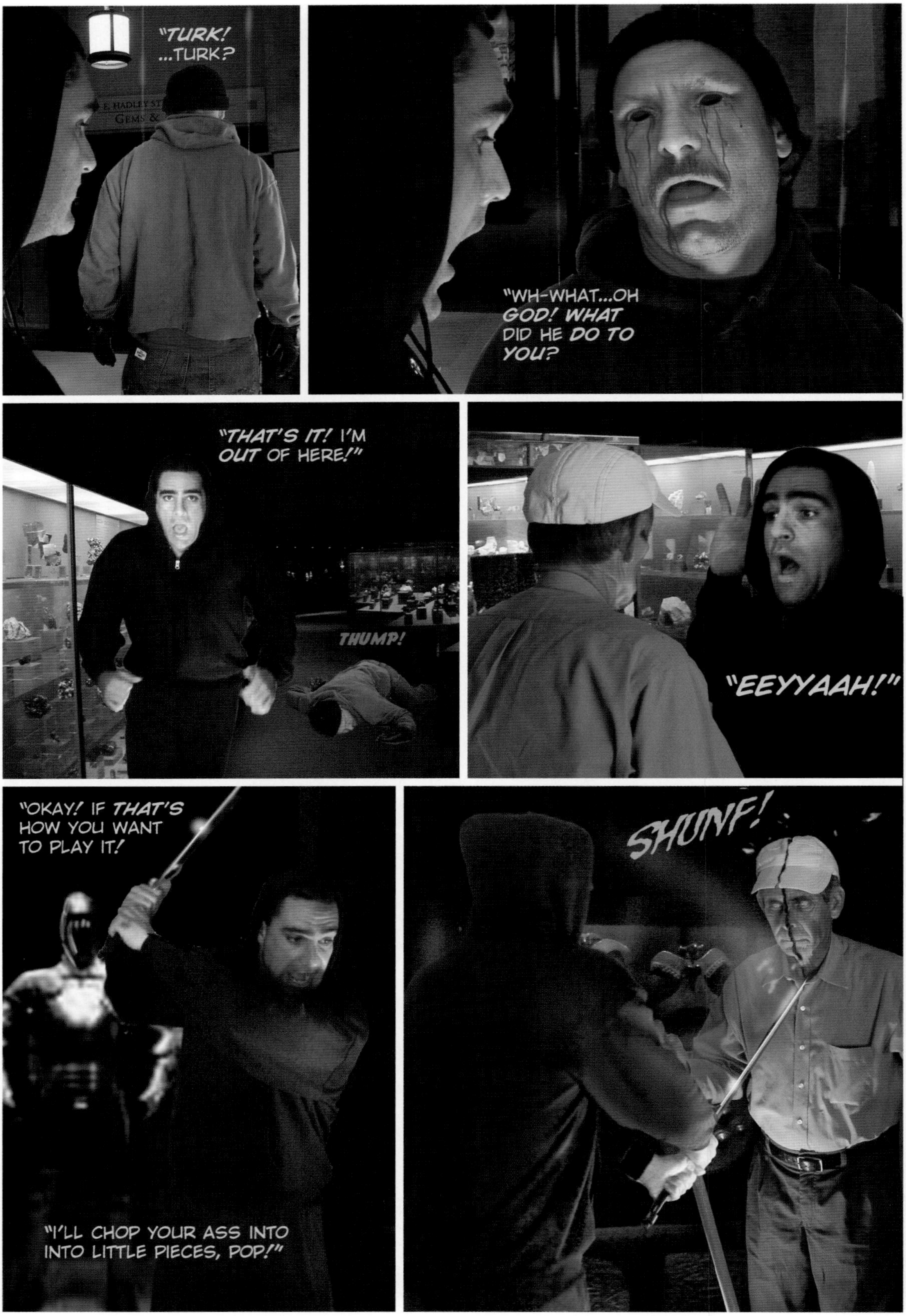
"TURK! ...TURK?
"WH-WHAT...OH GOD! WHAT DID HE DO TO YOU?
"THAT'S IT! I'M OUT OF HERE!"
THUMP!
"EEYYAAH!"
"OKAY! IF THAT'S HOW YOU WANT TO PLAY IT!
"I'LL CHOP YOUR ASS INTO INTO LITTLE PIECES, POP!"
SHUNF!

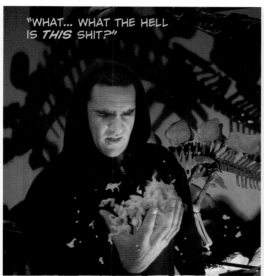

"WHAT... WHAT THE HELL IS *THIS* SHIT?"

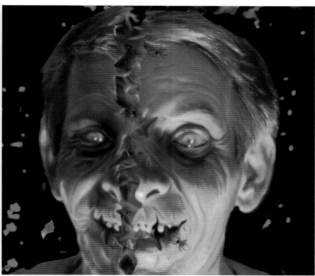

"TURK? JAIME? WHO IS THAT?"

"DON'T MESS WITH ME, YOU ASSHOLES! I'LL..."

"I'LL... I--

"I UHHHH..."

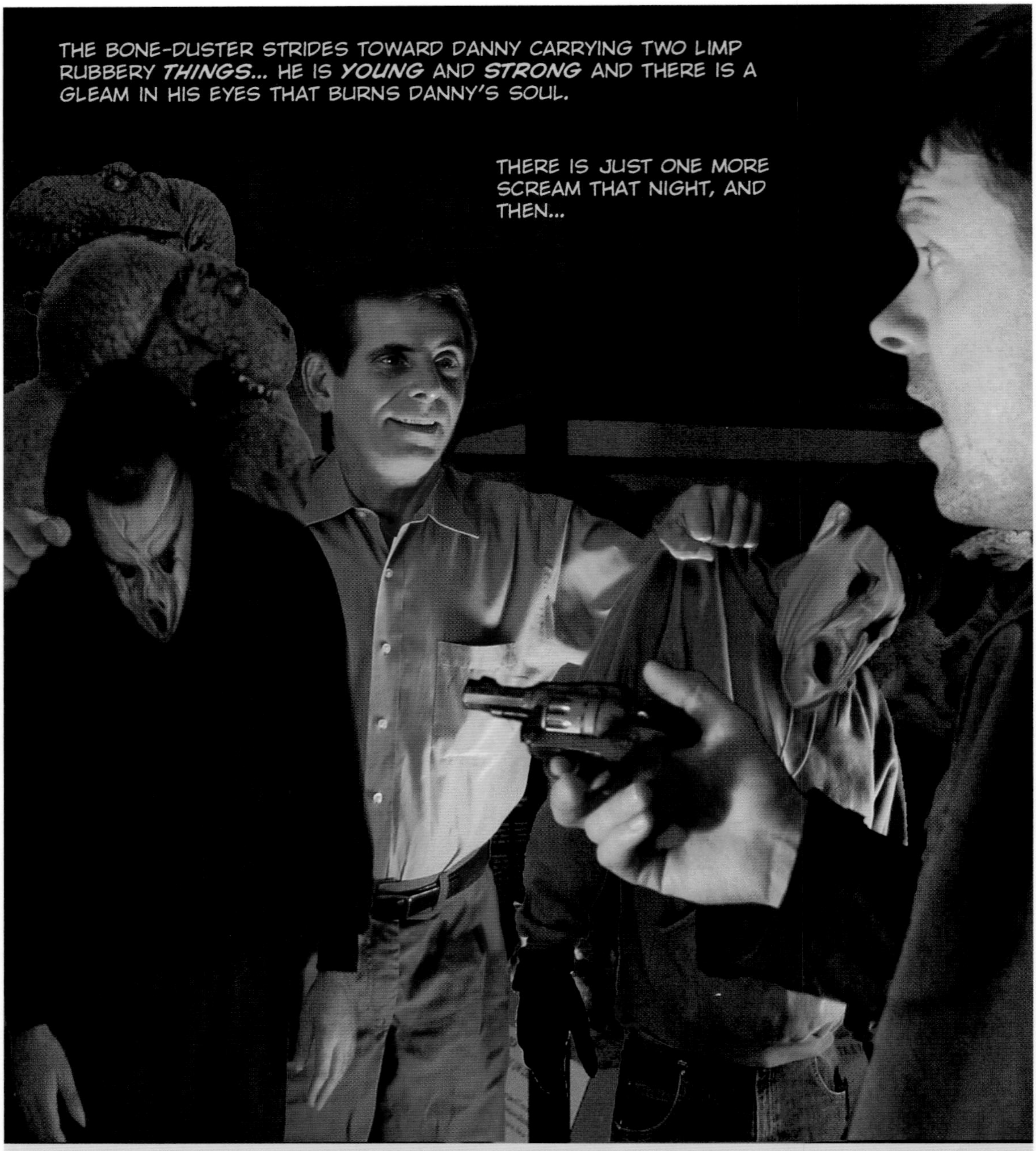
THE BONE-DUSTER STRIDES TOWARD DANNY CARRYING TWO LIMP RUBBERY *THINGS*... HE IS *YOUNG* AND *STRONG* AND THERE IS A GLEAM IN HIS EYES THAT BURNS DANNY'S SOUL.
THERE IS JUST ONE MORE SCREAM THAT NIGHT, AND THEN...

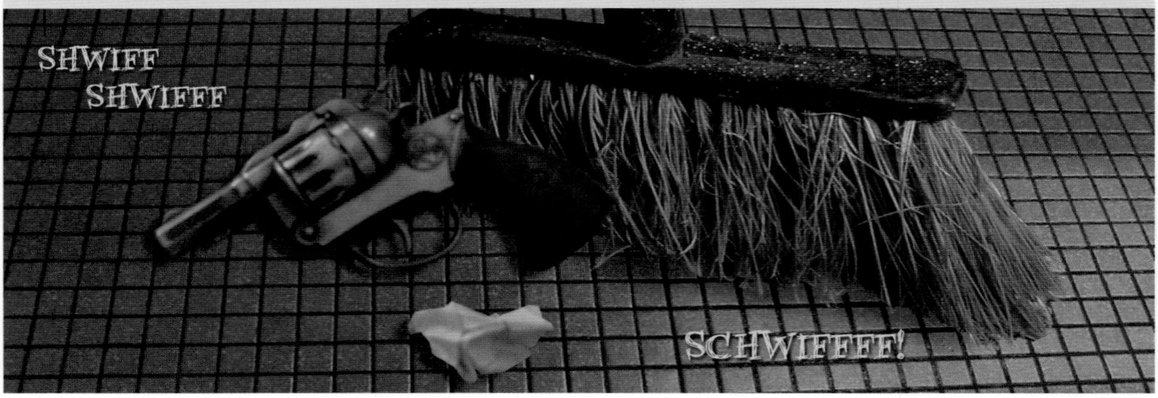
SHWIFF
SHWIFFF
SCHWIFFFF!

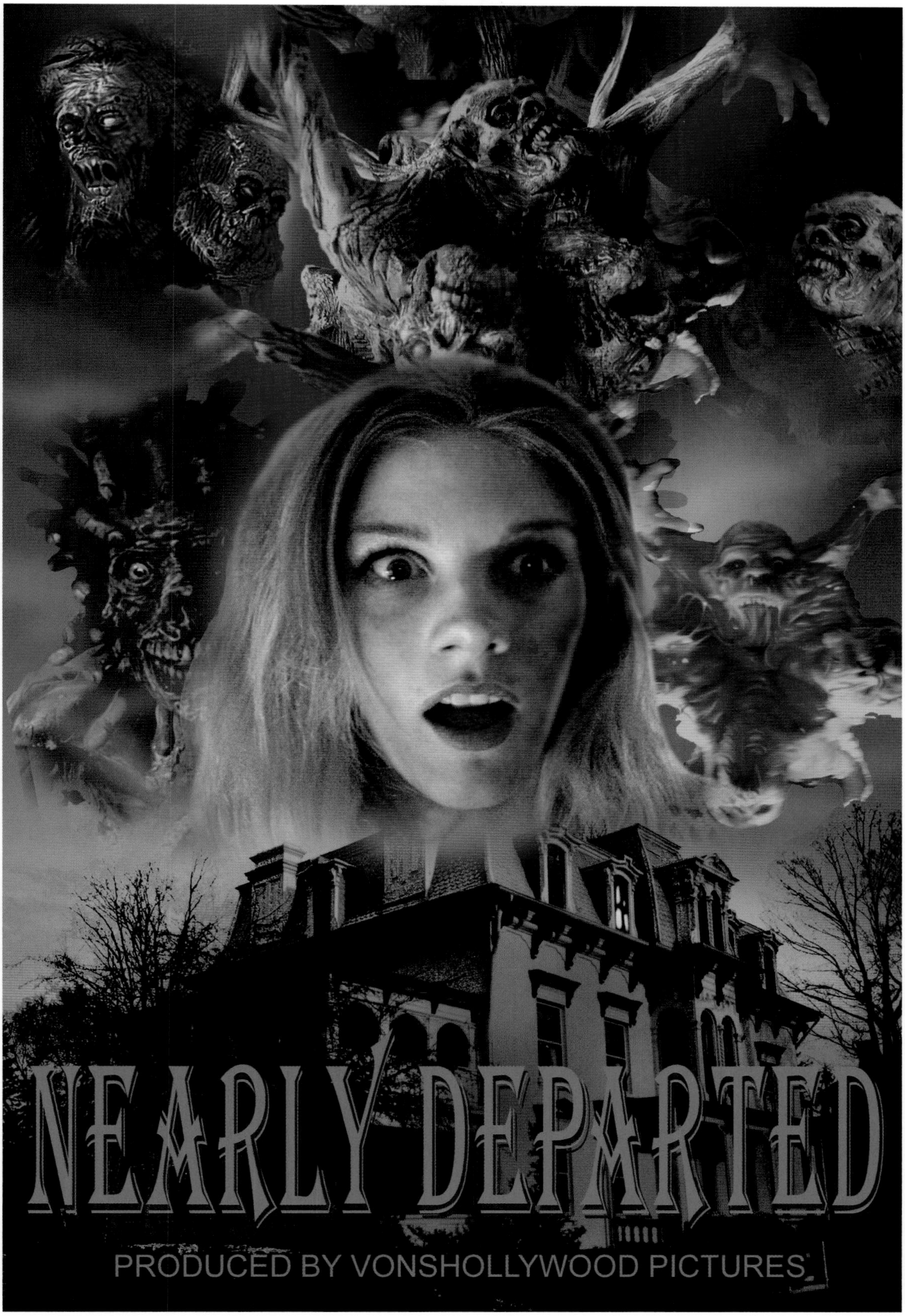
NEARLY DEPARTED
PRODUCED BY VONSHOLLYWOOD PICTURES

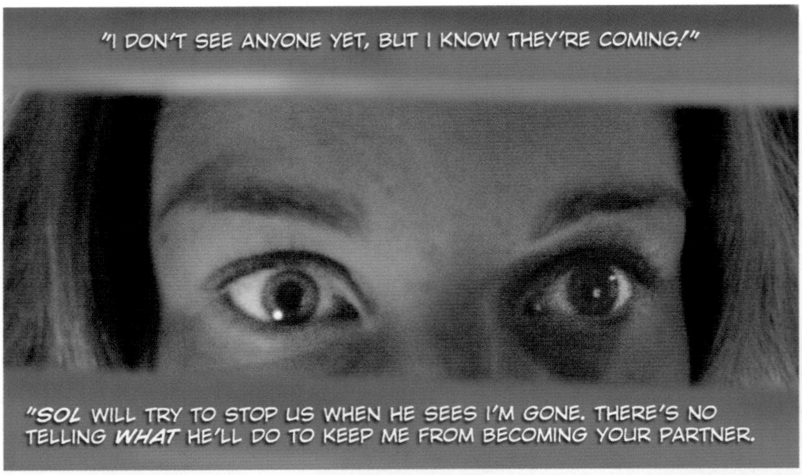
"I DON'T SEE ANYONE YET, BUT I KNOW THEY'RE COMING!"
"SOL WILL TRY TO STOP US WHEN HE SEES I'M GONE. THERE'S NO TELLING WHAT HE'LL DO TO KEEP ME FROM BECOMING YOUR PARTNER.

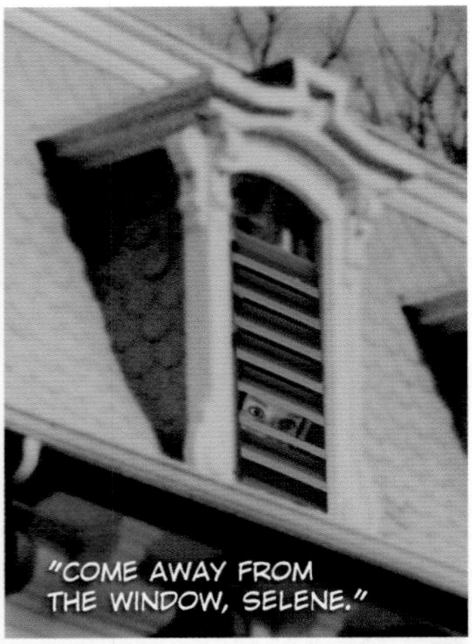
"COME AWAY FROM THE WINDOW, SELENE."

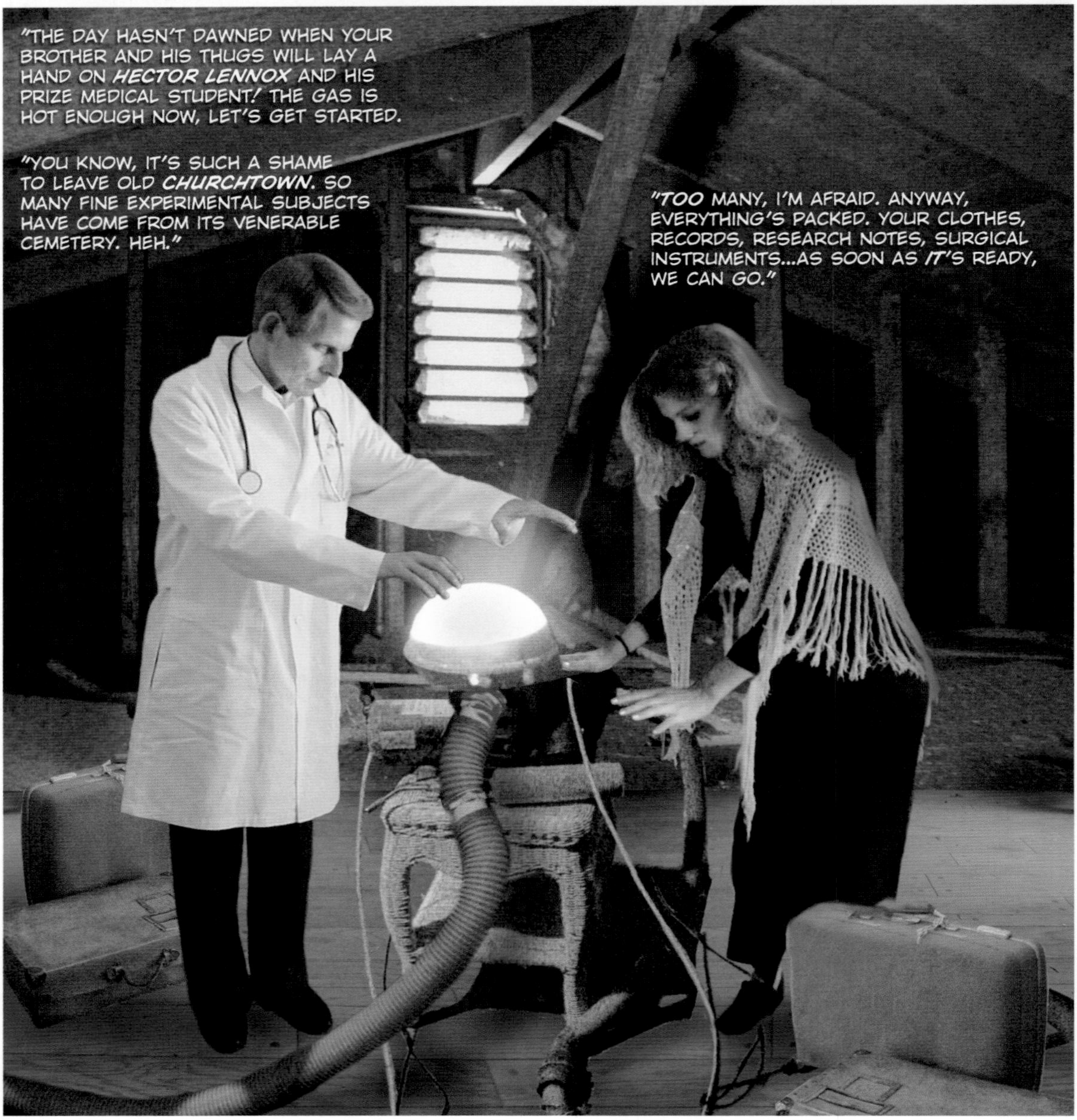
"THE DAY HASN'T DAWNED WHEN YOUR BROTHER AND HIS THUGS WILL LAY A HAND ON HECTOR LENNOX AND HIS PRIZE MEDICAL STUDENT! THE GAS IS HOT ENOUGH NOW, LET'S GET STARTED.
"YOU KNOW, IT'S SUCH A SHAME TO LEAVE OLD CHURCHTOWN. SO MANY FINE EXPERIMENTAL SUBJECTS HAVE COME FROM ITS VENERABLE CEMETERY. HEH."
"TOO MANY, I'M AFRAID. ANYWAY, EVERYTHING'S PACKED. YOUR CLOTHES, RECORDS, RESEARCH NOTES, SURGICAL INSTRUMENTS...AS SOON AS IT'S READY, WE CAN GO."

"IF OLD UNCLE HENRY HADN'T GOTTEN *OUT* AND GONE TO VISIT HIS FAMILY OUR SECRET WOULD STILL BE SAFE."

"COME ON, *HERBERT*. WE'RE GOING ON A LITTLE JOURNEY, SON.

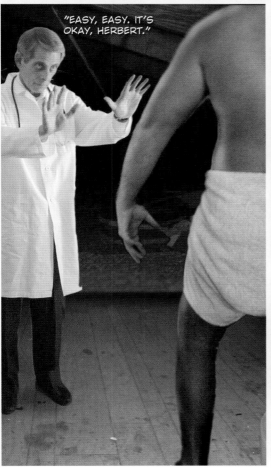

"EASY, EASY. IT'S OKAY, HERBERT."

"NGAAAA!

"NO GO! NOOO!"

"WE'LL BE WITH YOU, HERBERT. WE'LL GO SOMEPLACE I CAN FIX YOUR EYES, MAKE YOU SEE.

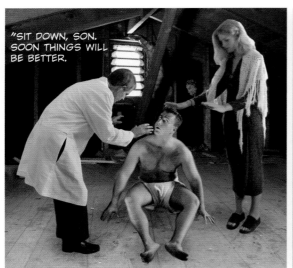

"SIT DOWN, SON. SOON THINGS WILL BE BETTER.

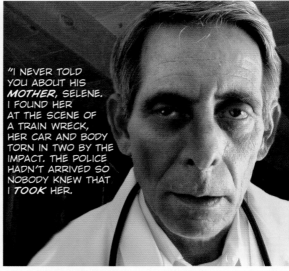

"I NEVER TOLD YOU ABOUT HIS *MOTHER*, SELENE. I FOUND HER AT THE SCENE OF A TRAIN WRECK, HER CAR AND BODY TORN IN TWO BY THE IMPACT. THE POLICE HADN'T ARRIVED SO NOBODY KNEW THAT I *TOOK* HER.

"BACK THEN I HAD ONLY SUCCEEDED IN RE-ANIMATING THE DEAD FOR LIMITED PERIODS.

"BUT COULD SUCH BEINGS *REPRODUCE*?

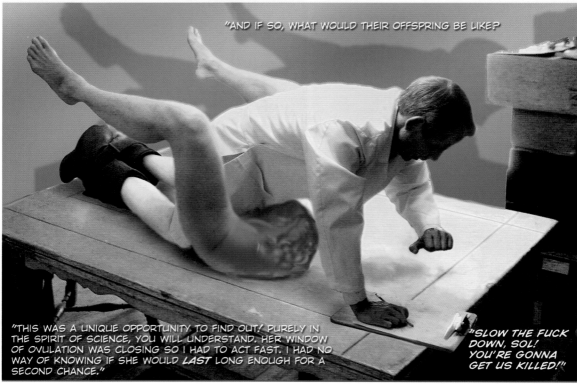

"AND IF SO, WHAT WOULD THEIR OFFSPRING BE LIKE?

"THIS WAS A UNIQUE OPPORTUNITY TO FIND OUT! PURELY IN THE SPIRIT OF SCIENCE, YOU WILL UNDERSTAND. HER WINDOW OF OVULATION WAS CLOSING SO I HAD TO ACT FAST. I HAD NO WAY OF KNOWING IF SHE WOULD *LAST* LONG ENOUGH FOR A SECOND CHANCE."

"SLOW THE FUCK DOWN, SOL! YOU'RE GONNA GET US KILLED!"

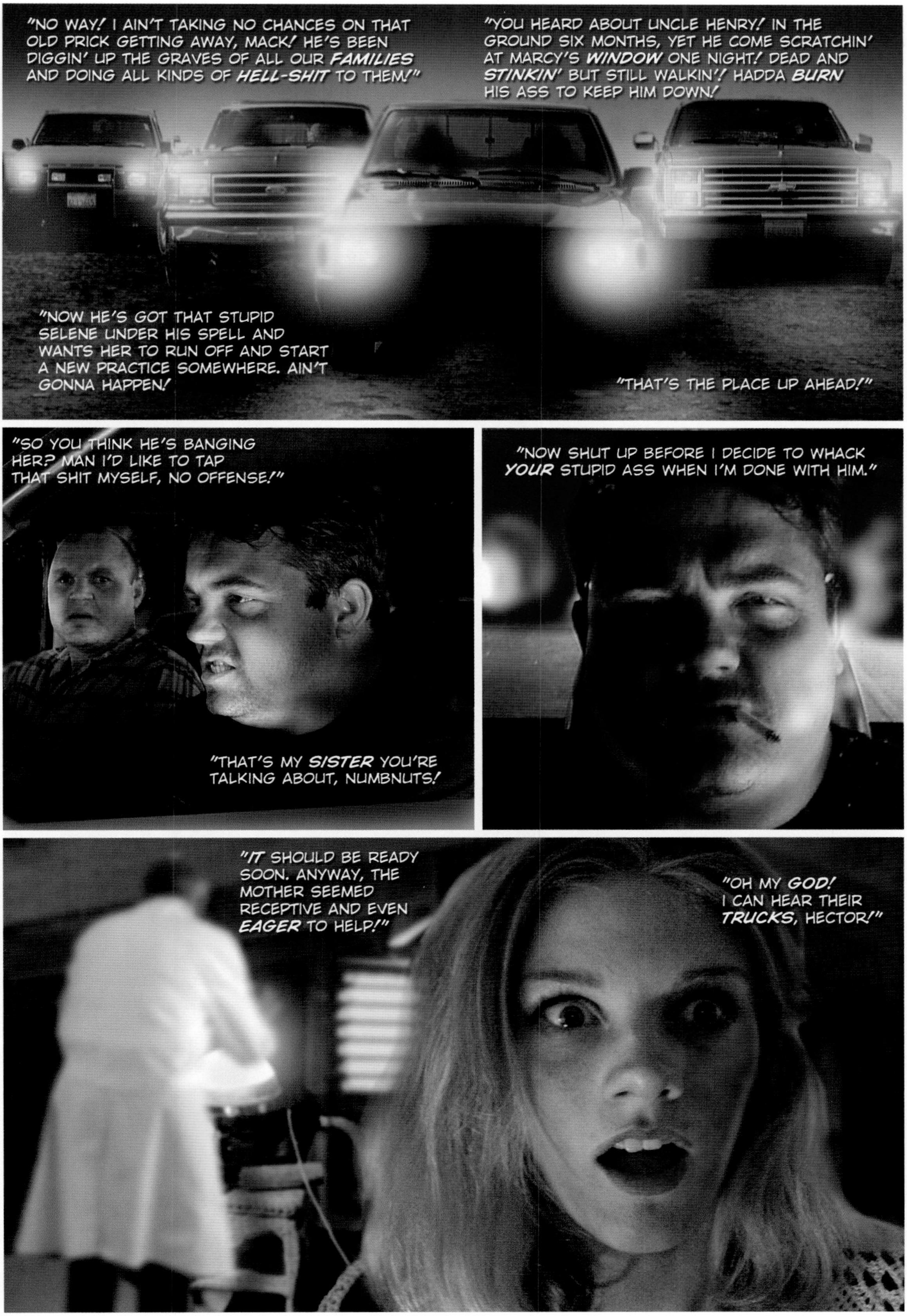
"NO WAY! I AIN'T TAKING NO CHANCES ON THAT OLD PRICK GETTING AWAY, MACK! HE'S BEEN DIGGIN' UP THE GRAVES OF ALL OUR FAMILIES AND DOING ALL KINDS OF HELL-SHIT TO THEM!"
"YOU HEARD ABOUT UNCLE HENRY! IN THE GROUND SIX MONTHS, YET HE COME SCRATCHIN' AT MARCY'S WINDOW ONE NIGHT! DEAD AND STINKIN' BUT STILL WALKIN'! HADDA BURN HIS ASS TO KEEP HIM DOWN!
"NOW HE'S GOT THAT STUPID SELENE UNDER HIS SPELL AND WANTS HER TO RUN OFF AND START A NEW PRACTICE SOMEWHERE. AIN'T GONNA HAPPEN!
"THAT'S THE PLACE UP AHEAD!"
"SO YOU THINK HE'S BANGING HER? MAN I'D LIKE TO TAP THAT SHIT MYSELF, NO OFFENSE!"
"THAT'S MY SISTER YOU'RE TALKING ABOUT, NUMBNUTS!
"NOW SHUT UP BEFORE I DECIDE TO WHACK YOUR STUPID ASS WHEN I'M DONE WITH HIM."
"IT SHOULD BE READY SOON. ANYWAY, THE MOTHER SEEMED RECEPTIVE AND EVEN EAGER TO HELP!"
"OH MY GOD! I CAN HEAR THEIR TRUCKS, HECTOR!"

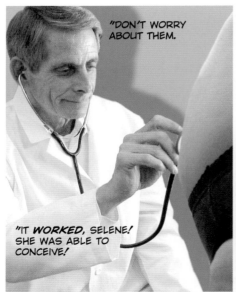

"DON'T WORRY ABOUT THEM.

"IT **WORKED**, SELENE! SHE WAS ABLE TO CONCEIVE!

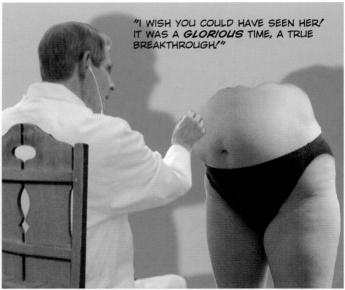

"I WISH YOU COULD HAVE SEEN HER! IT WAS A **GLORIOUS** TIME, A TRUE BREAKTHROUGH!"

"YEEEE-HAAAAW!"

"LENNOX! WHERE YOU AT, ASSHOLE? COME ON OUT 'CAUSE WE'RE COMIN' IN!"

"GODDAM LIGHTS AIN'T WORKING!"

"NO KIDDING. TAKE IT SLOW AND EASY, BOYS. THEY CAN'T GET PAST US!"

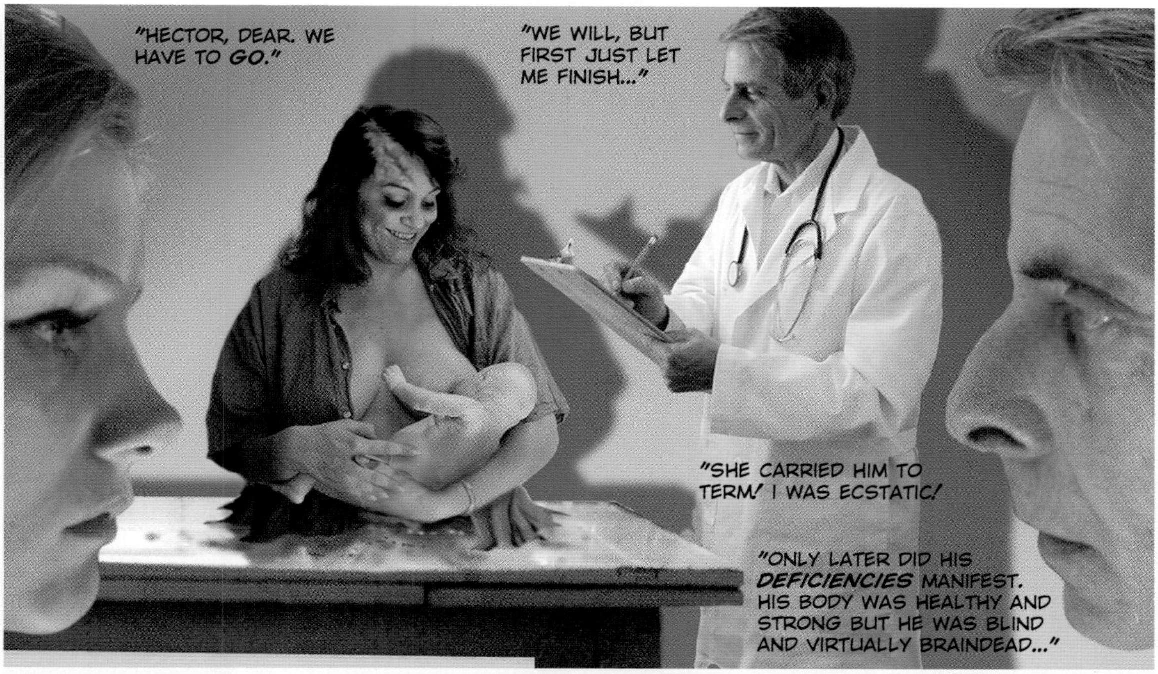
"HECTOR, DEAR. WE HAVE TO GO."
"WE WILL, BUT FIRST JUST LET ME FINISH..."
"SHE CARRIED HIM TO TERM! I WAS ECSTATIC!
"ONLY LATER DID HIS DEFICIENCIES MANIFEST. HIS BODY WAS HEALTHY AND STRONG BUT HE WAS BLIND AND VIRTUALLY BRAINDEAD..."

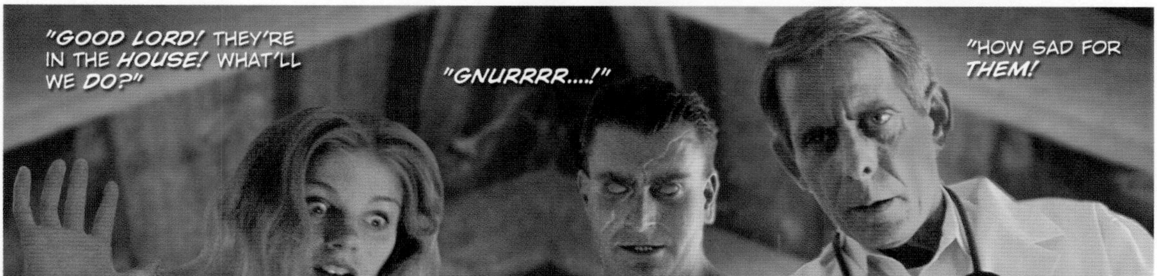
"GOOD LORD! THEY'RE IN THE HOUSE! WHAT'LL WE DO?"
"GNURRRR....!"
"HOW SAD FOR THEM!
"NOW THEY'LL HAVE TO DEAL WITH SECURITY, WHICH MAY INCLUDE SOME FAMILIAR FACES!"

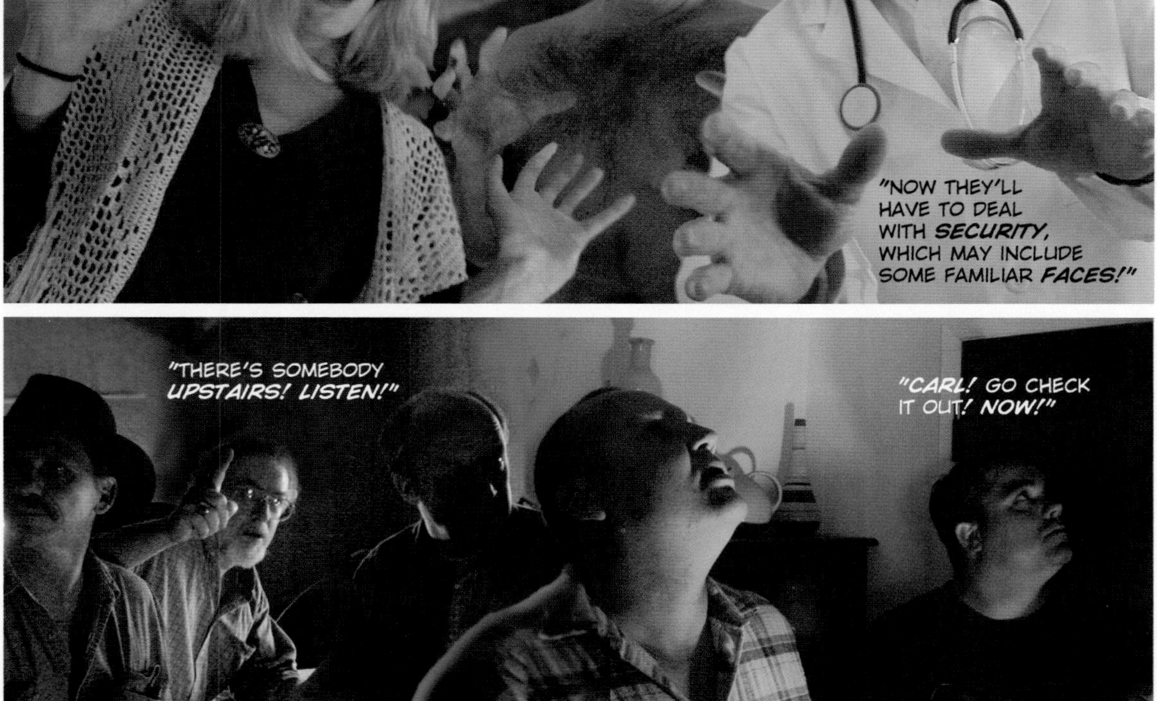
"THERE'S SOMEBODY UPSTAIRS! LISTEN!"
"CARL! GO CHECK IT OUT! NOW!"

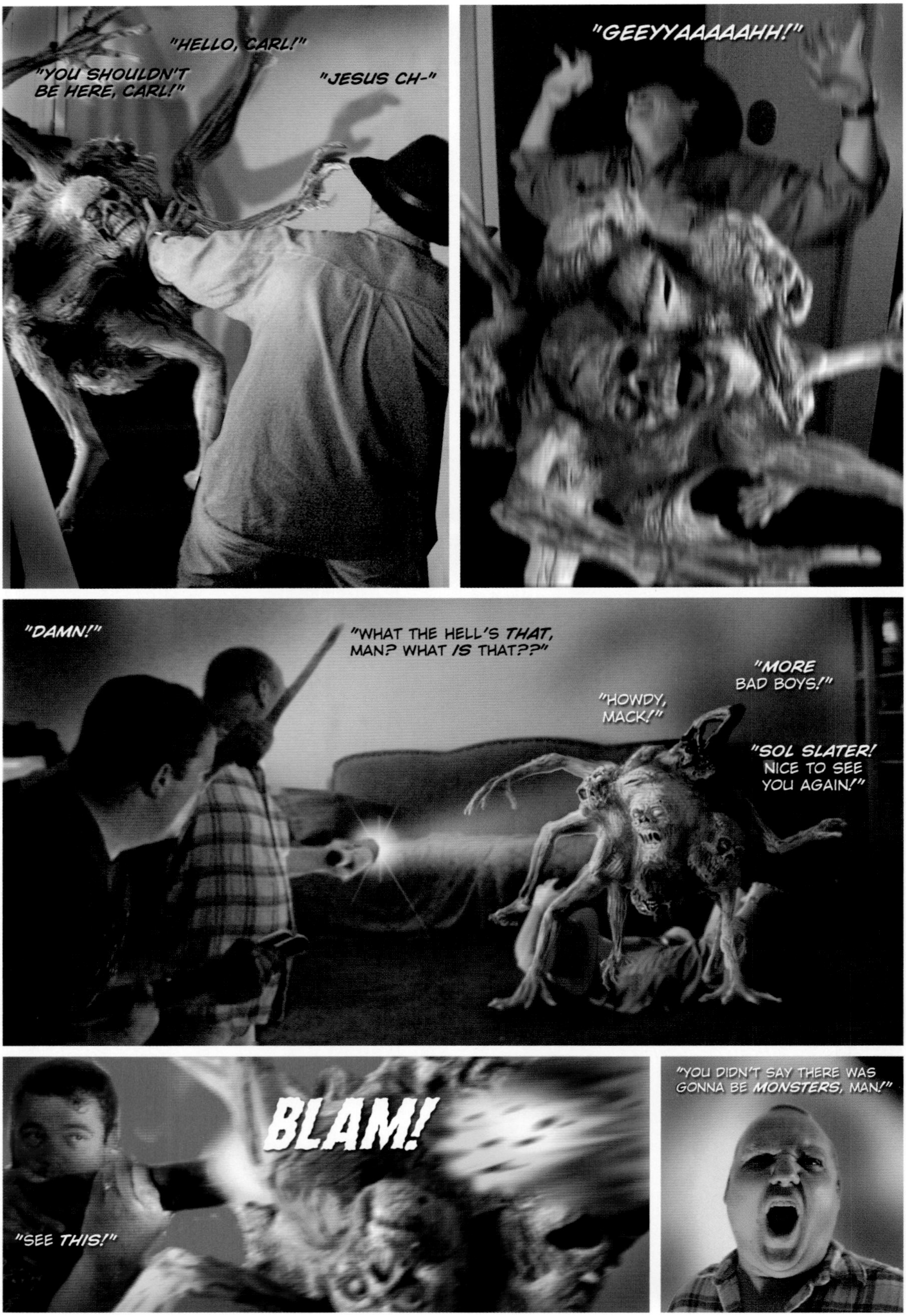
"HELLO, CARL!"
"YOU SHOULDN'T BE HERE, CARL!"
"JESUS CH-"
"GEEYYAAAAAHH!"
"DAMN!"
"WHAT THE HELL'S *THAT*, MAN? WHAT *IS* THAT??"
"HOWDY, MACK!"
"MORE BAD BOYS!"
"SOL SLATER! NICE TO SEE YOU AGAIN!"
BLAM!
"SEE *THIS!*"
"YOU DIDN'T SAY THERE WAS GONNA BE *MONSTERS*, MAN!"

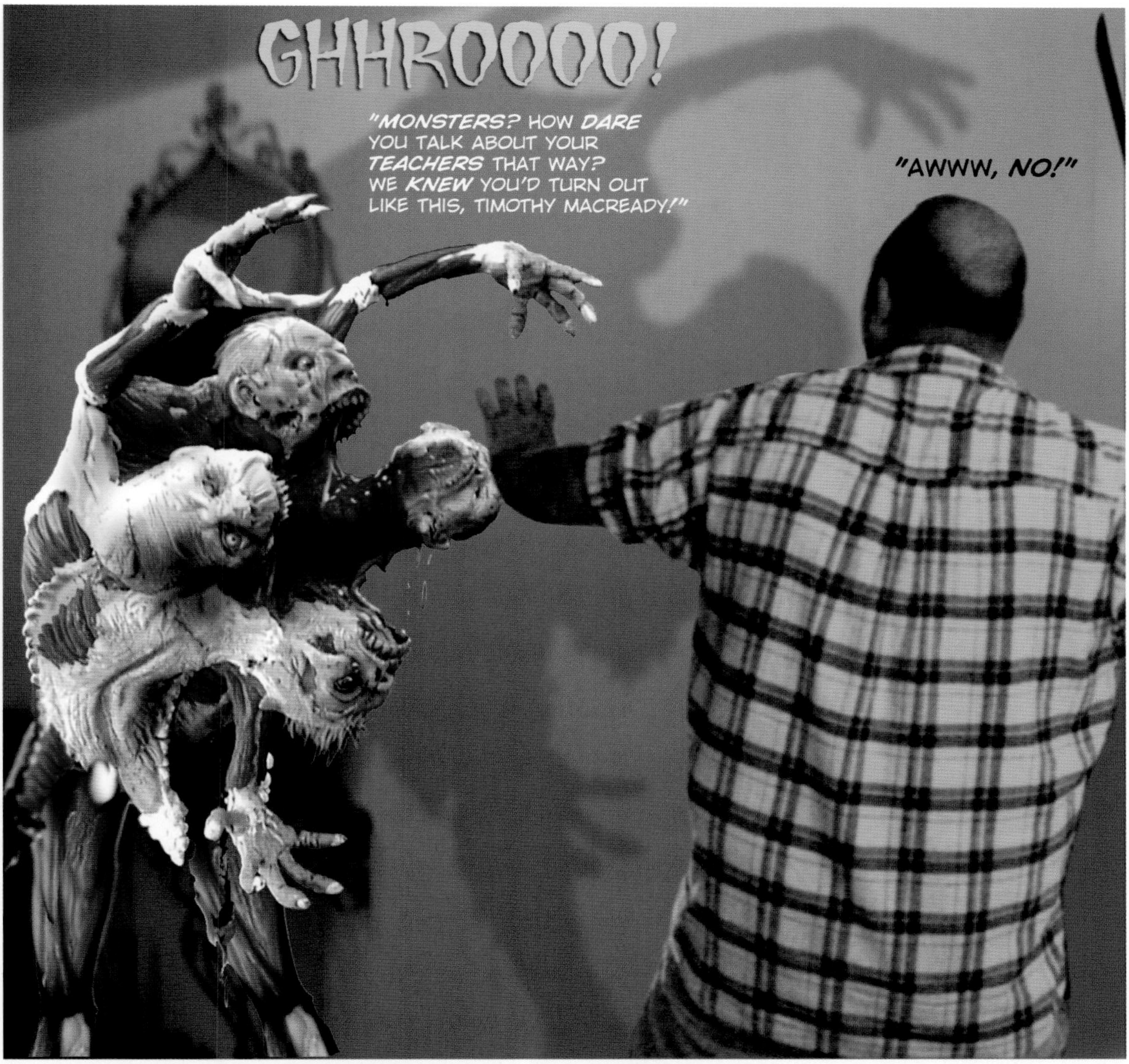
GHHROOOO!
"MONSTERS? HOW DARE YOU TALK ABOUT YOUR TEACHERS THAT WAY? WE KNEW YOU'D TURN OUT LIKE THIS, TIMOTHY MACREADY!"
"AWWW, NO!"

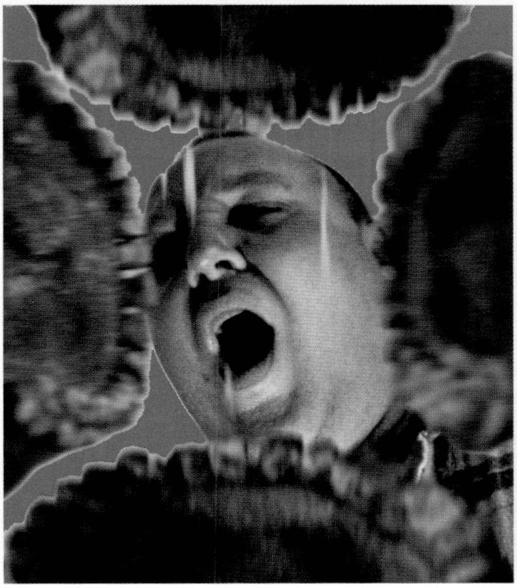

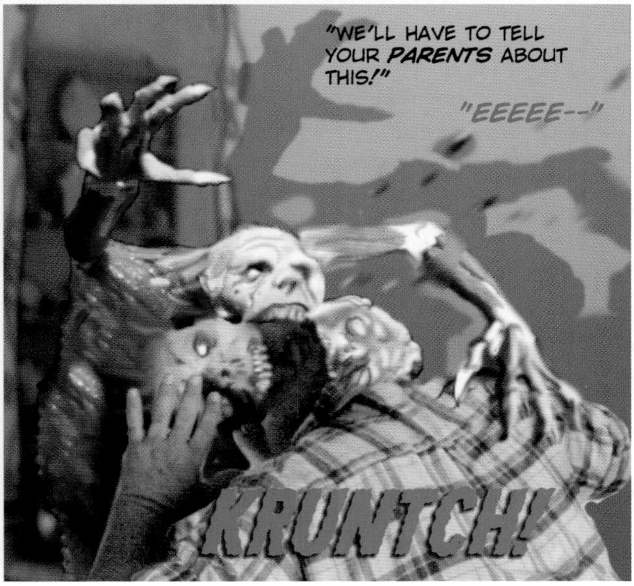
"WE'LL HAVE TO TELL YOUR PARENTS ABOUT THIS!"
"EEEEE--"
KRUNTCH!

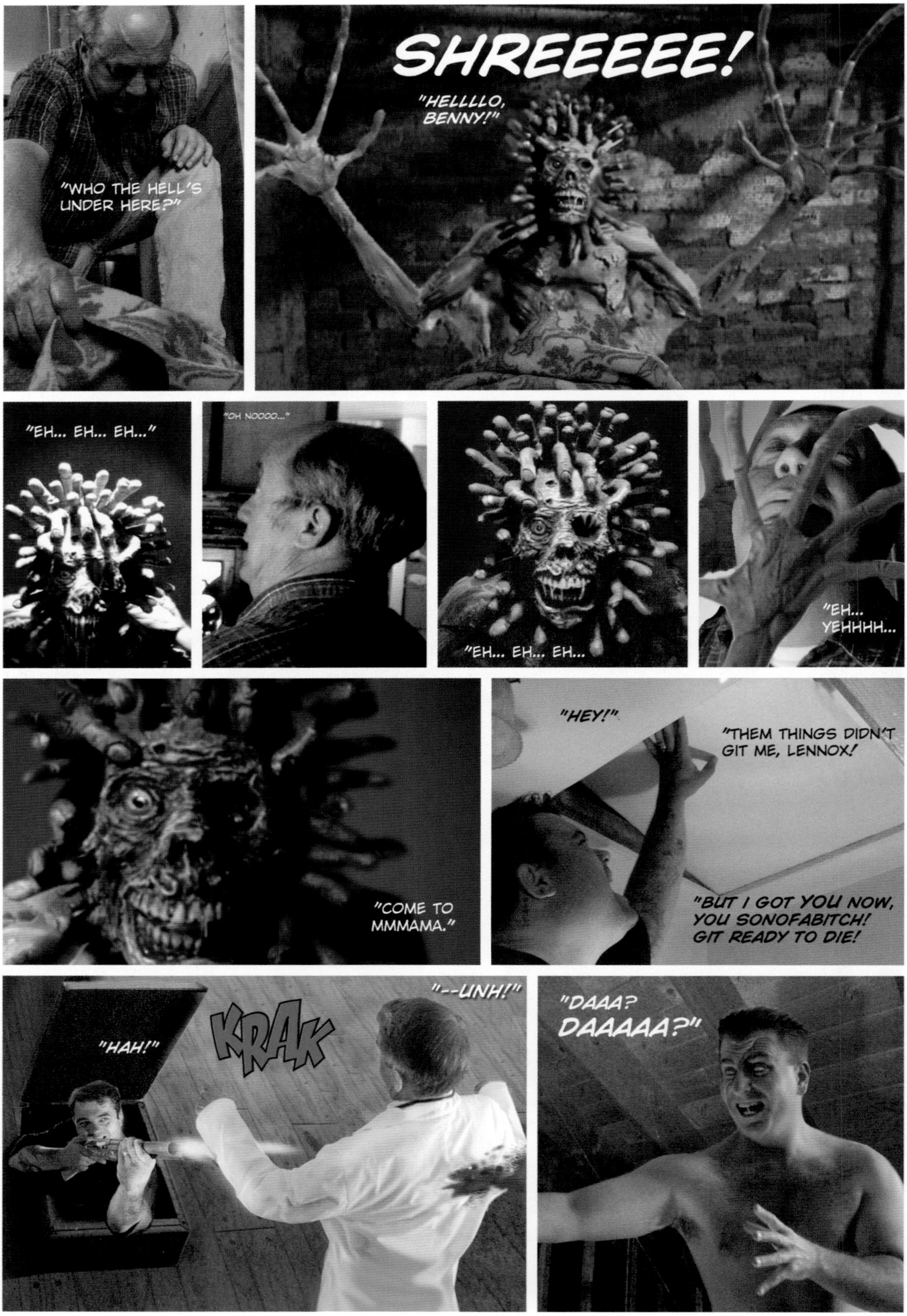
"WHO THE HELL'S UNDER HERE?"
SHREEEEEE!
"HELLLLO, BENNY!"
"EH... EH... EH..."
"OH NOOOO..."
"EH... EH... EH...
"EH... YEHHHH...
"COME TO MMMAMA."
"HEY!"
"THEM THINGS DIDN'T GIT ME, LENNOX!
"BUT I GOT YOU NOW, YOU SONOFABITCH! GIT READY TO DIE!
"HAH!"
KRAK
"--UNH!"
"DAAA? DAAAAA?"

"WHO THE HELL...?"
"DAAAAA!!!"
"NO, SOL! PLEASE DON'T! THAT'S MY SON!"
"IZZAT SO? WELL STEP RIGHT UP, SONNY BOY!"
BLAM!
splurtch!
"SPLUCK! GURGLE!"
"G-GET... GCCHH! KUH!
"--SKEEEEEEE..."

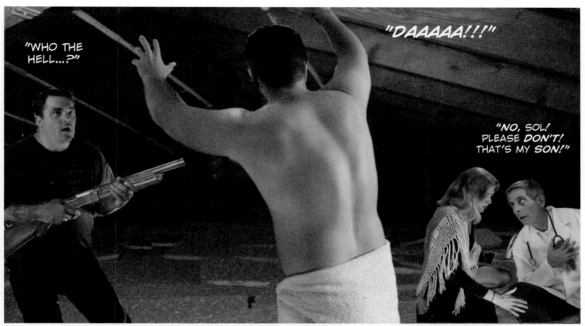

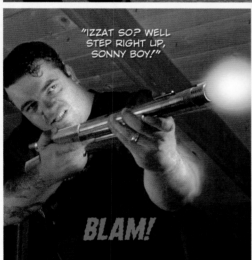

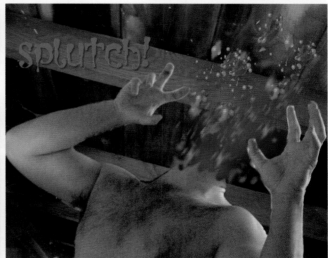

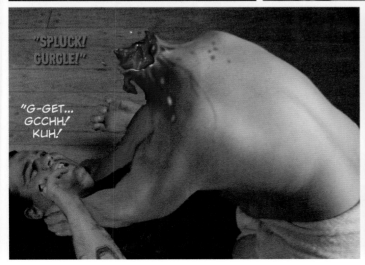

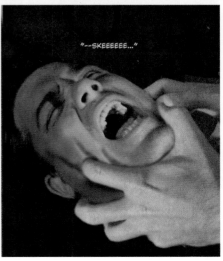

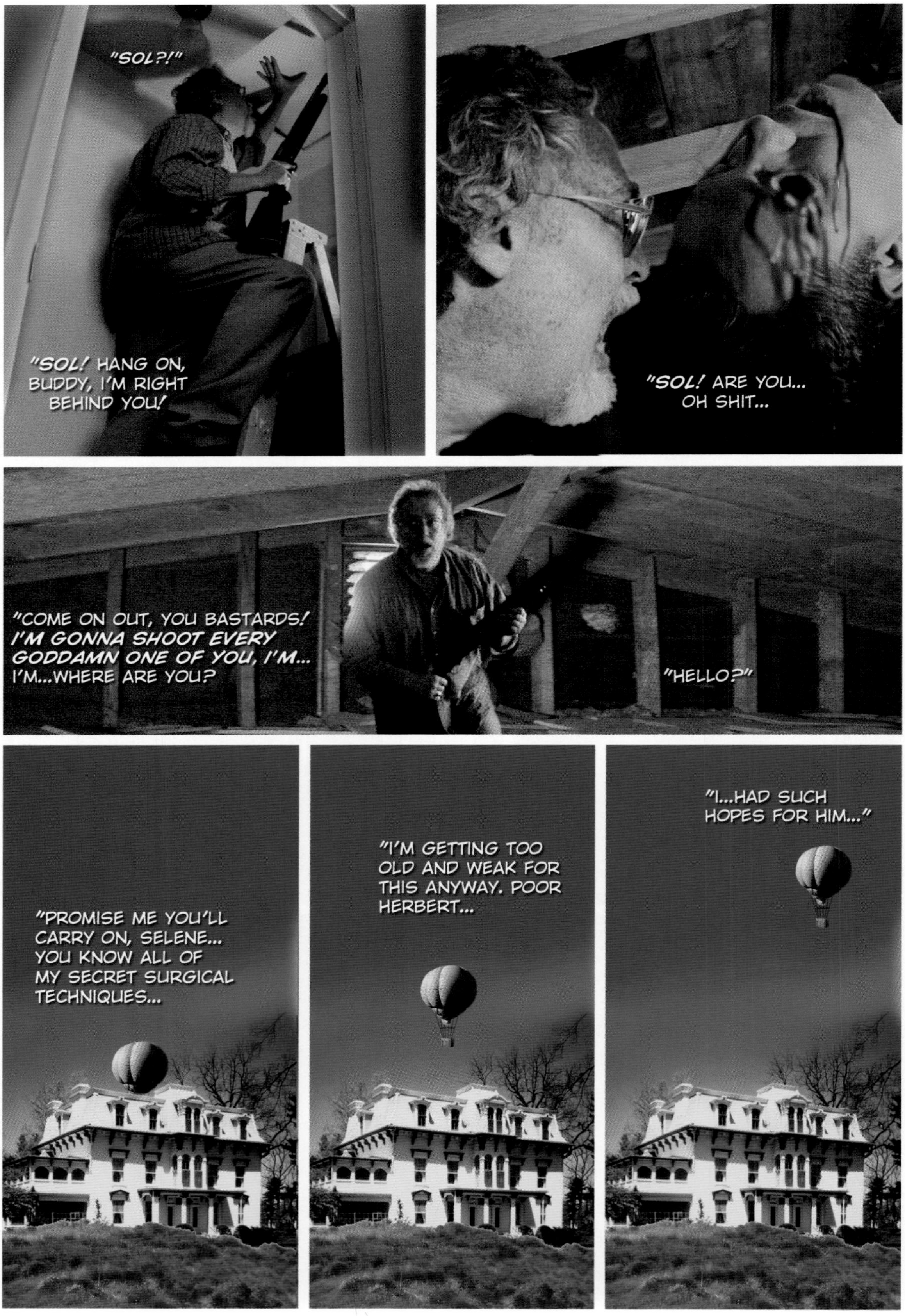
"SOL?!"
"SOL! HANG ON, BUDDY, I'M RIGHT BEHIND YOU!
"SOL! ARE YOU... OH SHIT...
"COME ON OUT, YOU BASTARDS! I'M GONNA SHOOT EVERY GODDAMN ONE OF YOU, I'M... I'M...WHERE ARE YOU?
"HELLO?"
"PROMISE ME YOU'LL CARRY ON, SELENE... YOU KNOW ALL OF MY SECRET SURGICAL TECHNIQUES...
"I'M GETTING TOO OLD AND WEAK FOR THIS ANYWAY. POOR HERBERT...
"I...HAD SUCH HOPES FOR HIM..."

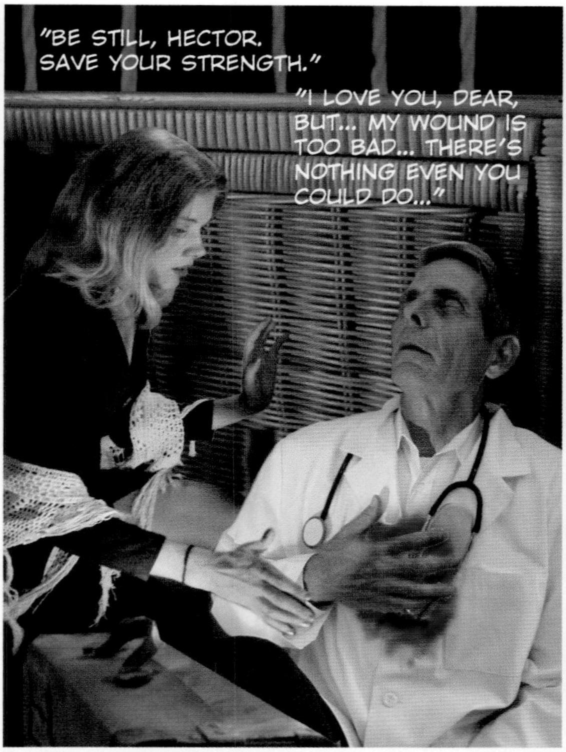
"BE STILL, HECTOR.
SAVE YOUR STRENGTH."
"I LOVE YOU, DEAR, BUT... MY WOUND IS TOO BAD... THERE'S NOTHING EVEN YOU COULD DO..."

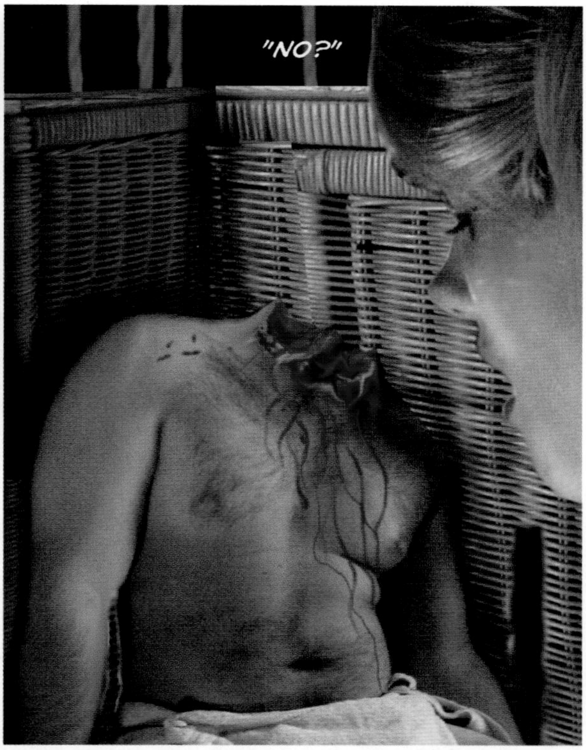
"NO?"

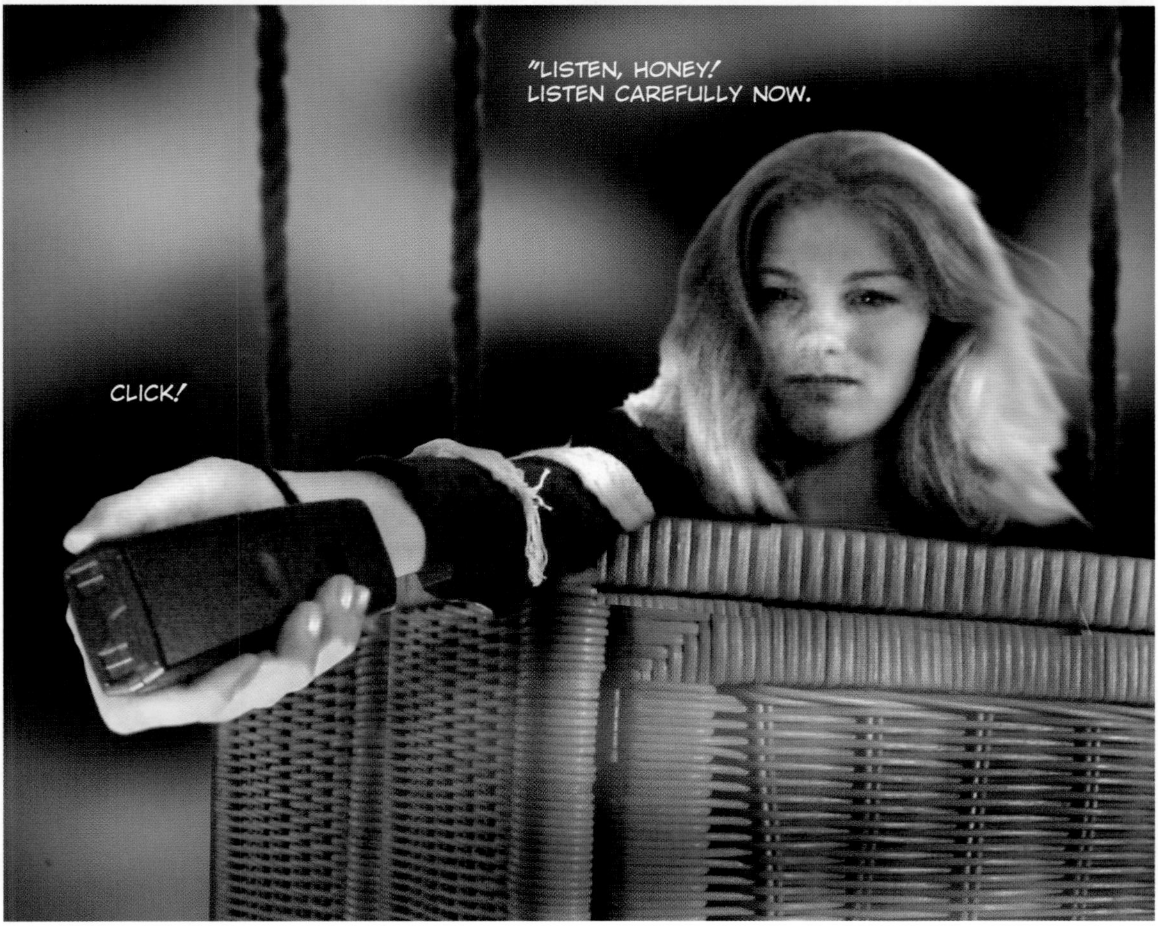
"LISTEN, HONEY!
LISTEN CAREFULLY NOW.
CLICK!

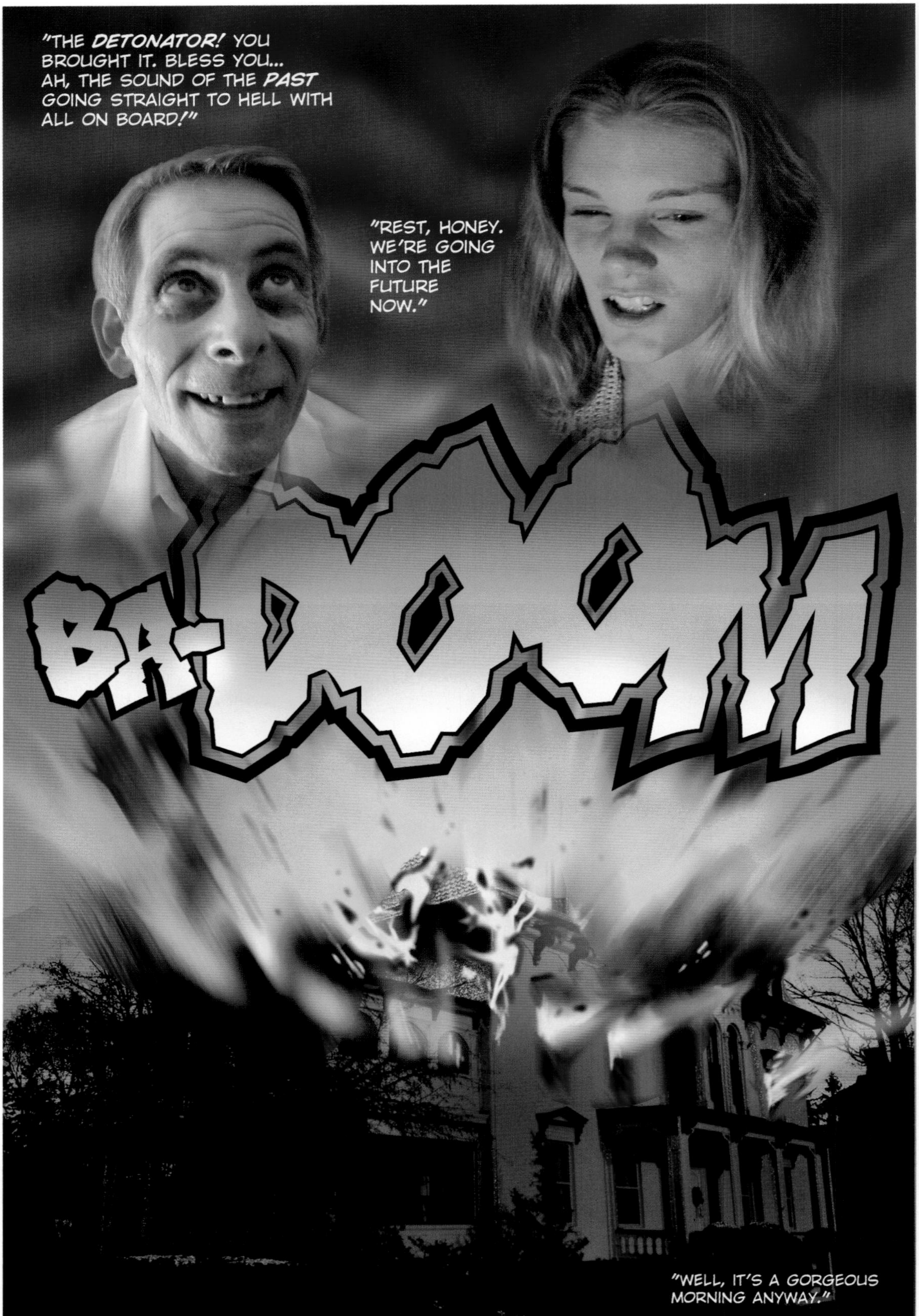
"THE DETONATOR! YOU BROUGHT IT. BLESS YOU... AH, THE SOUND OF THE PAST GOING STRAIGHT TO HELL WITH ALL ON BOARD!"
"REST, HONEY. WE'RE GOING INTO THE FUTURE NOW."
BA-DOOM
"WELL, IT'S A GORGEOUS MORNING ANYWAY."

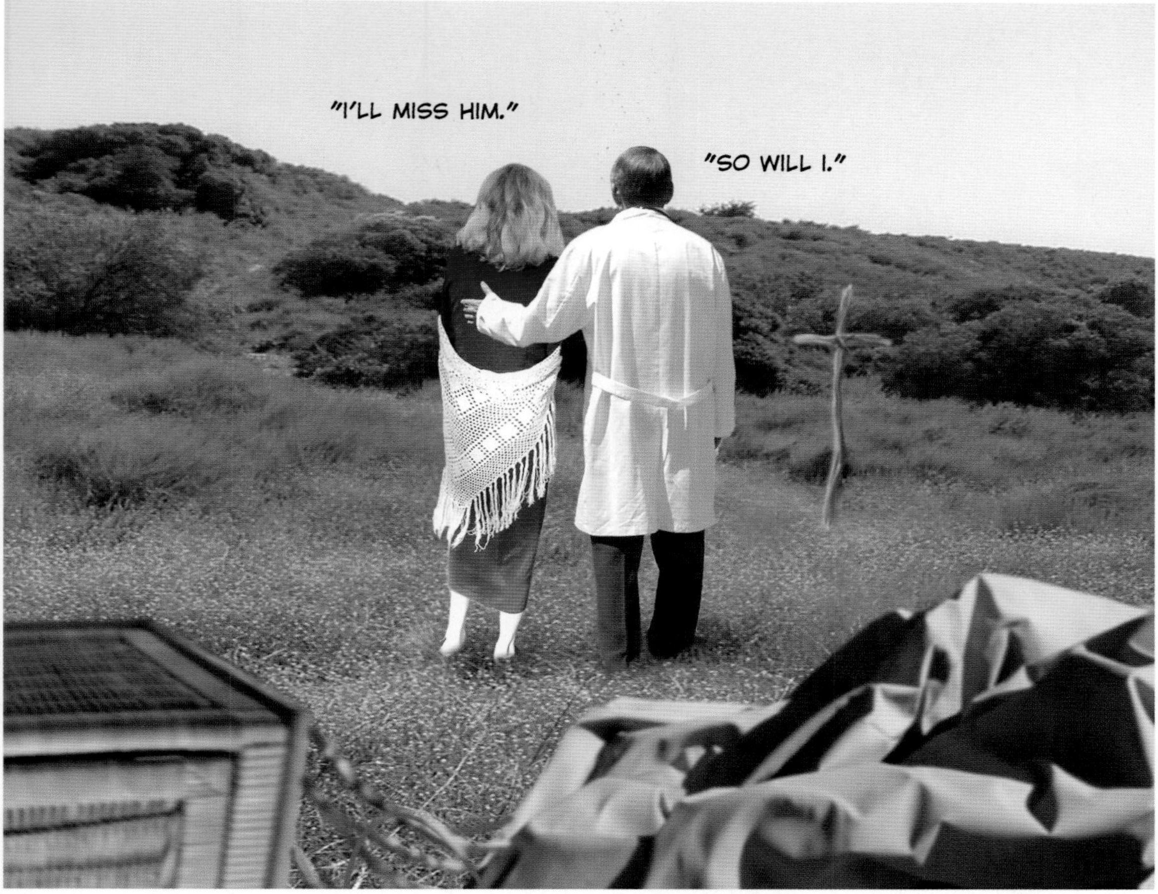
"I'LL MISS HIM."
"SO WILL I."

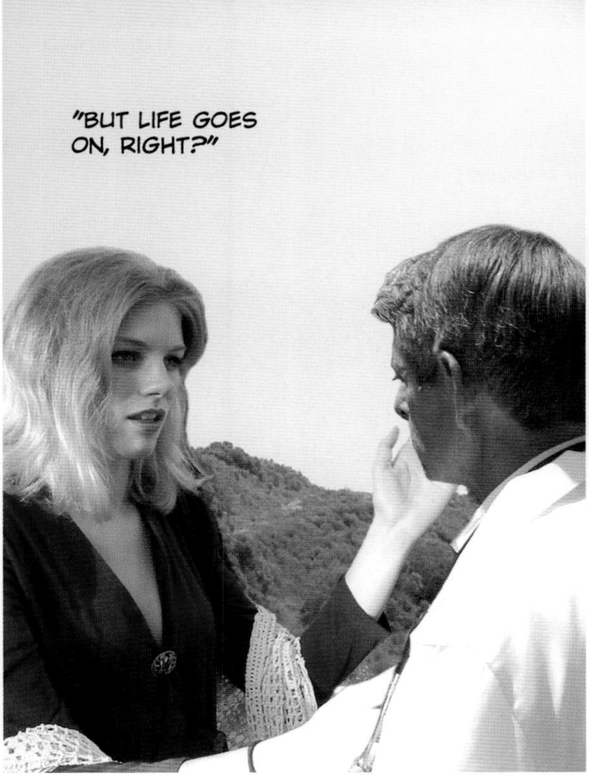
"BUT LIFE GOES ON, RIGHT?"

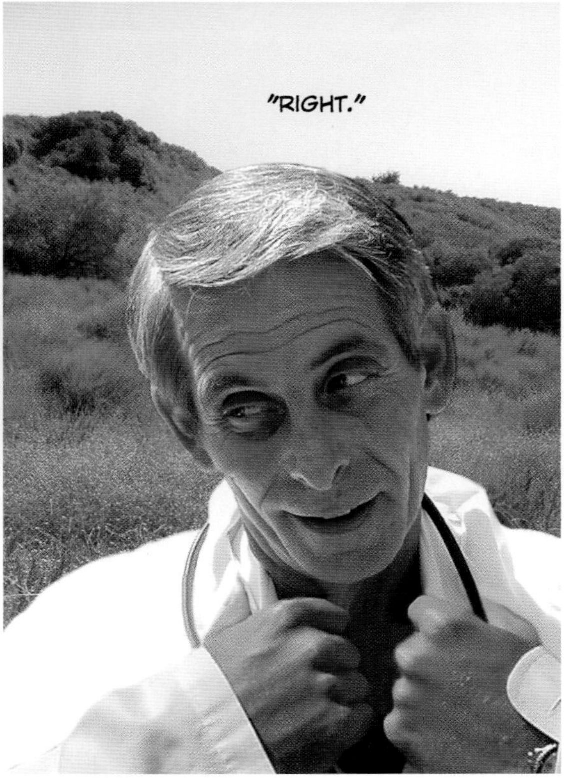
"RIGHT."

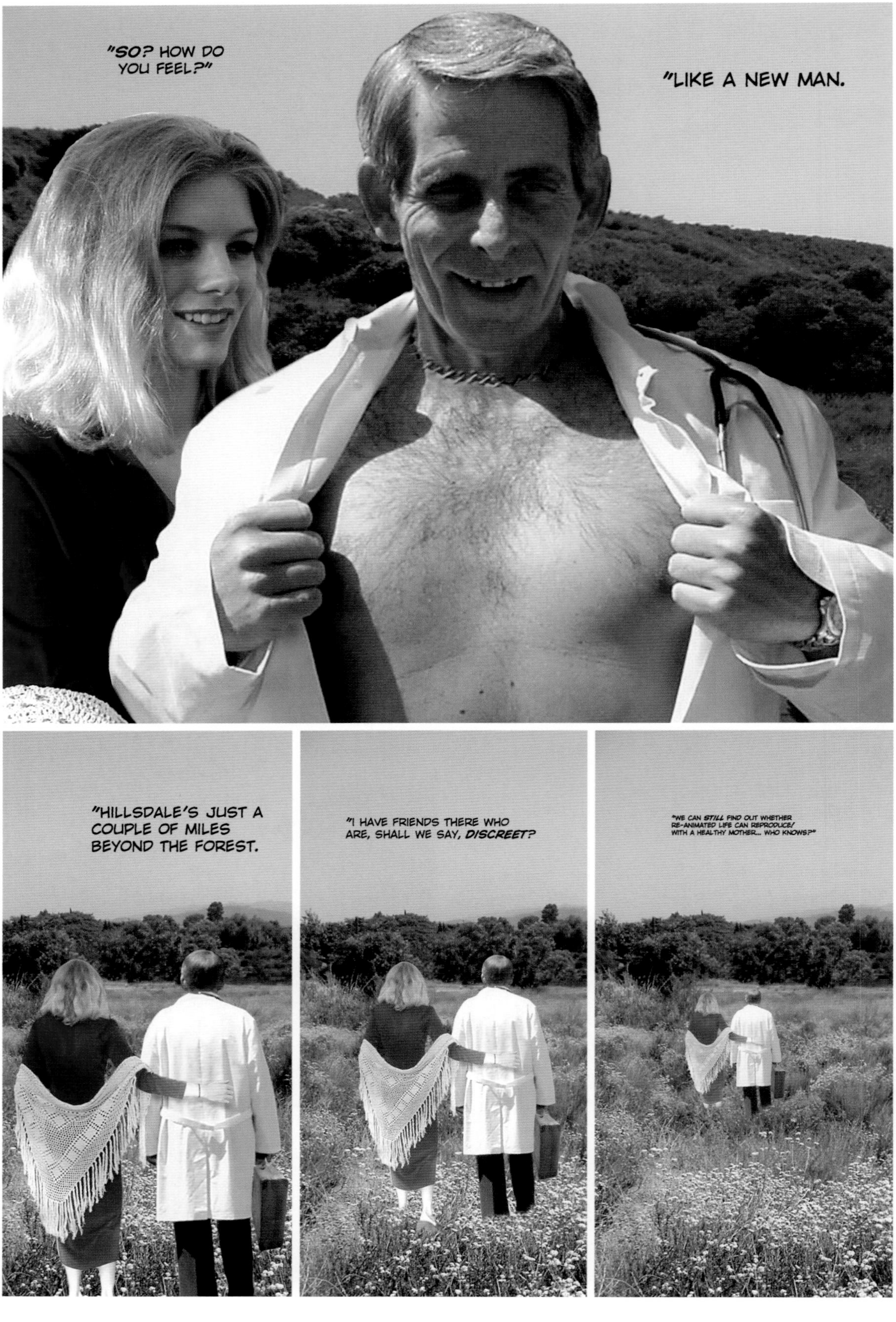
"SO? HOW DO YOU FEEL?"
"LIKE A NEW MAN.
"HILLSDALE'S JUST A COUPLE OF MILES BEYOND THE FOREST.
"I HAVE FRIENDS THERE WHO ARE, SHALL WE SAY, DISCREET?
"WE CAN STILL FIND OUT WHETHER RE-ANIMATED LIFE CAN REPRODUCE! WITH A HEALTHY MOTHER... WHO KNOWS?"

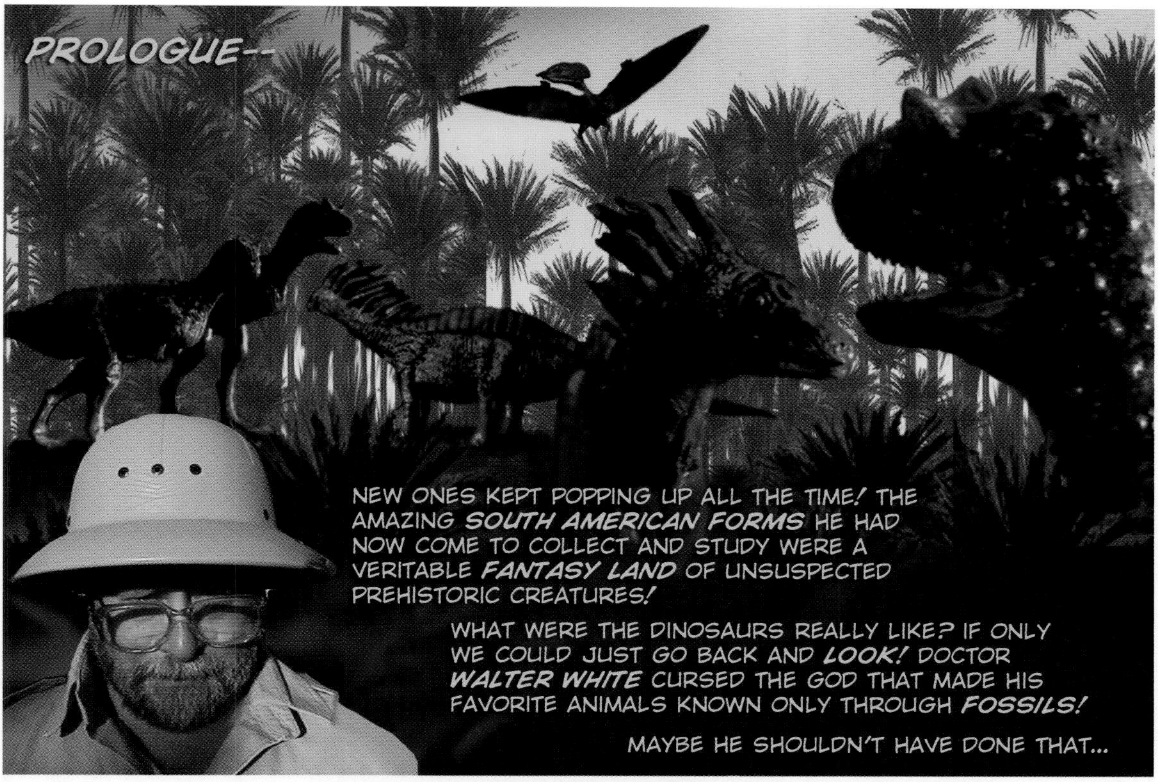
PROLOGUE--
NEW ONES KEPT POPPING UP ALL THE TIME! THE AMAZING SOUTH AMERICAN FORMS HE HAD NOW COME TO COLLECT AND STUDY WERE A VERITABLE FANTASY LAND OF UNSUSPECTED PREHISTORIC CREATURES!
WHAT WERE THE DINOSAURS REALLY LIKE? IF ONLY WE COULD JUST GO BACK AND LOOK! DOCTOR WALTER WHITE CURSED THE GOD THAT MADE HIS FAVORITE ANIMALS KNOWN ONLY THROUGH FOSSILS!
MAYBE HE SHOULDN'T HAVE DONE THAT...
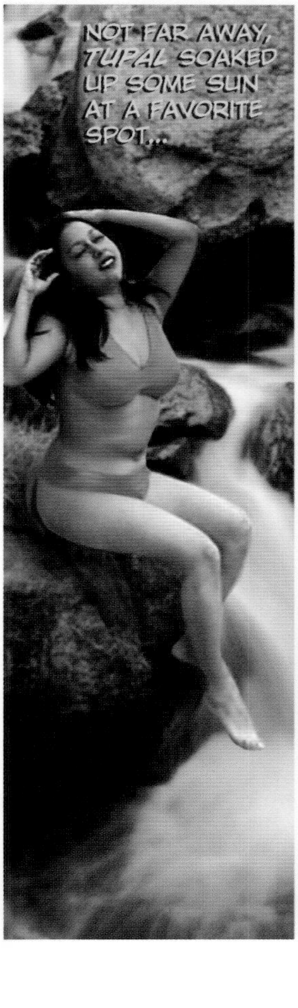
NOT FAR AWAY, TUPAL SOAKED UP SOME SUN AT A FAVORITE SPOT...
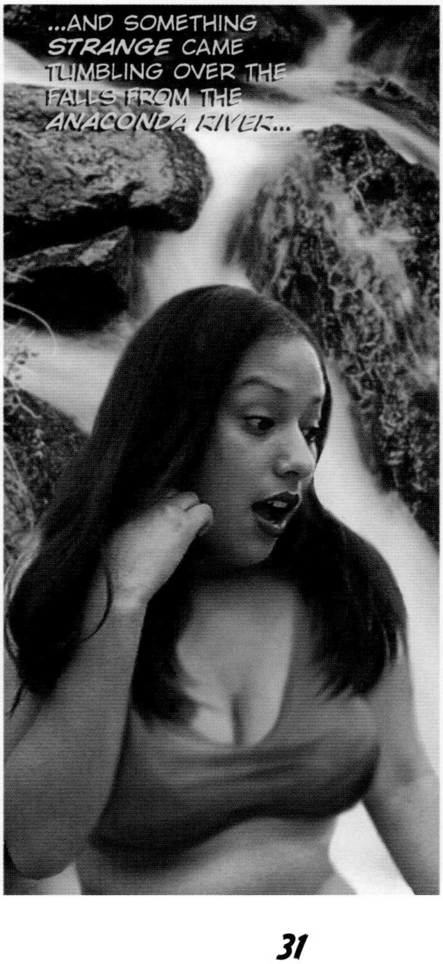
...AND SOMETHING STRANGE CAME TUMBLING OVER THE FALLS FROM THE ANACONDA RIVER...
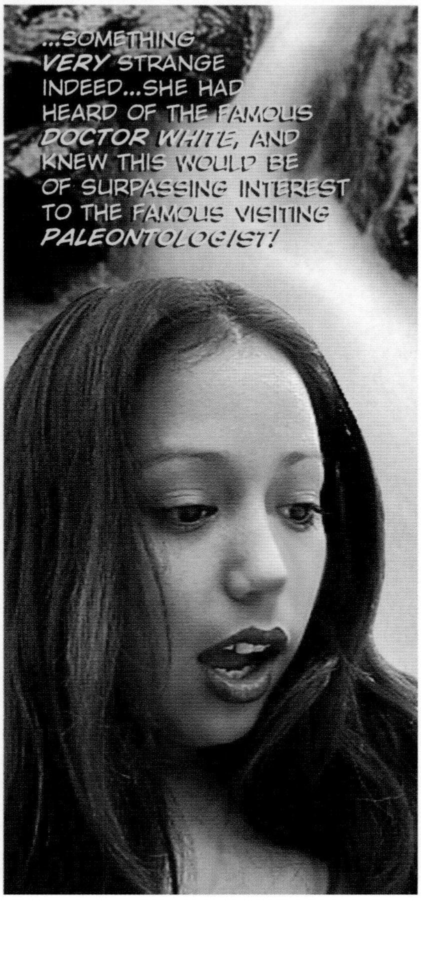
...SOMETHING VERY STRANGE INDEED...SHE HAD HEARD OF THE FAMOUS DOCTOR WHITE, AND KNEW THIS WOULD BE OF SURPASSING INTEREST TO THE FAMOUS VISITING PALEONTOLOGIST!

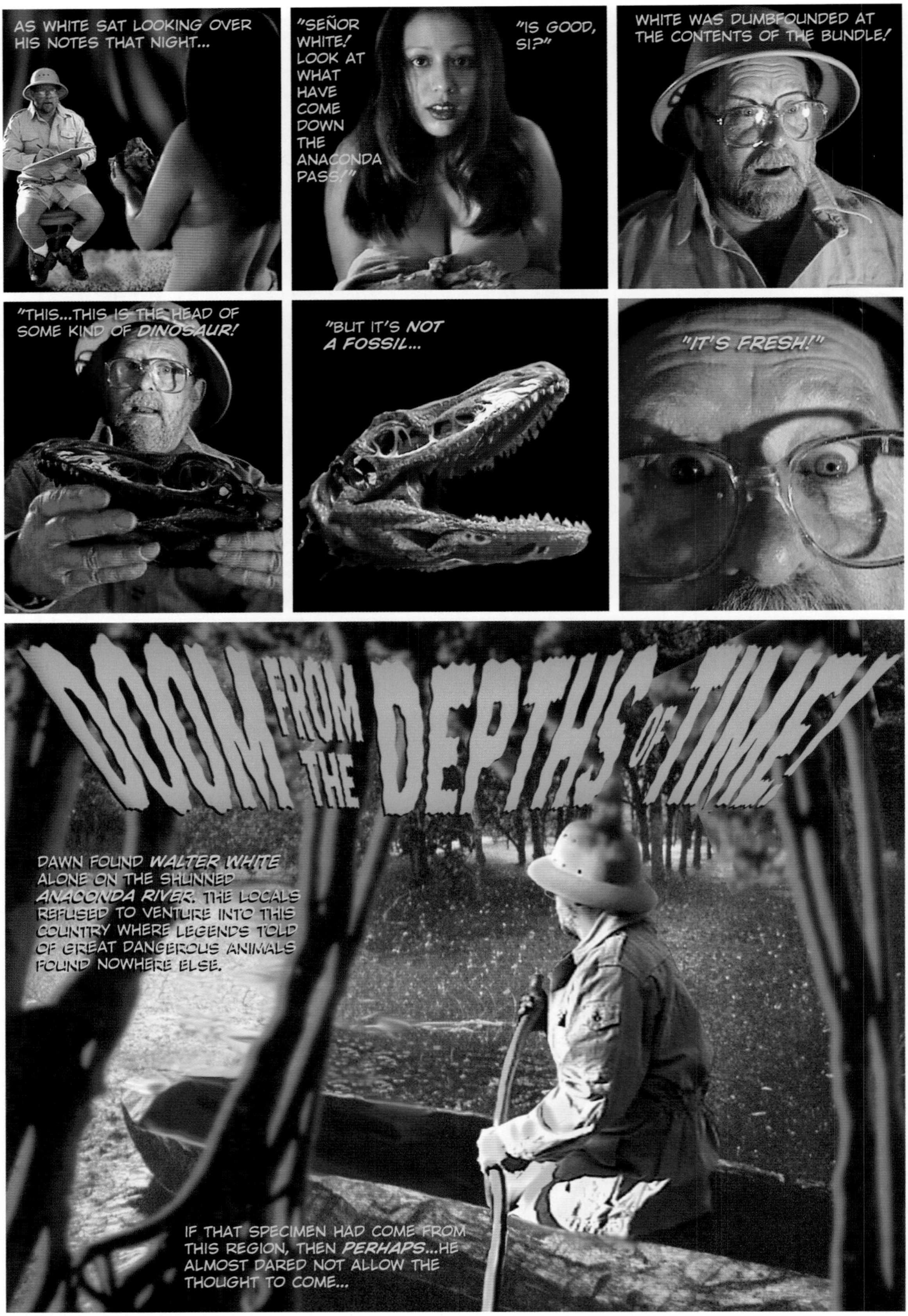
AS WHITE SAT LOOKING OVER HIS NOTES THAT NIGHT...
"SEÑOR WHITE! LOOK AT WHAT HAVE COME DOWN THE ANACONDA PASS!"
"IS GOOD, SI?"
WHITE WAS DUMBFOUNDED AT THE CONTENTS OF THE BUNDLE!
"THIS...THIS IS THE HEAD OF SOME KIND OF *DINOSAUR!*
"BUT IT'S *NOT A FOSSIL...*
"IT'S FRESH!"
DOOM FROM THE DEPTHS OF TIME!
DAWN FOUND *WALTER WHITE* ALONE ON THE SHUNNED *ANACONDA RIVER.* THE LOCALS REFUSED TO VENTURE INTO THIS COUNTRY WHERE LEGENDS TOLD OF GREAT DANGEROUS ANIMALS FOUND NOWHERE ELSE.
IF THAT SPECIMEN HAD COME FROM THIS REGION, THEN *PERHAPS...*HE ALMOST DARED NOT ALLOW THE THOUGHT TO COME...

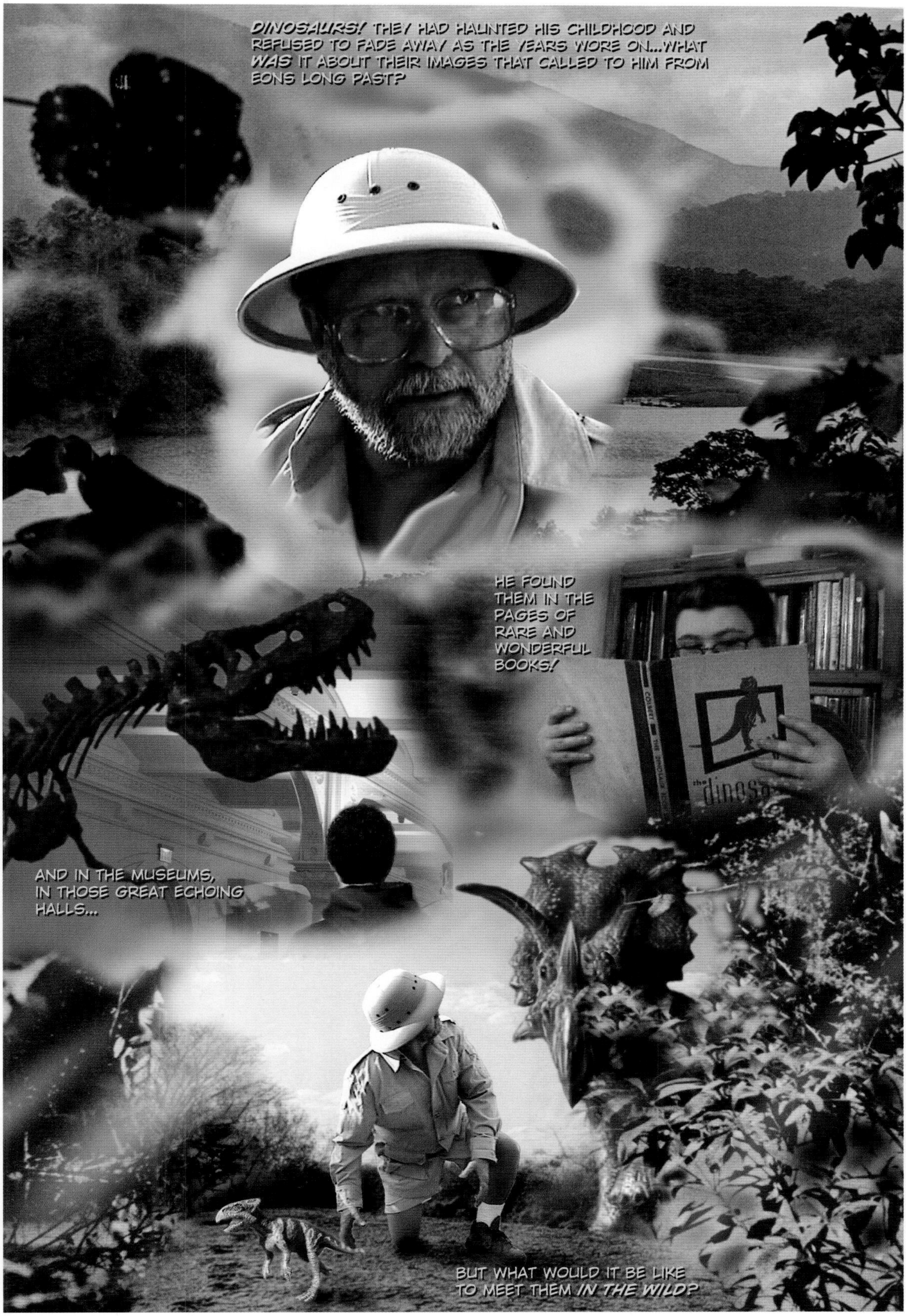
DINOSAURS! THEY HAD HAUNTED HIS CHILDHOOD AND REFUSED TO FADE AWAY AS THE YEARS WORE ON...WHAT WAS IT ABOUT THEIR IMAGES THAT CALLED TO HIM FROM EONS LONG PAST?
HE FOUND THEM IN THE PAGES OF RARE AND WONDERFUL BOOKS!
AND IN THE MUSEUMS, IN THOSE GREAT ECHOING HALLS...
BUT WHAT WOULD IT BE LIKE TO MEET THEM IN THE WILD?

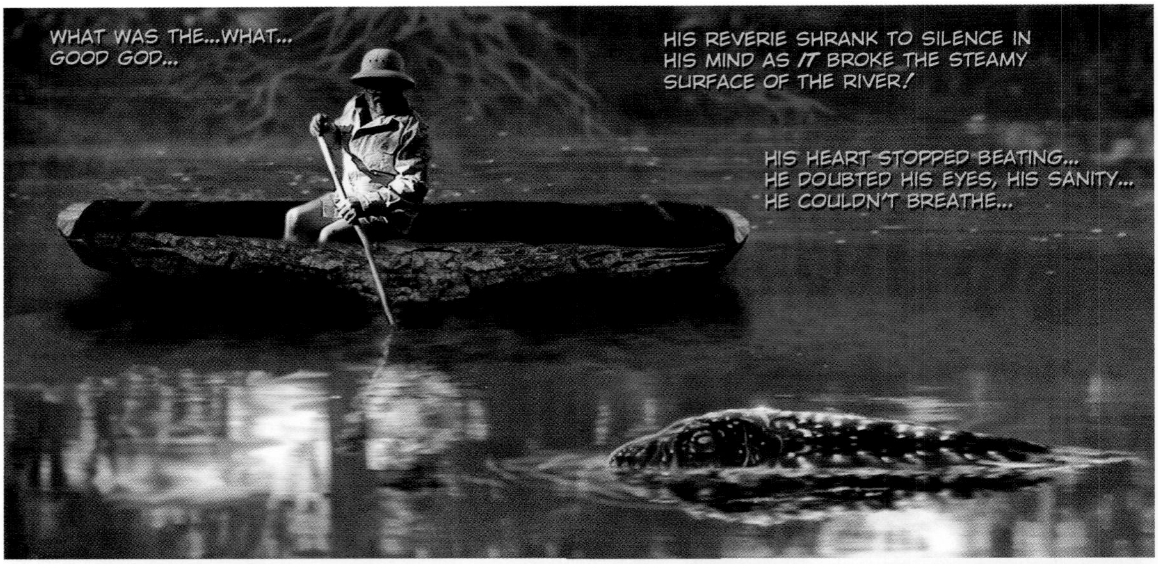
WHAT WAS THE...WHAT...
GOOD GOD...
HIS REVERIE SHRANK TO SILENCE IN HIS MIND AS *IT* BROKE THE STEAMY SURFACE OF THE RIVER!
HIS HEART STOPPED BEATING... HE DOUBTED HIS EYES, HIS SANITY... HE COULDN'T BREATHE...

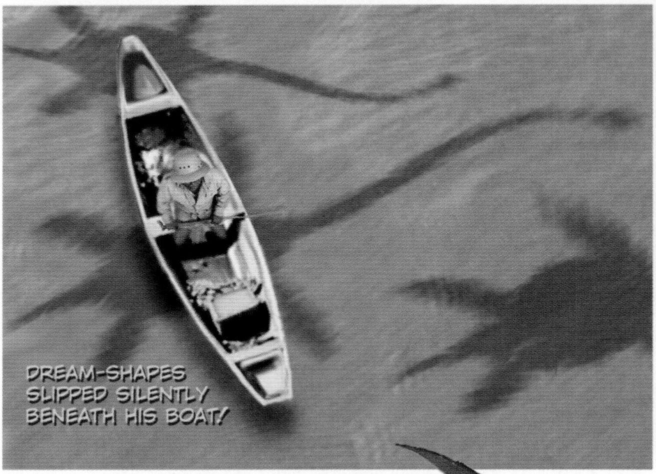
DREAM-SHAPES SLIPPED SILENTLY BENEATH HIS BOAT!

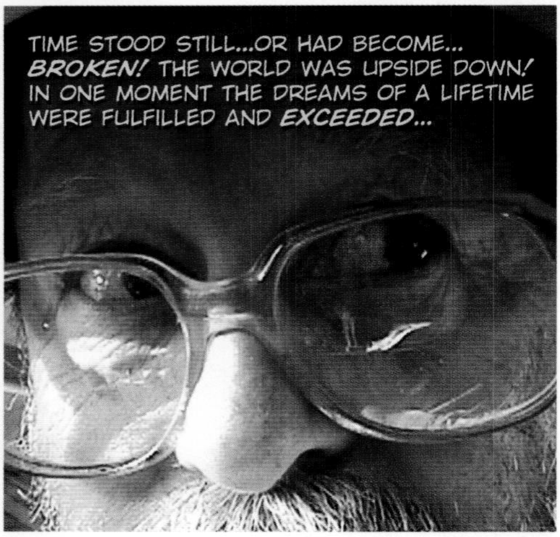
TIME STOOD STILL...OR HAD BECOME... ***BROKEN!*** THE WORLD WAS UPSIDE DOWN! IN ONE MOMENT THE DREAMS OF A LIFETIME WERE FULFILLED AND ***EXCEEDED...***

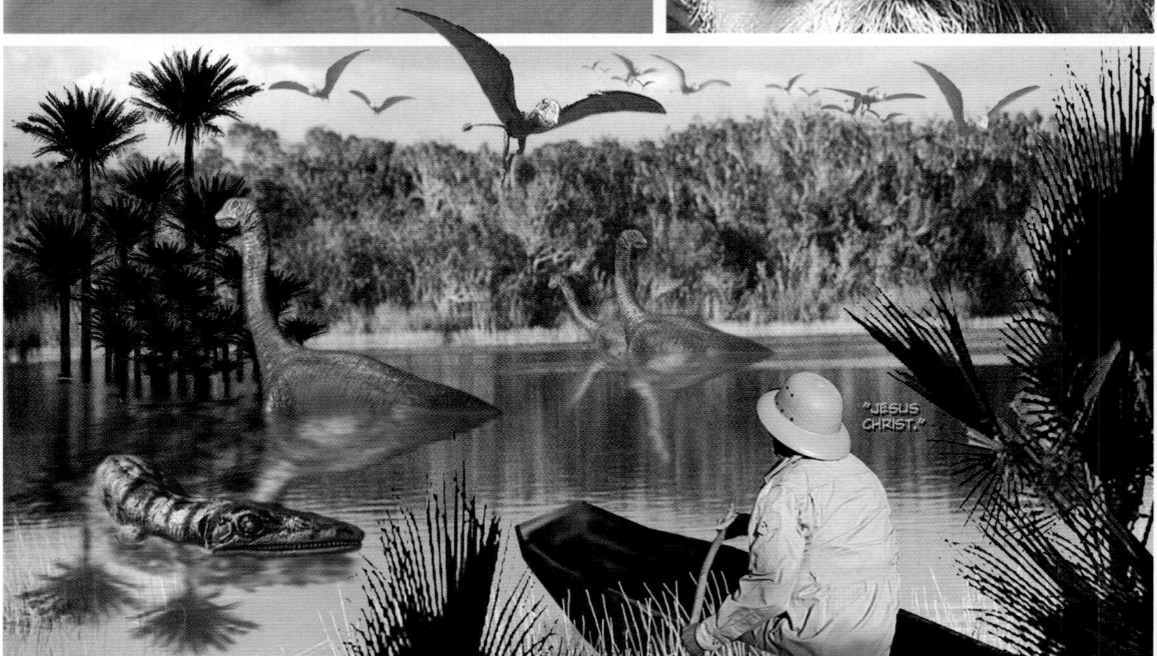
"JESUS CHRIST."

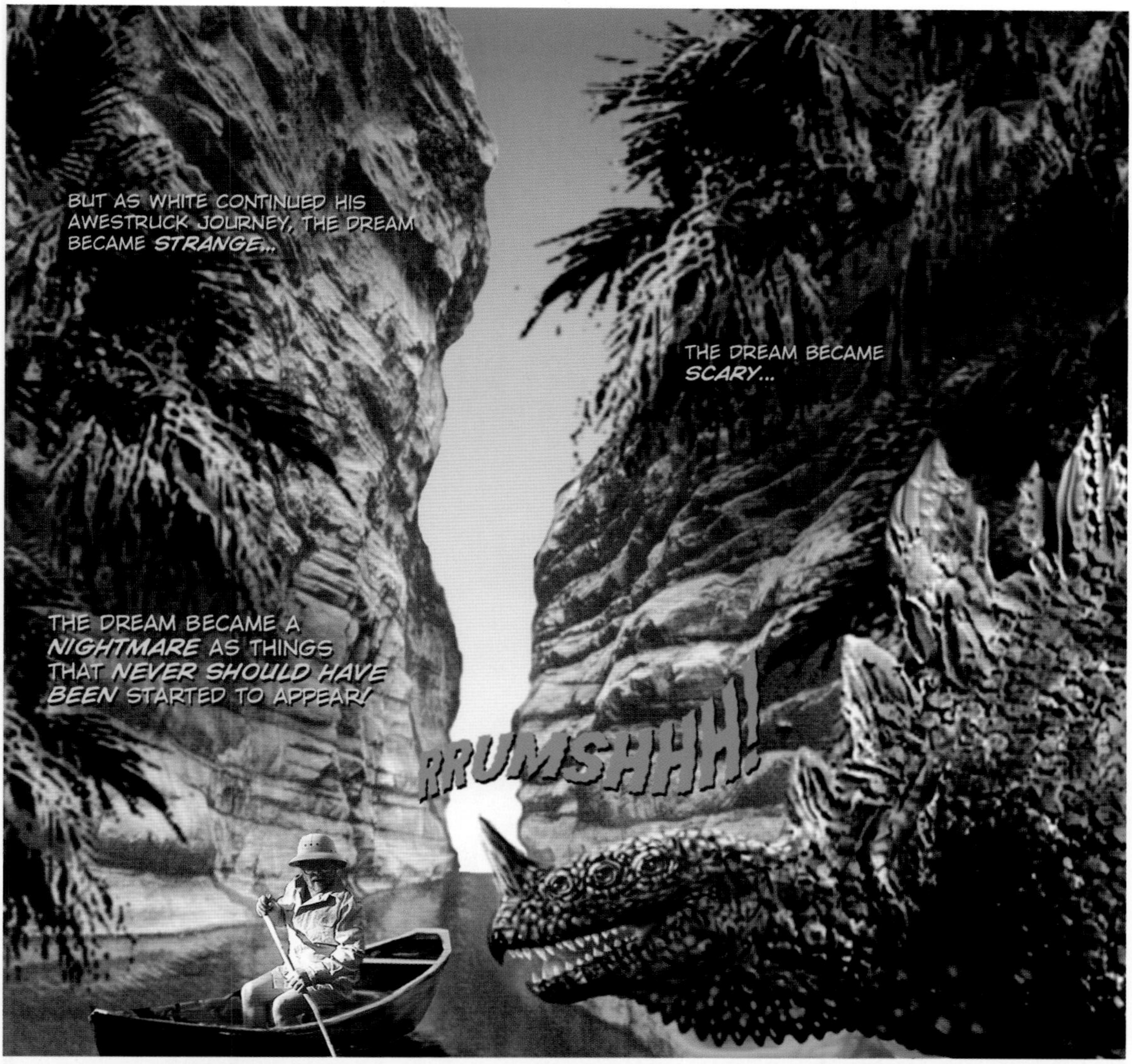
BUT AS WHITE CONTINUED HIS AWESTRUCK JOURNEY, THE DREAM BECAME *STRANGE*...
THE DREAM BECAME *SCARY*...
THE DREAM BECAME A *NIGHTMARE* AS THINGS THAT *NEVER SHOULD HAVE BEEN* STARTED TO APPEAR!
RRUMSHHH!

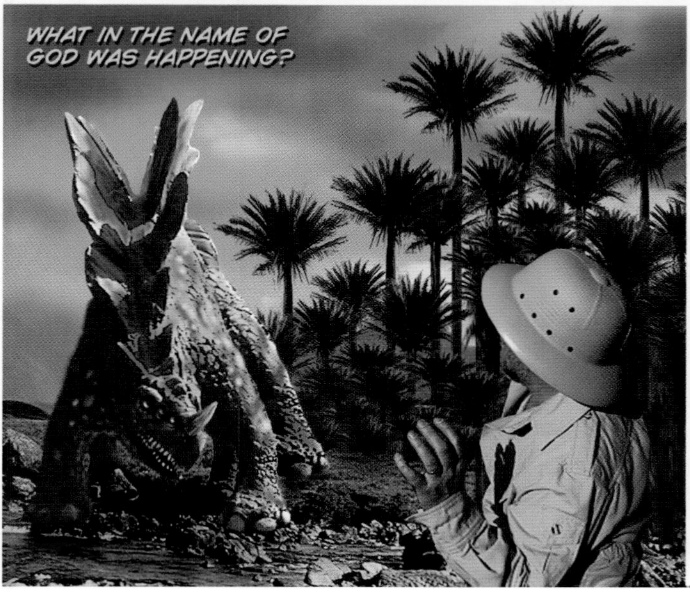
WHAT IN THE NAME OF GOD WAS HAPPENING?

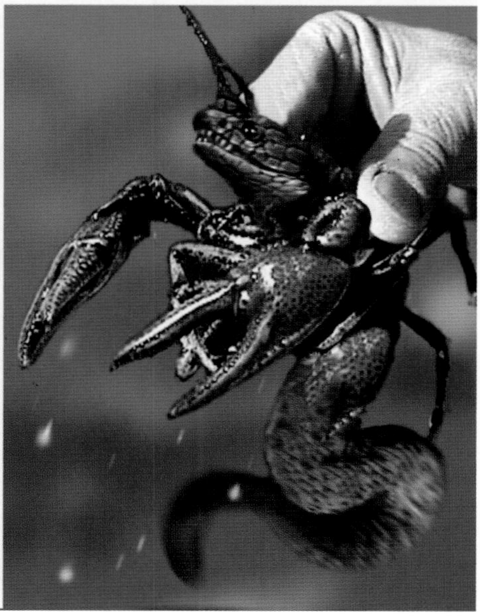

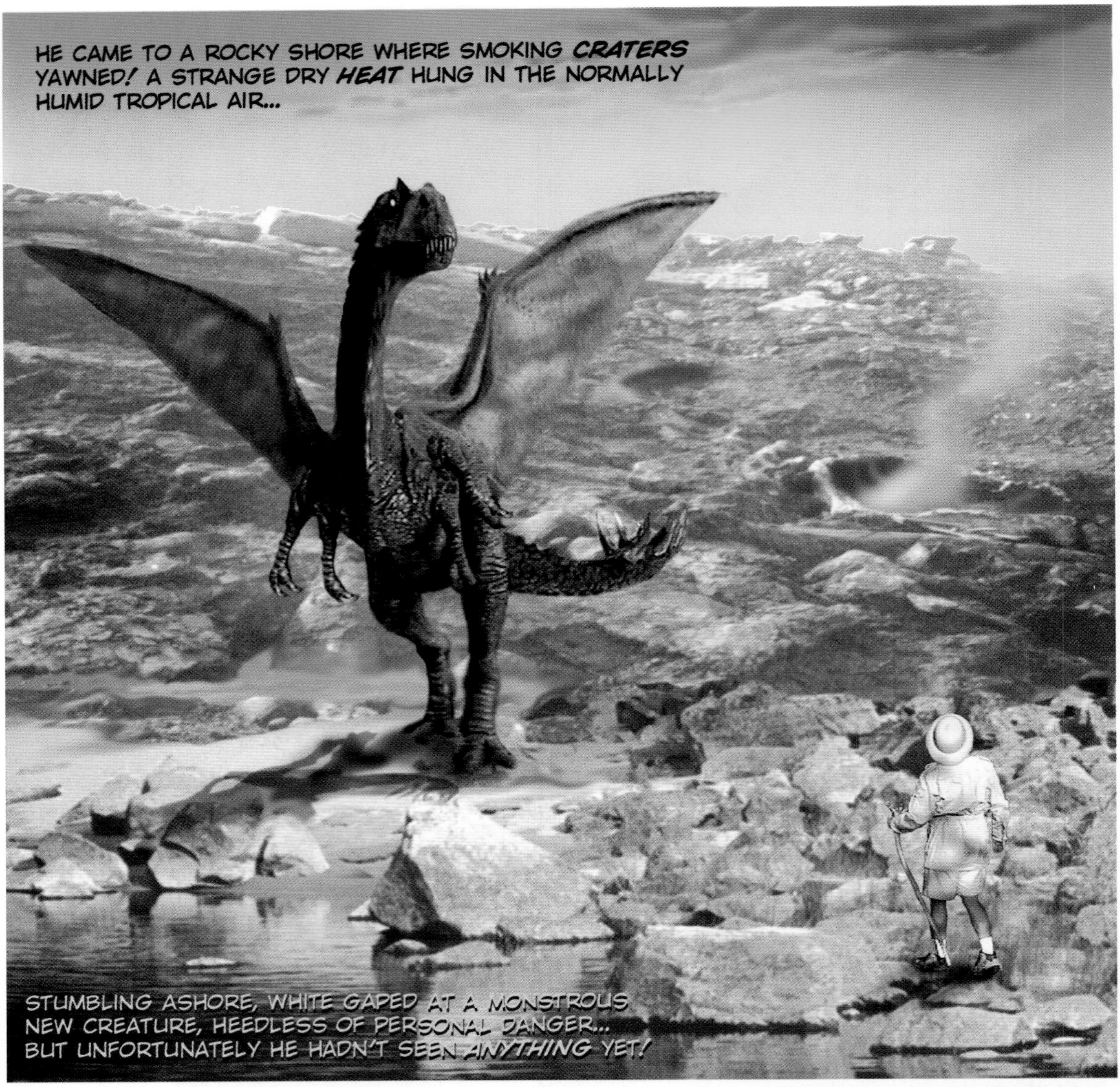
HE CAME TO A ROCKY SHORE WHERE SMOKING *CRATERS* YAWNED! A STRANGE DRY *HEAT* HUNG IN THE NORMALLY HUMID TROPICAL AIR...
STUMBLING ASHORE, WHITE GAPED AT A MONSTROUS NEW CREATURE, HEEDLESS OF PERSONAL DANGER... BUT UNFORTUNATELY HE HADN'T SEEN *ANYTHING* YET!

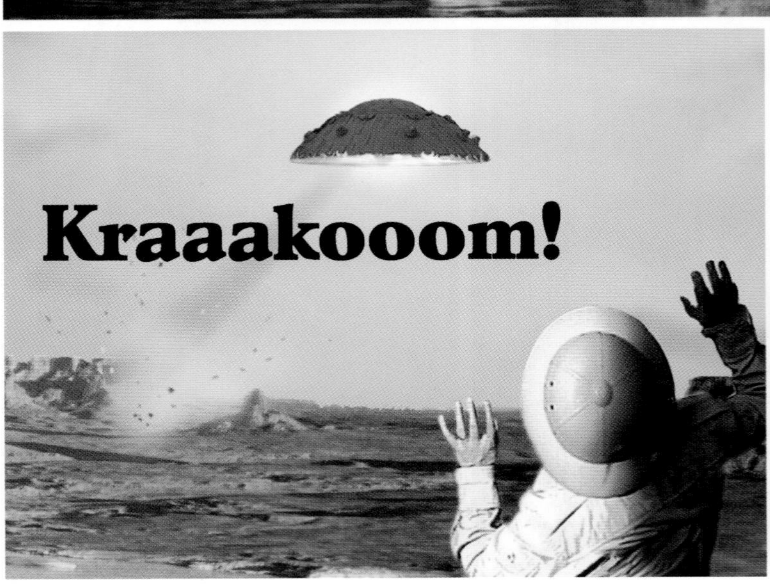
Kraaakooom!

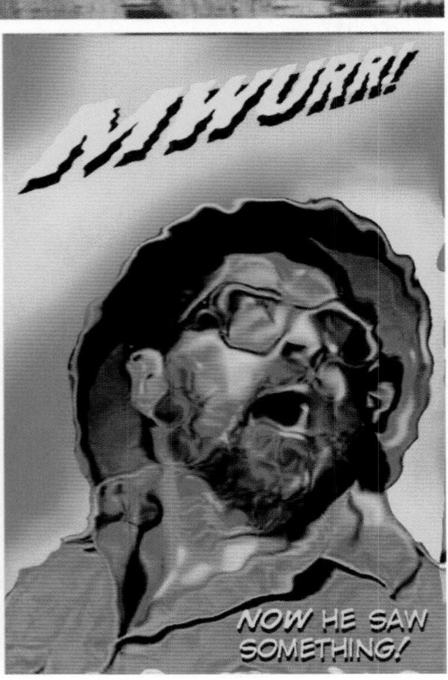
NOW HE SAW SOMETHING!

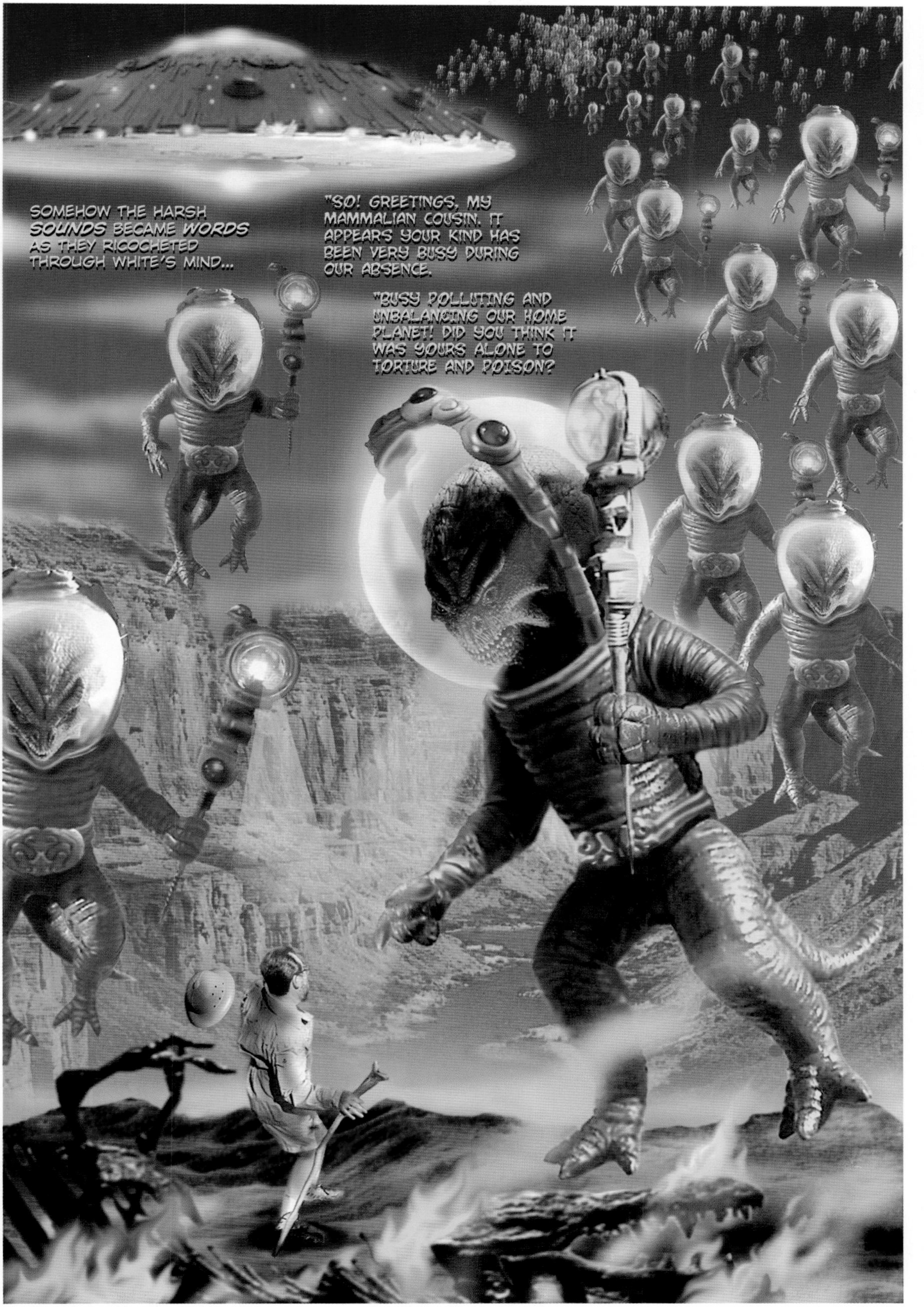
SOMEHOW THE HARSH *SOUNDS* BECAME *WORDS* AS THEY RICOCHETED THROUGH WHITE'S MIND...
"SO! GREETINGS, MY MAMMALIAN COUSIN. IT APPEARS YOUR KIND HAS BEEN VERY BUSY DURING OUR ABSENCE.
"BUSY POLLUTING AND UNBALANCING OUR HOME PLANET! DID YOU THINK IT WAS YOURS ALONE TO TORTURE AND POISON?

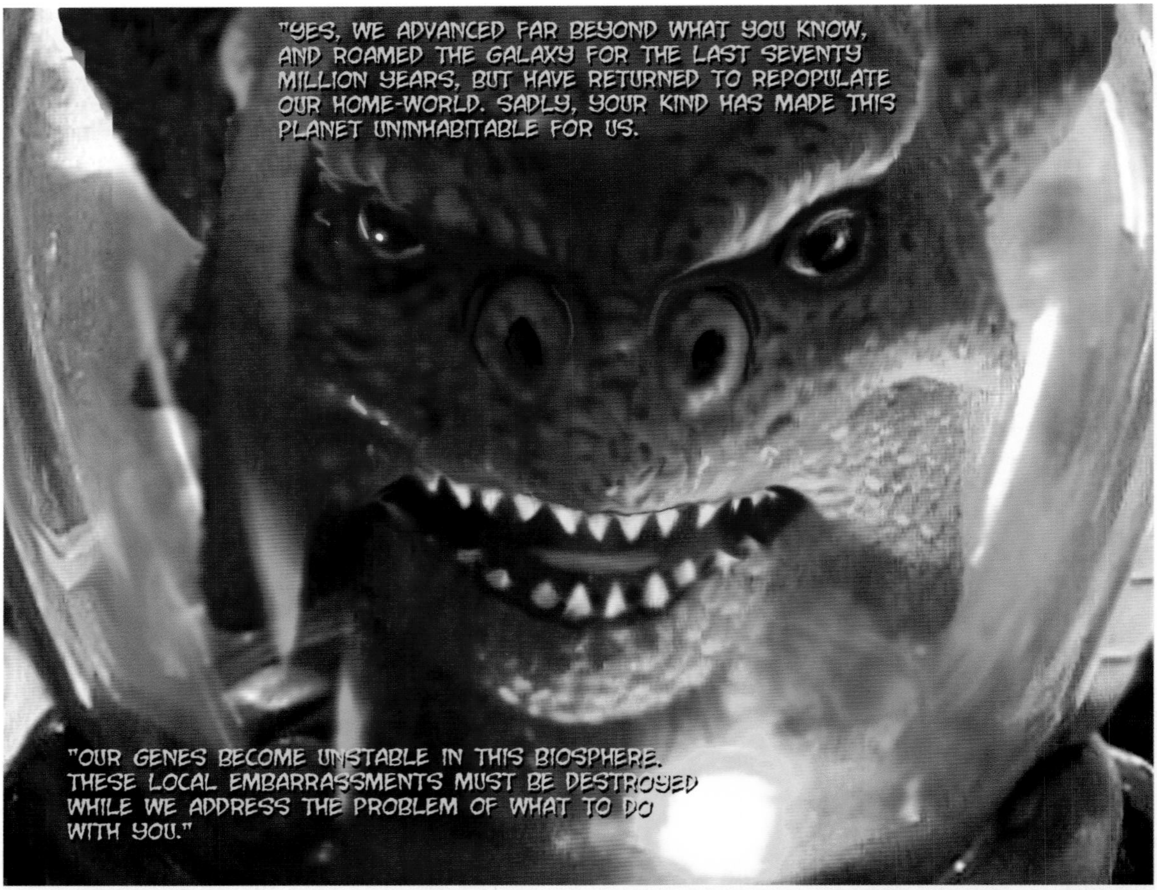
"YES, WE ADVANCED FAR BEYOND WHAT YOU KNOW, AND ROAMED THE GALAXY FOR THE LAST SEVENTY MILLION YEARS, BUT HAVE RETURNED TO REPOPULATE OUR HOME-WORLD. SADLY, YOUR KIND HAS MADE THIS PLANET UNINHABITABLE FOR US.
"OUR GENES BECOME UNSTABLE IN THIS BIOSPHERE. THESE LOCAL EMBARRASSMENTS MUST BE DESTROYED WHILE WE ADDRESS THE PROBLEM OF WHAT TO DO WITH YOU."

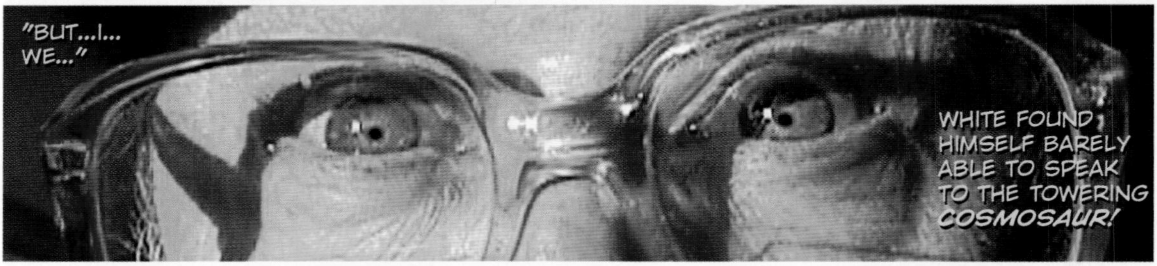
"BUT...I... WE..."
WHITE FOUND HIMSELF BARELY ABLE TO SPEAK TO THE TOWERING *COSMOSAUR!*

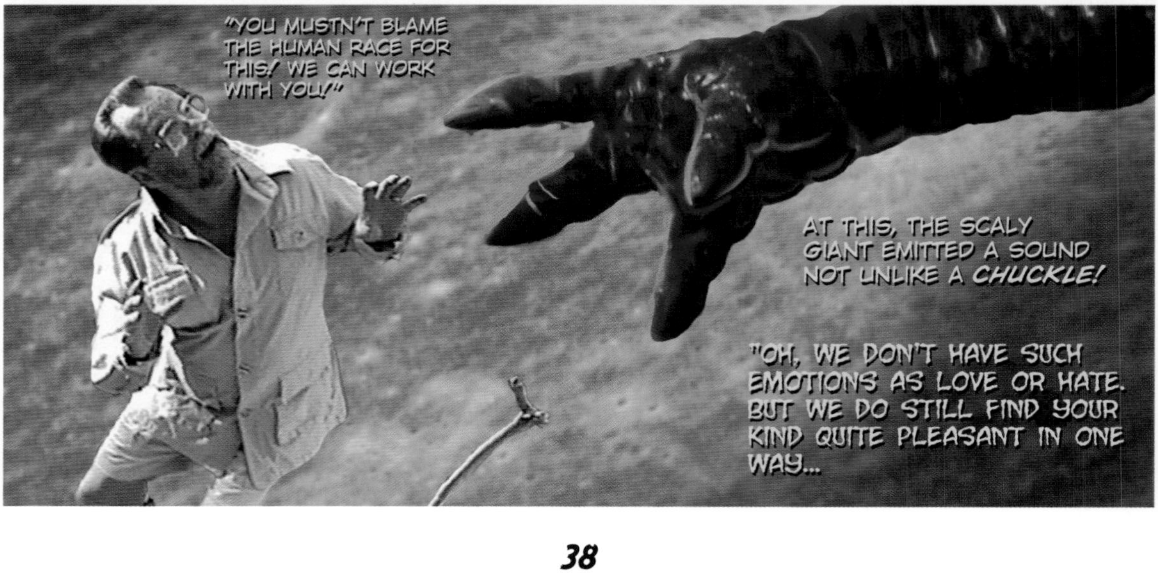
"YOU MUSTN'T BLAME THE HUMAN RACE FOR THIS! WE CAN WORK WITH YOU!"
AT THIS, THE SCALY GIANT EMITTED A SOUND NOT UNLIKE A *CHUCKLE!*
"OH, WE DON'T HAVE SUCH EMOTIONS AS LOVE OR HATE. BUT WE DO STILL FIND YOUR KIND QUITE PLEASANT IN ONE WAY...

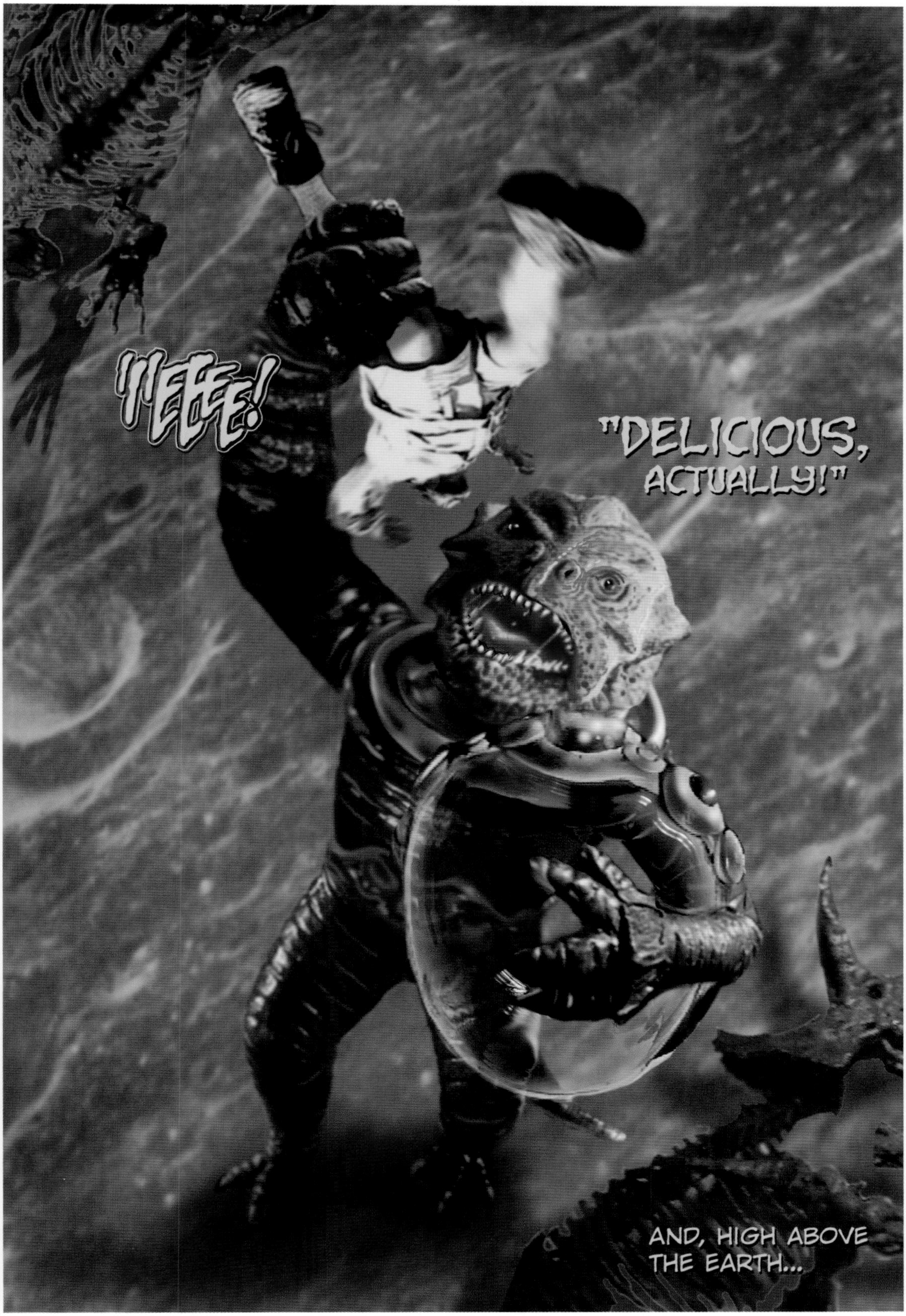

"EEEE!
"DELICIOUS, ACTUALLY!"
AND, HIGH ABOVE THE EARTH...

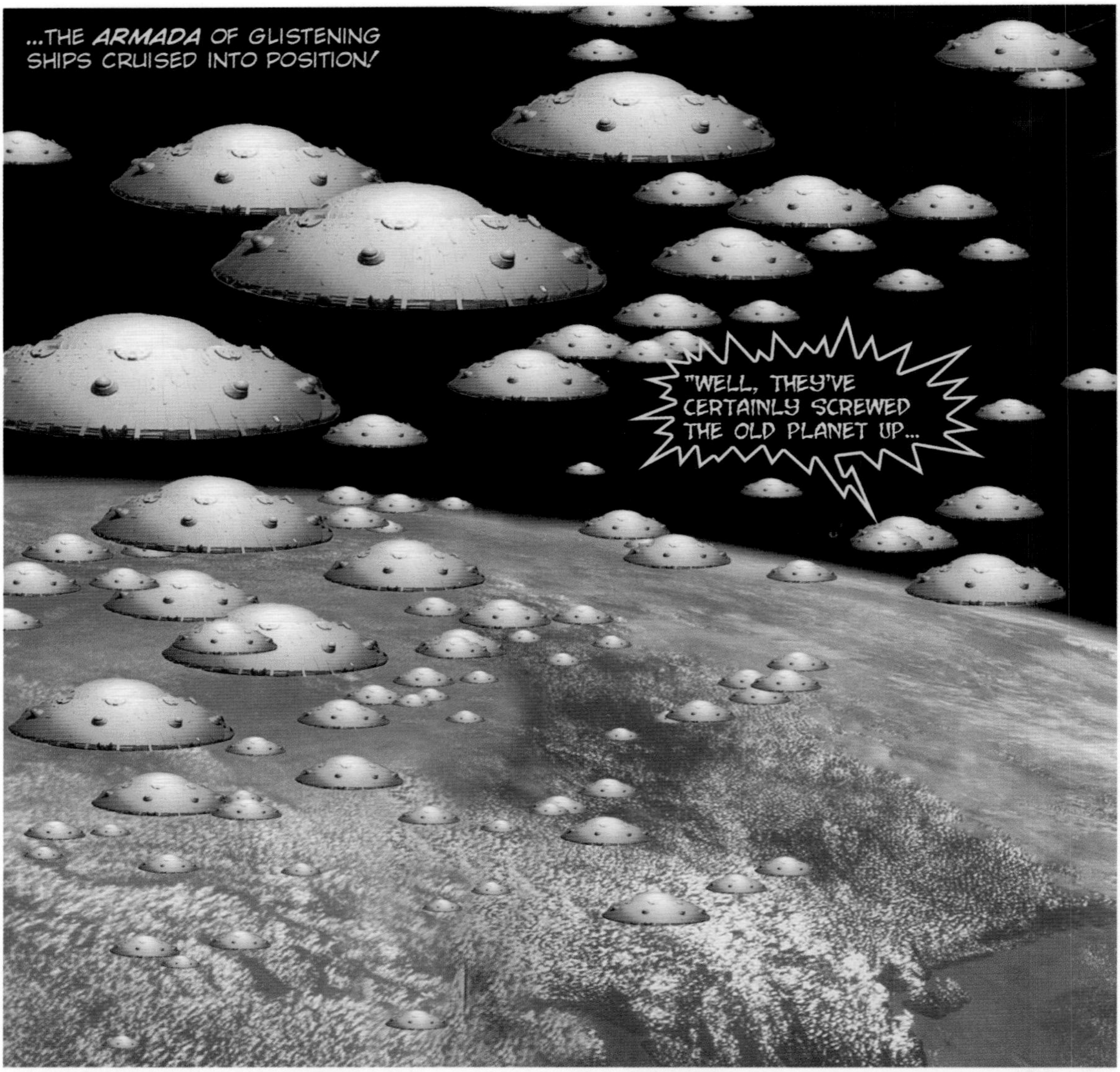
...THE *ARMADA* OF GLISTENING SHIPS CRUISED INTO POSITION!
"WELL, THEY'VE CERTAINLY SCREWED THE OLD PLANET UP...

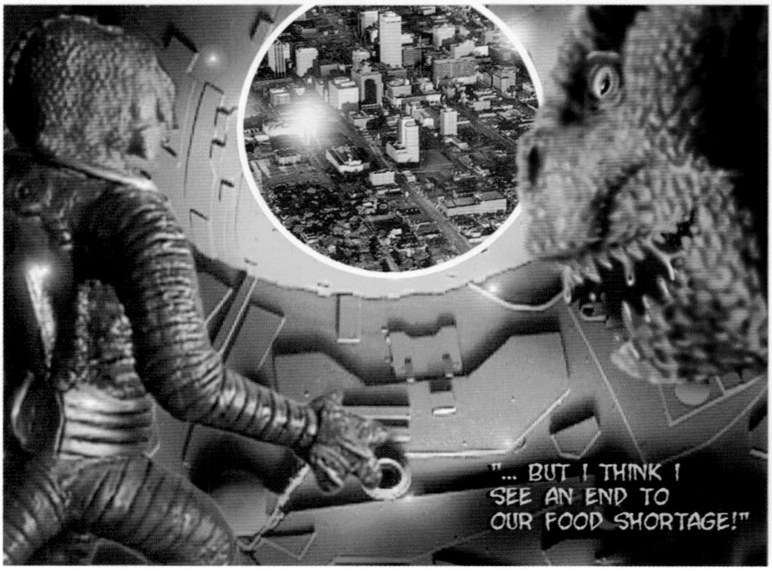
"... BUT I THINK I SEE AN END TO OUR FOOD SHORTAGE!"

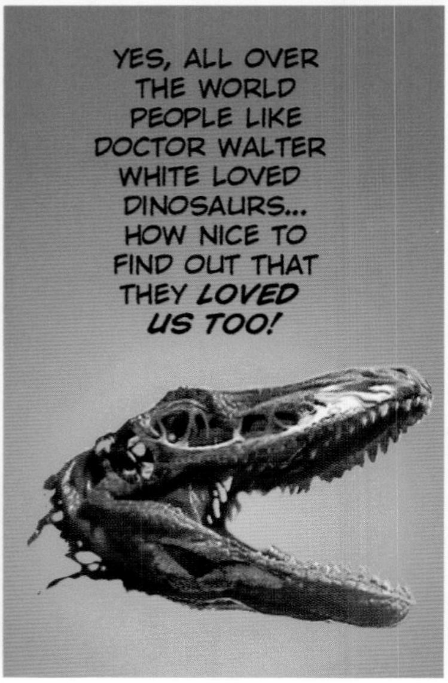
YES, ALL OVER THE WORLD PEOPLE LIKE DOCTOR WALTER WHITE LOVED DINOSAURS... HOW NICE TO FIND OUT THAT THEY *LOVED US TOO!*

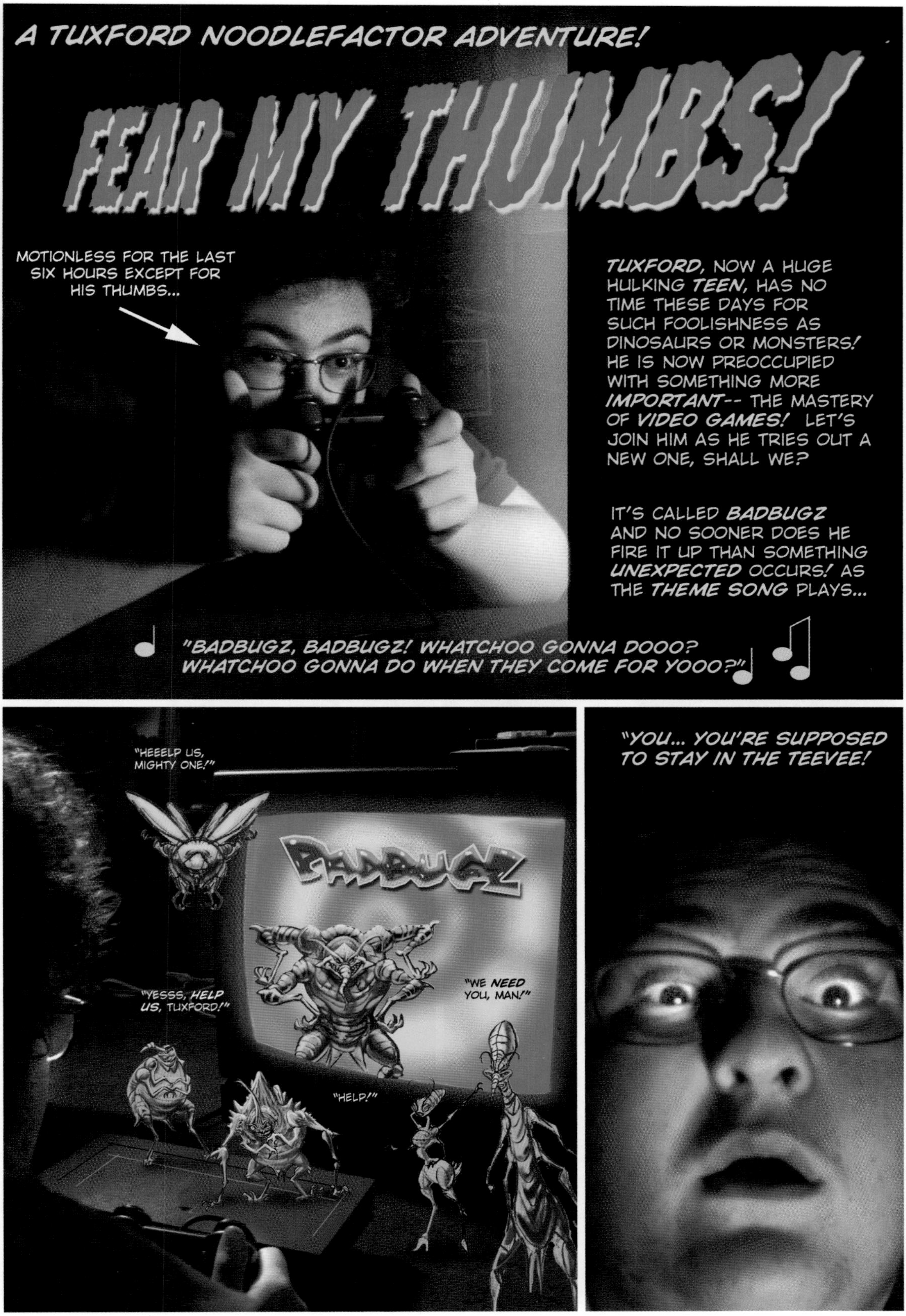
A TUXFORD NOODLEFACTOR ADVENTURE!
FEAR MY THUMBS!
MOTIONLESS FOR THE LAST SIX HOURS EXCEPT FOR HIS THUMBS...
TUXFORD, NOW A HUGE HULKING TEEN, HAS NO TIME THESE DAYS FOR SUCH FOOLISHNESS AS DINOSAURS OR MONSTERS! HE IS NOW PREOCCUPIED WITH SOMETHING MORE IMPORTANT-- THE MASTERY OF VIDEO GAMES! LET'S JOIN HIM AS HE TRIES OUT A NEW ONE, SHALL WE?
IT'S CALLED BADBUGZ AND NO SOONER DOES HE FIRE IT UP THAN SOMETHING UNEXPECTED OCCURS! AS THE THEME SONG PLAYS...
"BADBUGZ, BADBUGZ! WHATCHOO GONNA DOOO? WHATCHOO GONNA DO WHEN THEY COME FOR YOOO?"
"HEEELP US, MIGHTY ONE!"
BADBUGZ
"YESSS, HELP US, TUXFORD!"
"WE NEED YOU, MAN!"
"HELP!"
"YOU... YOU'RE SUPPOSED TO STAY IN THE TEEVEE!

"I MUST BE GOING MAD! HOW CAN THIS BE?"
"BUUGS IN THE SYSTEM!"
"BUUGS IN THE SYSTEM!"
"BUUGS IN THE SYSTEM!"
"COME INSIDE THE GAME AND SAVE US!"
"THE BOSS IS OUT OF CONTROL!"
"LOOK, BIG BOY! JUST PRESS THESE LIKE THIS!"
CLICK! CLICK!
"NOW WAIT JUST A SECOND YOU GUYS..."
"INTO THE TUBE, HURRY!"
"BUT... BUT..."
BVVVVT!
"EEEYOW!"
"HUP!"
"ALLEY OOP!"

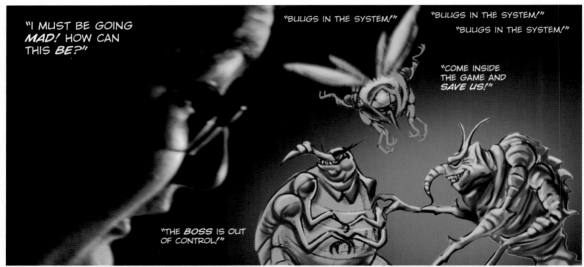

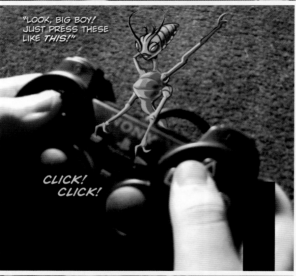

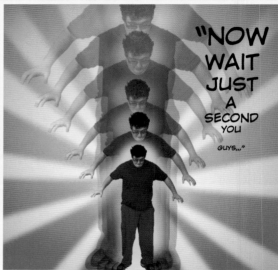

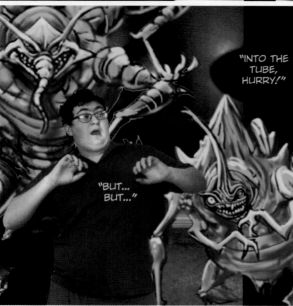

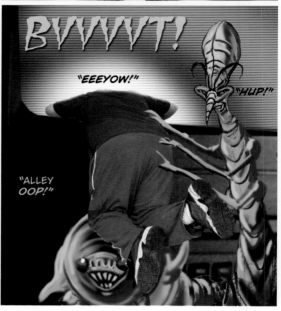

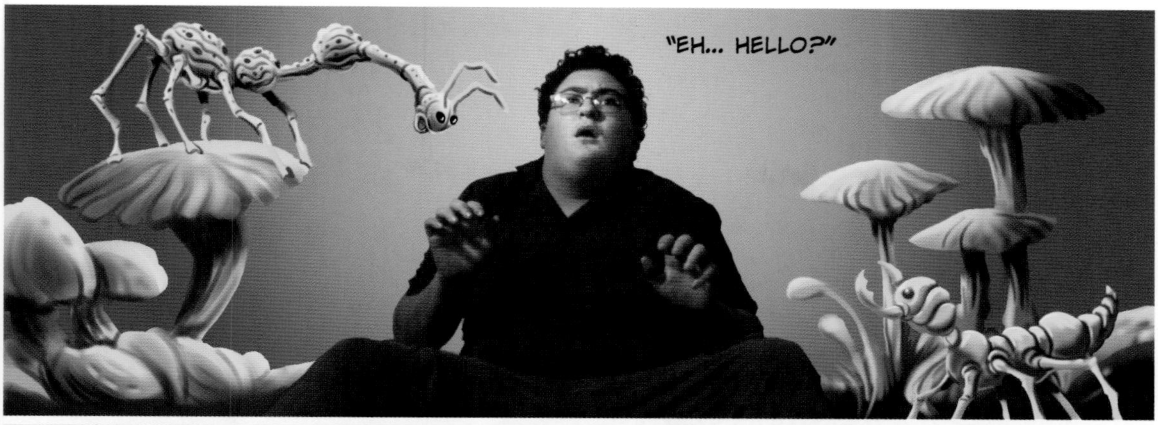
"EH... HELLO?"

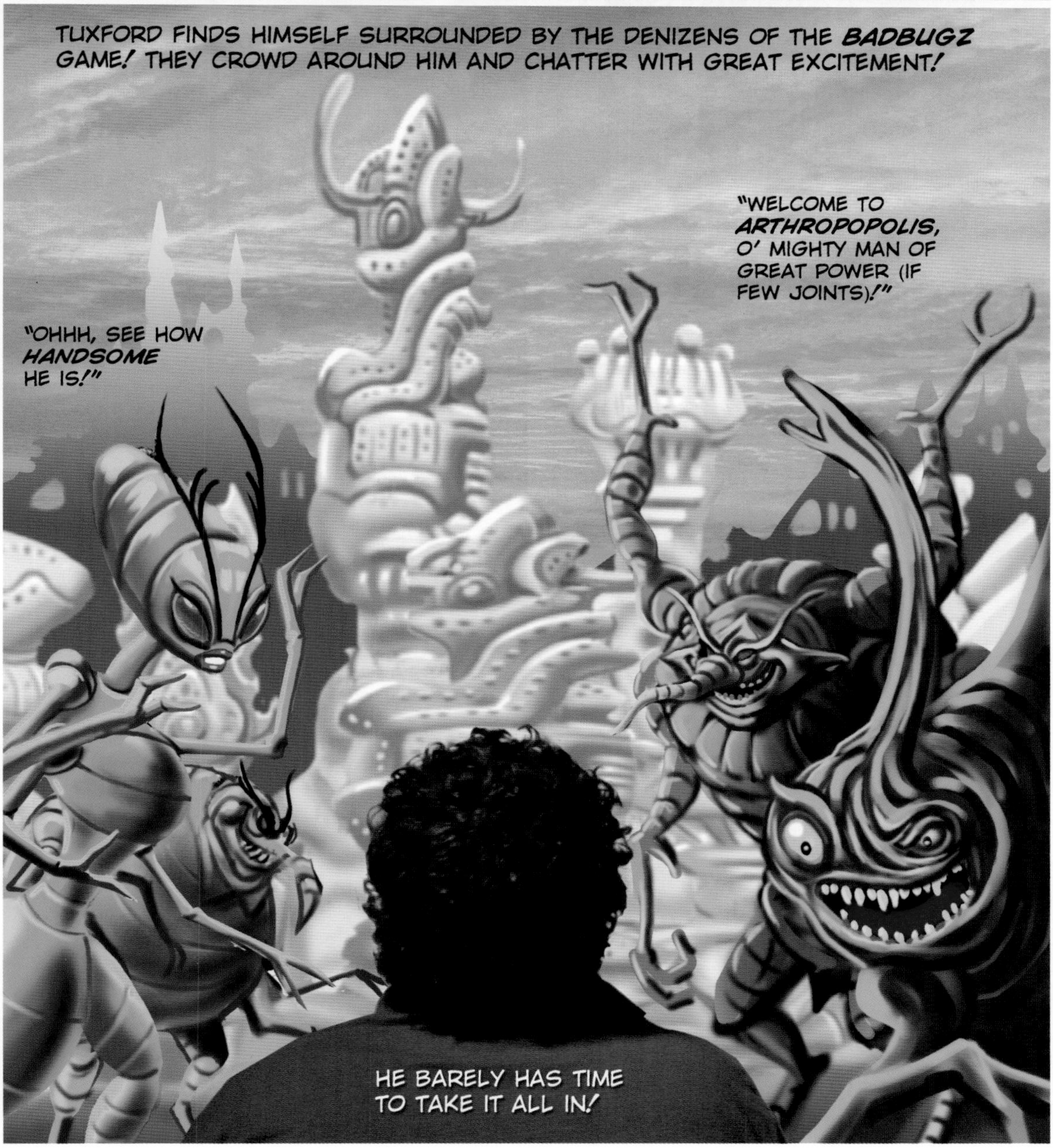
TUXFORD FINDS HIMSELF SURROUNDED BY THE DENIZENS OF THE BADBUGZ GAME! THEY CROWD AROUND HIM AND CHATTER WITH GREAT EXCITEMENT!
"WELCOME TO ARTHROPOPOLIS, O' MIGHTY MAN OF GREAT POWER (IF FEW JOINTS)!"
"OHHH, SEE HOW HANDSOME HE IS!"
HE BARELY HAS TIME TO TAKE IT ALL IN!

THEY TELL HIM OF THE *SLAG BEETLE* WHO'S TERRORIZED THEM FOR YEARS.

AND HOW THE GREAT *CECIL B. DE MILLIPEDE* WEIGHED IN-- "FIND US A *CHAMPION!*"

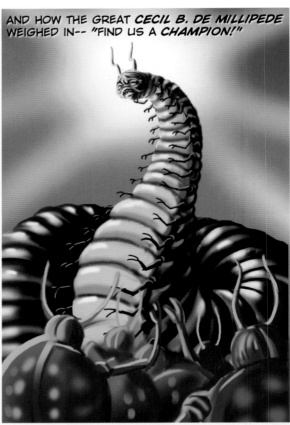

FAR AND WIDE THE *MOSQUITOPOIDS* FLEW, SCANNING THE HORIZONS...

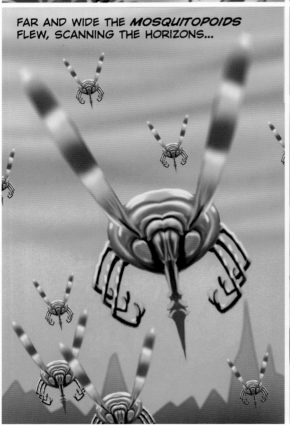

EVEN THE *STILTSPIDERS* JOINED THE QUEST...

FINALLY THEY SPOTTED *TUXFORD* AND SENT THE DELEGATION OUT TO *BRING HIM IN!*

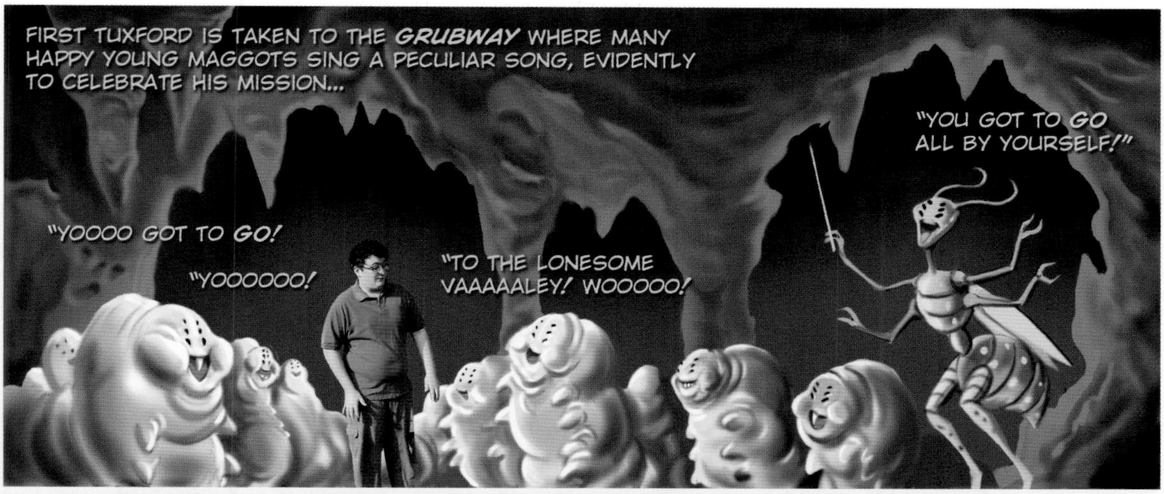
FIRST TUXFORD IS TAKEN TO THE *GRUBWAY* WHERE MANY HAPPY YOUNG MAGGOTS SING A PECULIAR SONG, EVIDENTLY TO CELEBRATE HIS MISSION...
"YOOOO GOT TO *GO!*
"YOOOOOO!
"TO THE LONESOME VAAAAALEY! WOOOOO!
"YOU GOT TO *GO* ALL BY YOURSELF!"

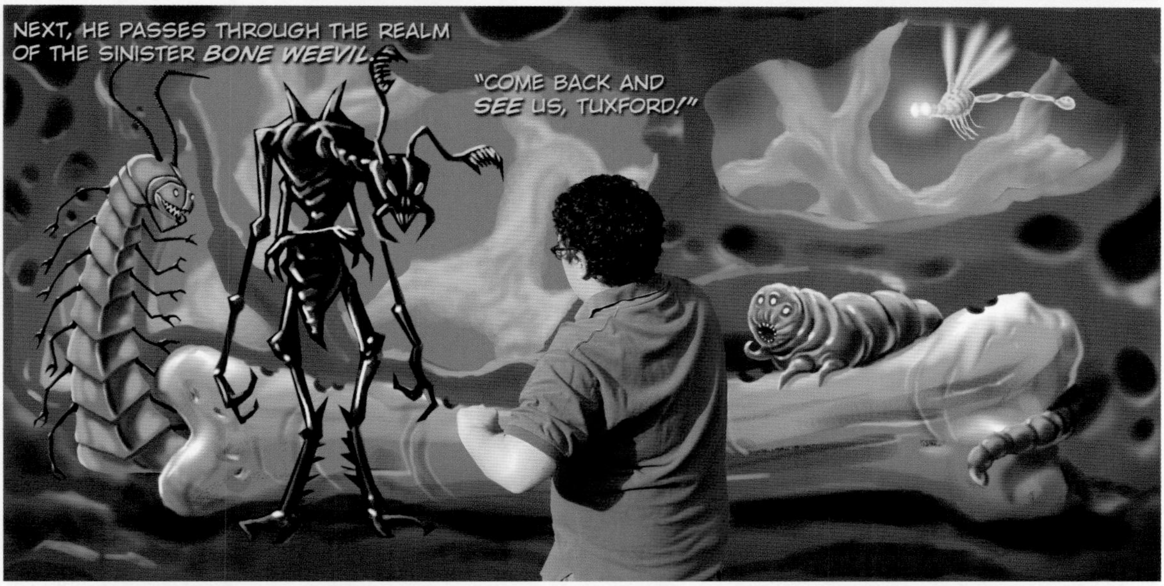
NEXT, HE PASSES THROUGH THE REALM OF THE SINISTER *BONE WEEVIL*...
"COME BACK AND *SEE* US, TUXFORD!"

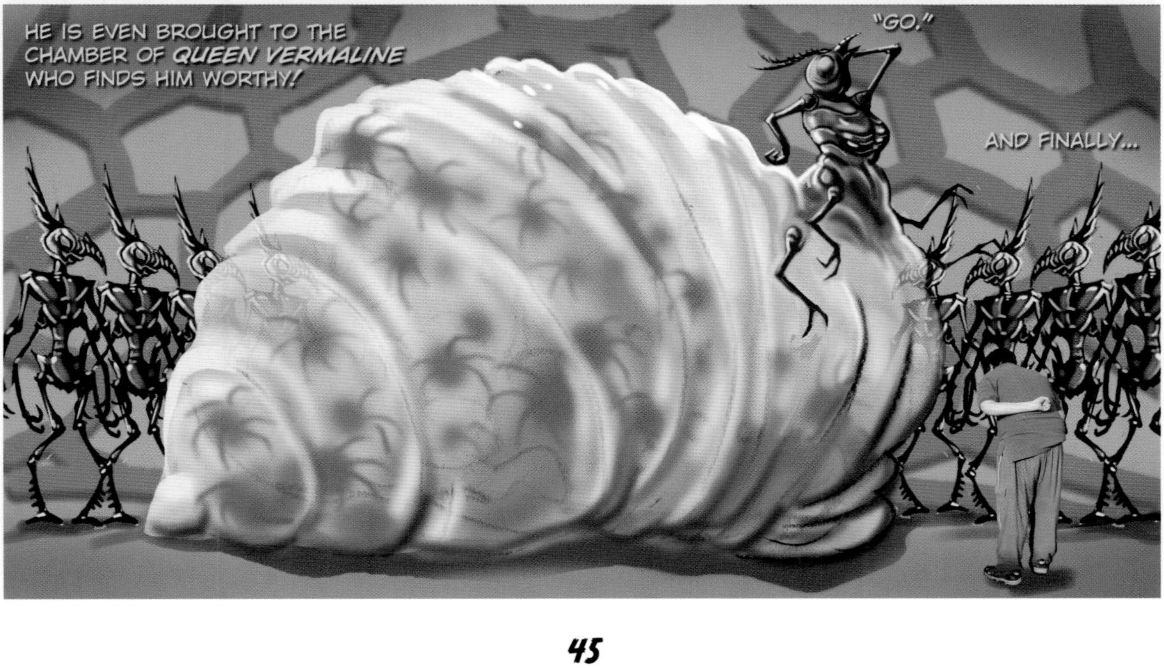
HE IS EVEN BROUGHT TO THE CHAMBER OF *QUEEN VERMALINE* WHO FINDS HIM WORTHY!
"GO."
AND FINALLY...

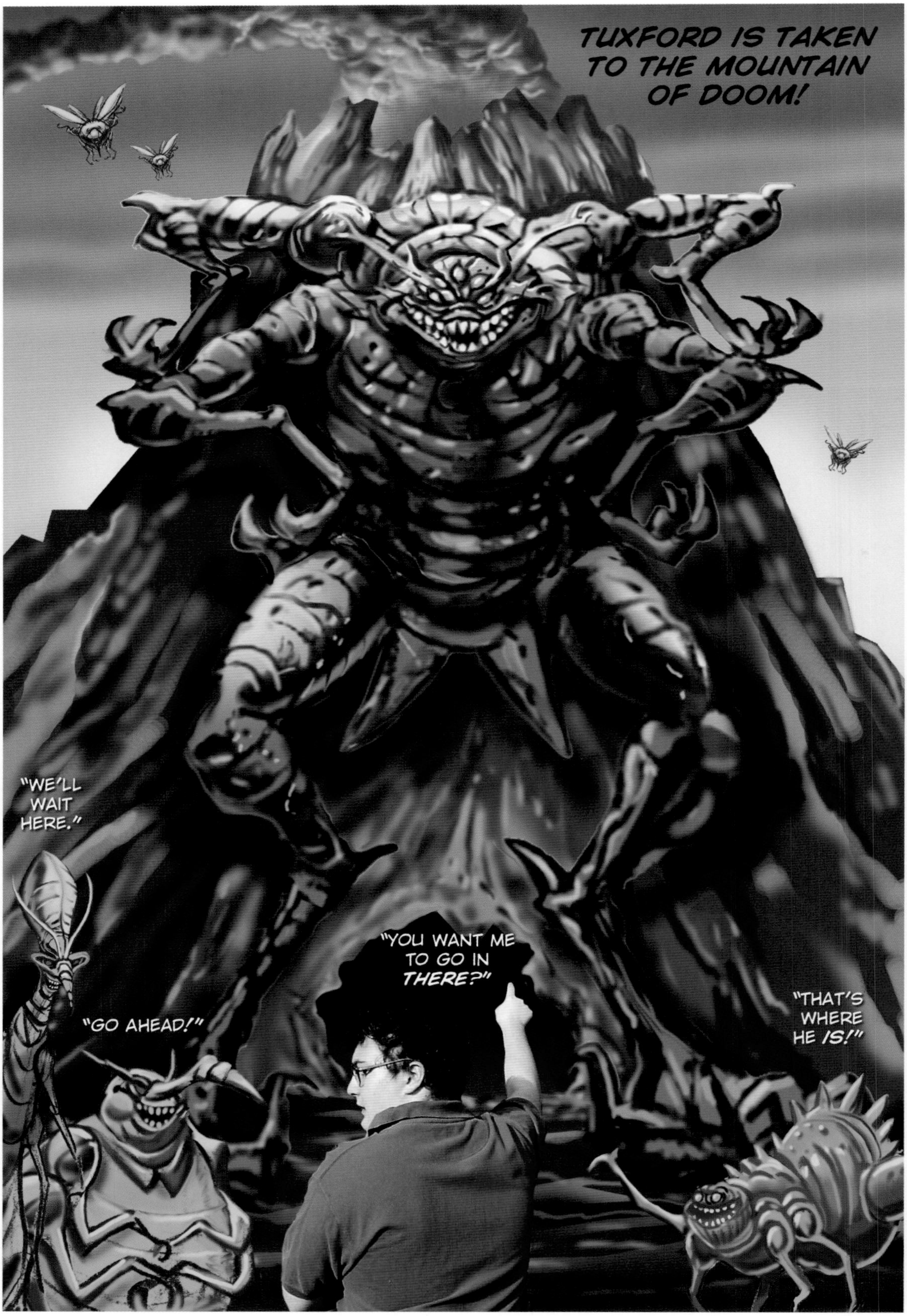
TUXFORD IS TAKEN TO THE MOUNTAIN OF DOOM!
"WE'LL WAIT HERE."
"GO AHEAD!"
"YOU WANT ME TO GO IN *THERE?*"
"THAT'S WHERE HE *IS!*"

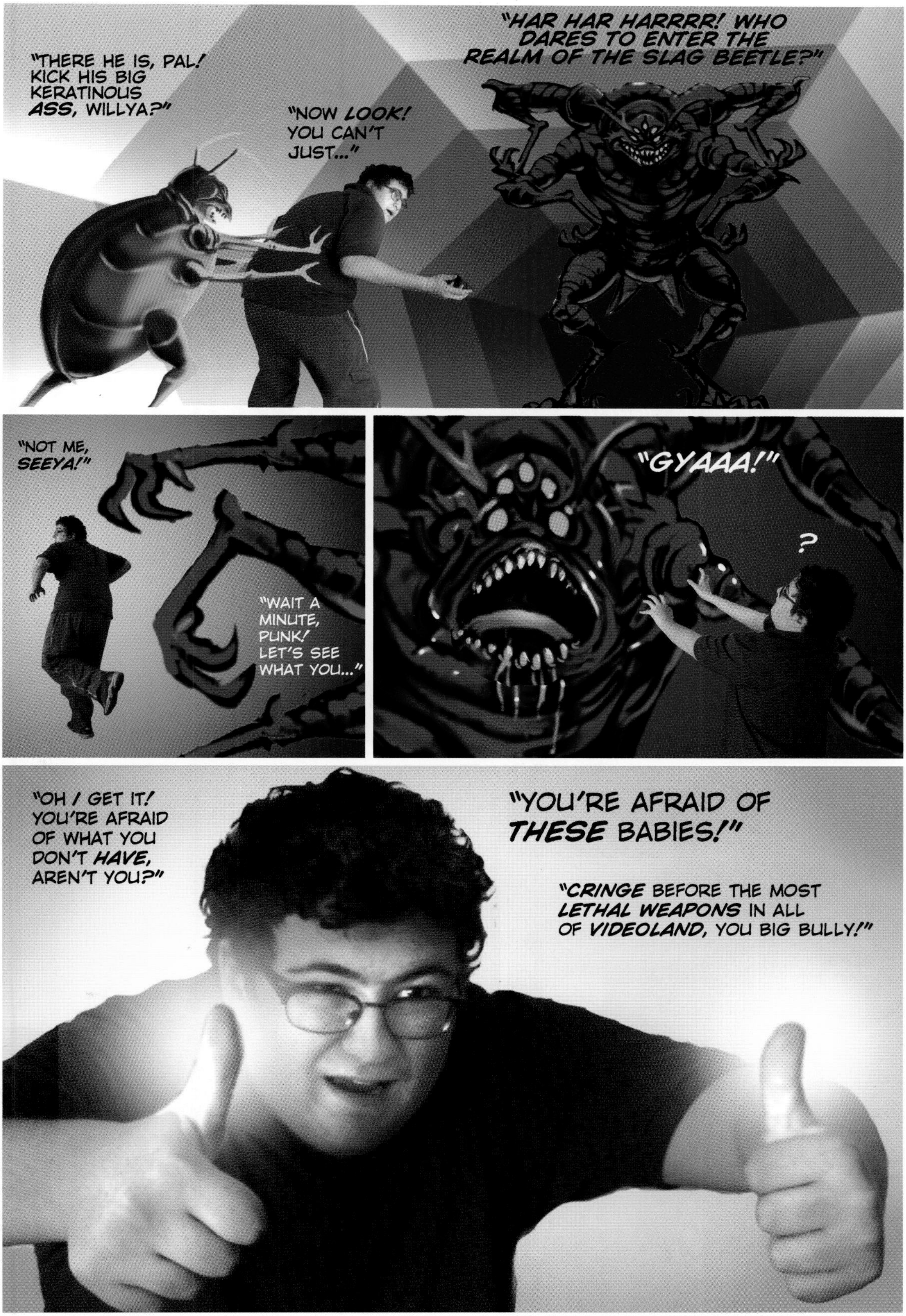

"THERE HE IS, PAL! KICK HIS BIG KERATINOUS ASS, WILLYA?"
"NOW LOOK! YOU CAN'T JUST..."
"HAR HAR HARRRR! WHO DARES TO ENTER THE REALM OF THE SLAG BEETLE?"
"NOT ME, SEEYA!"
"WAIT A MINUTE, PUNK! LET'S SEE WHAT YOU..."
"GYAAA!"
?
"OH I GET IT! YOU'RE AFRAID OF WHAT YOU DON'T HAVE, AREN'T YOU?"
"YOU'RE AFRAID OF THESE BABIES!"
"CRINGE BEFORE THE MOST LETHAL WEAPONS IN ALL OF VIDEOLAND, YOU BIG BULLY!"

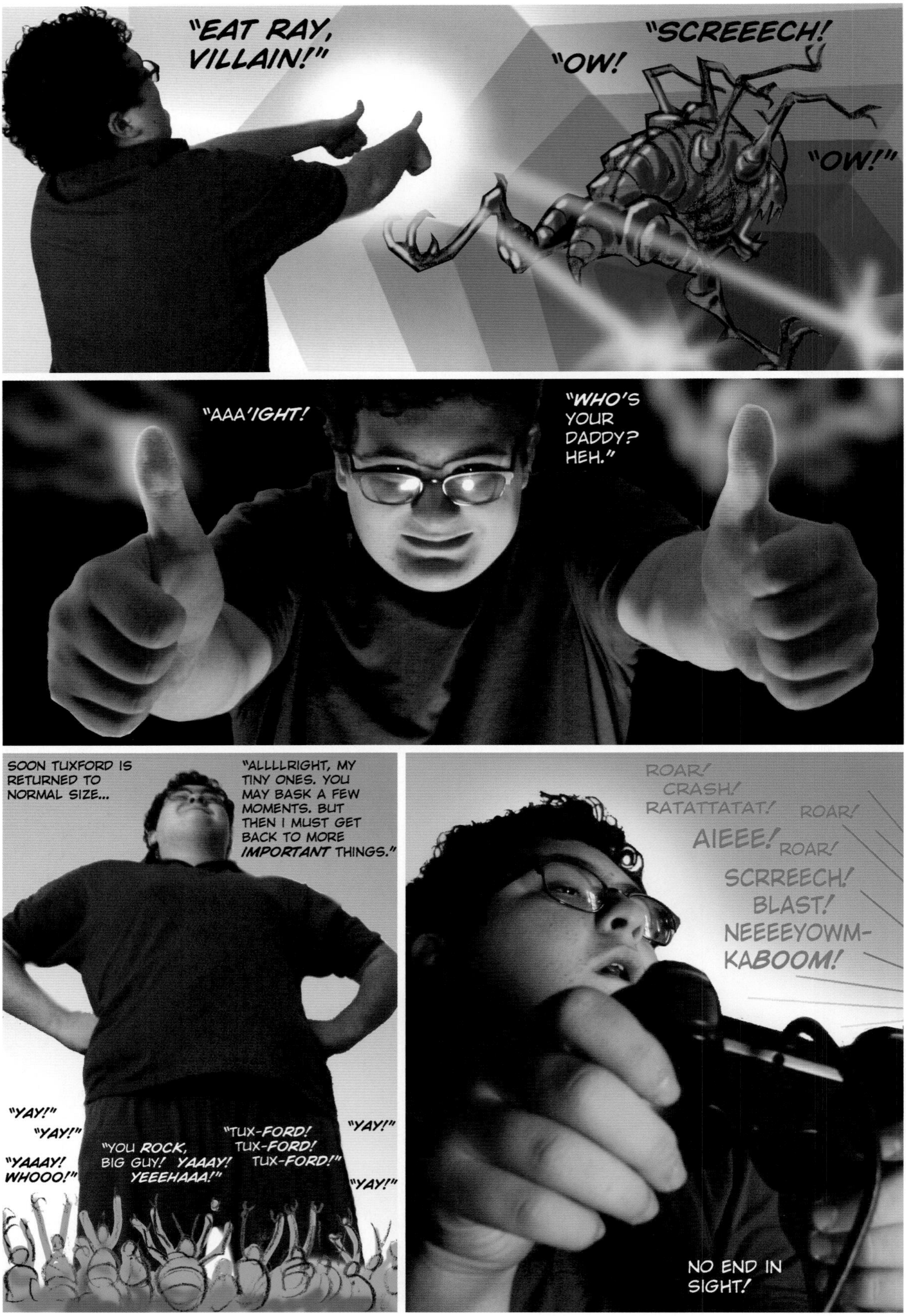
"EAT RAY, VILLAIN!"
"OW!
"SCREEECH!
"OW!"
"AAA'IGHT!
"WHO'S YOUR DADDY? HEH."
SOON TUXFORD IS RETURNED TO NORMAL SIZE...
"ALLLLRIGHT, MY TINY ONES. YOU MAY BASK A FEW MOMENTS. BUT THEN I MUST GET BACK TO MORE IMPORTANT THINGS."
"YAY!"
"YAY!"
"YAAAY! WHOOO!"
"YOU ROCK, BIG GUY! YAAAY! YEEEHAAA!"
"TUX-FORD! TUX-FORD! TUX-FORD!"
"YAY!"
"YAY!"
ROAR! CRASH! RATATTATAT!
ROAR!
AIEEE!
ROAR!
SCRREECH!
BLAST!
NEEEEYOWM-KABOOM!
NO END IN SIGHT!

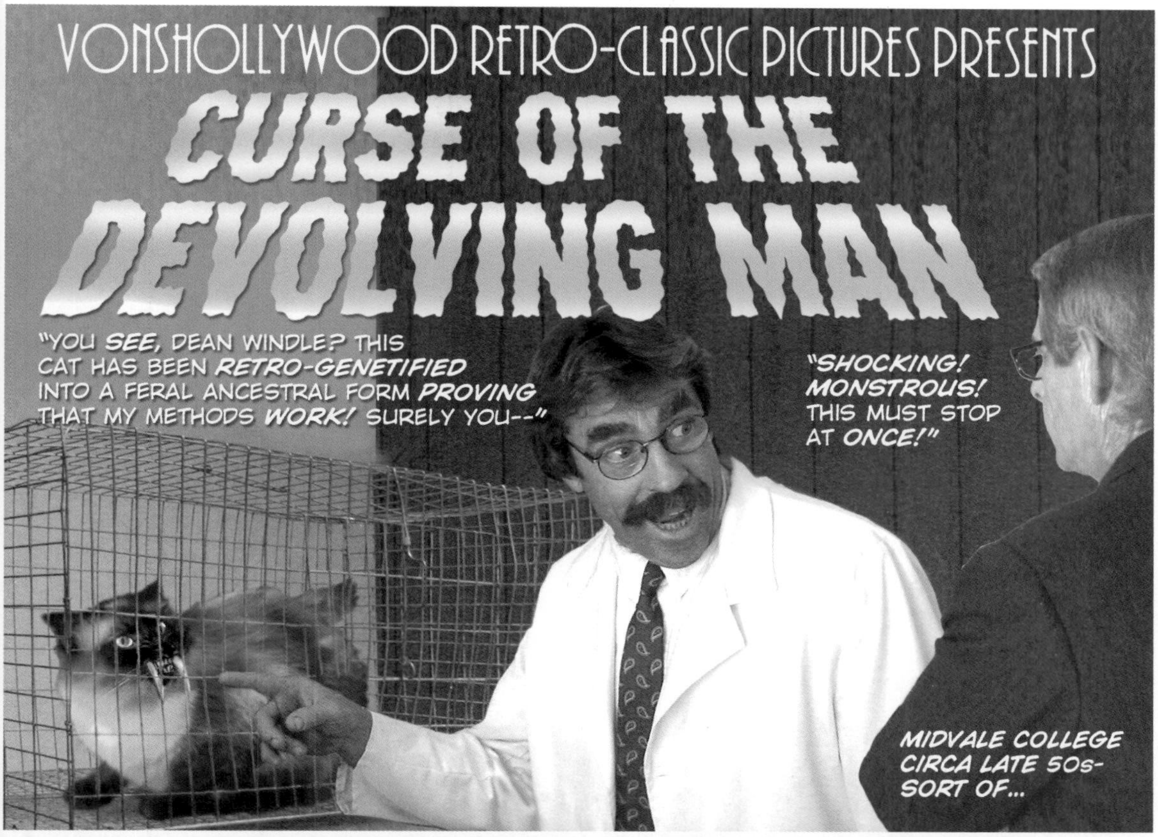
VONSHOLLYWOOD RETRO-CLASSIC PICTURES PRESENTS
CURSE OF THE DEVOLVING MAN
"YOU SEE, DEAN WINDLE? THIS CAT HAS BEEN RETRO-GENETIFIED INTO A FERAL ANCESTRAL FORM PROVING THAT MY METHODS WORK! SURELY YOU--"
"SHOCKING! MONSTROUS! THIS MUST STOP AT ONCE!"
MIDVALE COLLEGE CIRCA LATE 50s-SORT OF...

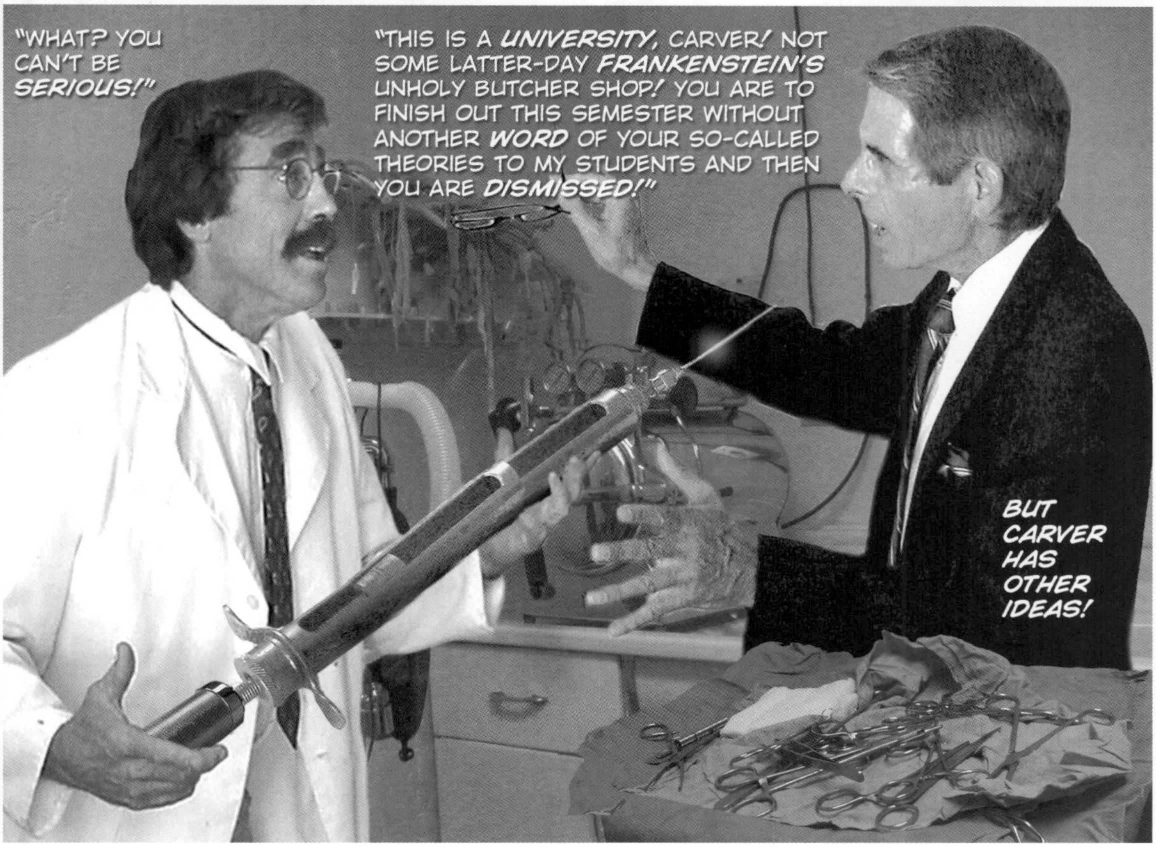
"WHAT? YOU CAN'T BE SERIOUS!"
"THIS IS A UNIVERSITY, CARVER! NOT SOME LATTER-DAY FRANKENSTEIN'S UNHOLY BUTCHER SHOP! YOU ARE TO FINISH OUT THIS SEMESTER WITHOUT ANOTHER WORD OF YOUR SO-CALLED THEORIES TO MY STUDENTS AND THEN YOU ARE DISMISSED!"
BUT CARVER HAS OTHER IDEAS!

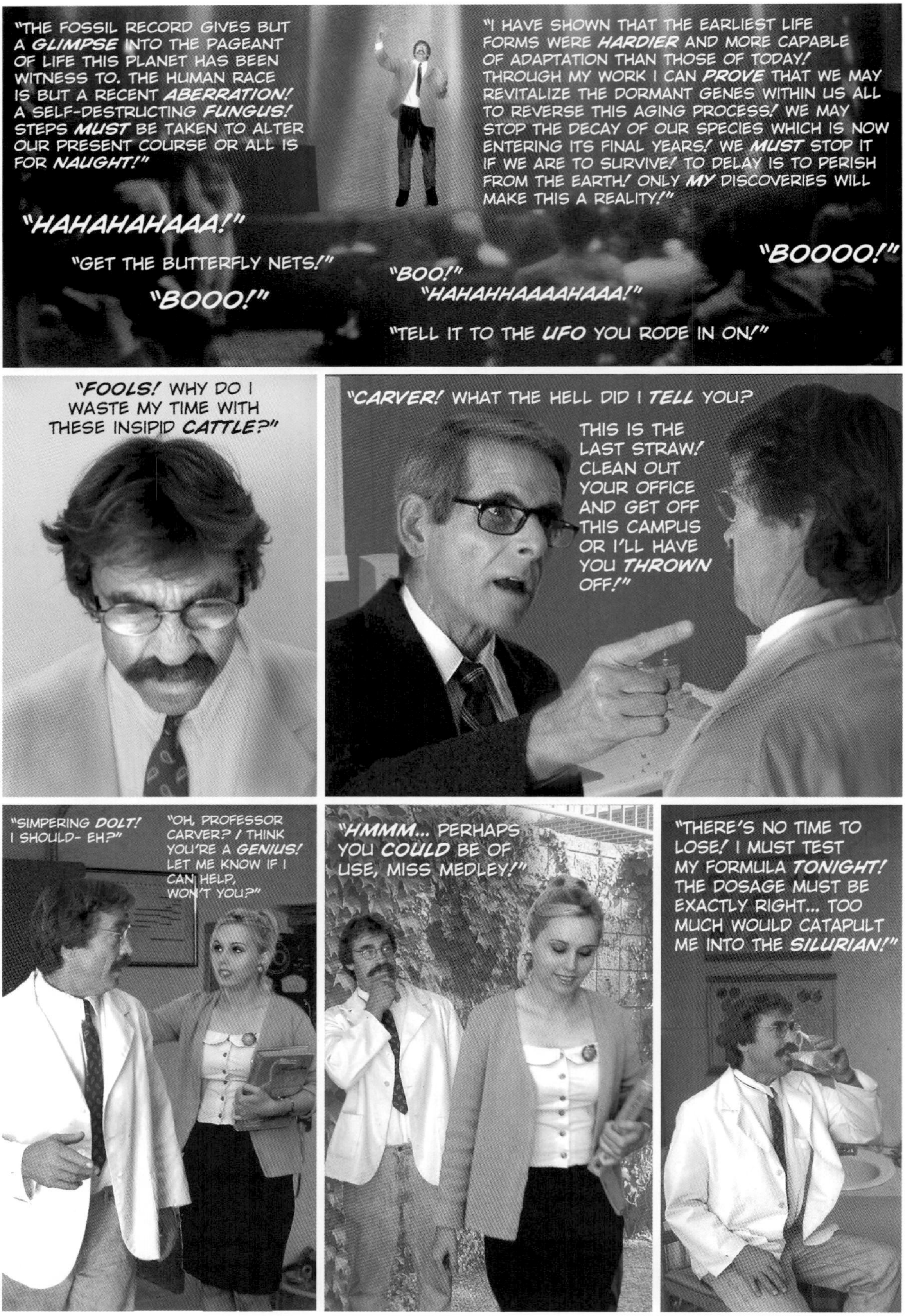
"THE FOSSIL RECORD GIVES BUT A GLIMPSE INTO THE PAGEANT OF LIFE THIS PLANET HAS BEEN WITNESS TO. THE HUMAN RACE IS BUT A RECENT ABERRATION! A SELF-DESTRUCTING FUNGUS! STEPS MUST BE TAKEN TO ALTER OUR PRESENT COURSE OR ALL IS FOR NAUGHT!"
"I HAVE SHOWN THAT THE EARLIEST LIFE FORMS WERE HARDIER AND MORE CAPABLE OF ADAPTATION THAN THOSE OF TODAY! THROUGH MY WORK I CAN PROVE THAT WE MAY REVITALIZE THE DORMANT GENES WITHIN US ALL TO REVERSE THIS AGING PROCESS! WE MAY STOP THE DECAY OF OUR SPECIES WHICH IS NOW ENTERING ITS FINAL YEARS! WE MUST STOP IT IF WE ARE TO SURVIVE! TO DELAY IS TO PERISH FROM THE EARTH! ONLY MY DISCOVERIES WILL MAKE THIS A REALITY!"
"HAHAHAHAAA!"
"GET THE BUTTERFLY NETS!"
"BOOO!"
"BOO!"
"HAHAHHAAAAHAAA!"
"BOOOO!"
"TELL IT TO THE UFO YOU RODE IN ON!"
"FOOLS! WHY DO I WASTE MY TIME WITH THESE INSIPID CATTLE?"
"CARVER! WHAT THE HELL DID I TELL YOU?
THIS IS THE LAST STRAW! CLEAN OUT YOUR OFFICE AND GET OFF THIS CAMPUS OR I'LL HAVE YOU THROWN OFF!"
"SIMPERING DOLT! I SHOULD- EH?"
"OH, PROFESSOR CARVER? I THINK YOU'RE A GENIUS! LET ME KNOW IF I CAN HELP, WON'T YOU?"
"HMMM... PERHAPS YOU COULD BE OF USE, MISS MEDLEY!"
"THERE'S NO TIME TO LOSE! I MUST TEST MY FORMULA TONIGHT! THE DOSAGE MUST BE EXACTLY RIGHT... TOO MUCH WOULD CATAPULT ME INTO THE SILURIAN!"

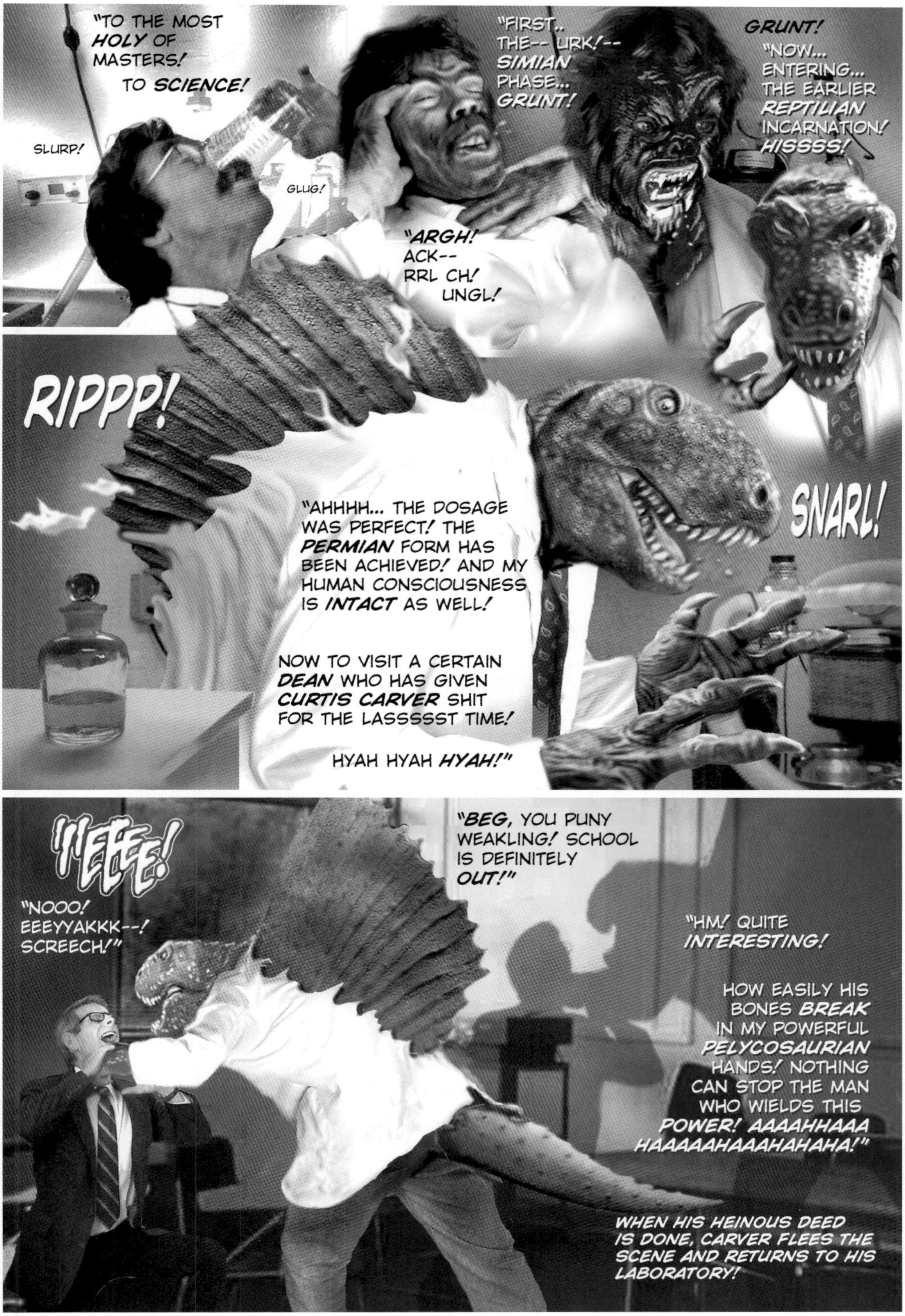
"TO THE MOST HOLY OF MASTERS! TO SCIENCE!
SLURP!
GLUG!
"FIRST.. THE-- URK!-- SIMIAN PHASE... GRUNT!
GRUNT!
"NOW... ENTERING... THE EARLIER REPTILIAN INCARNATION! HISSSS!
"ARGH! ACK-- RRL CH! UNGL!
RIPPP!
SNARL!
"AHHHH... THE DOSAGE WAS PERFECT! THE PERMIAN FORM HAS BEEN ACHIEVED! AND MY HUMAN CONSCIOUSNESS IS INTACT AS WELL!
NOW TO VISIT A CERTAIN DEAN WHO HAS GIVEN CURTIS CARVER SHIT FOR THE LASSSSST TIME!
HYAH HYAH HYAH!"
"BEG, YOU PUNY WEAKLING! SCHOOL IS DEFINITELY OUT!"
"NOOO! EEEYYAKKK--! SCREECH!"
"HM! QUITE INTERESTING!
HOW EASILY HIS BONES BREAK IN MY POWERFUL PELYCOSAURIAN HANDS! NOTHING CAN STOP THE MAN WHO WIELDS THIS POWER! AAAAHHAAA HAAAAAHAAAHAHAHA!"
WHEN HIS HEINOUS DEED IS DONE, CARVER FLEES THE SCENE AND RETURNS TO HIS LABORATORY!

"UUUUNNNNGGGGHHHHH.....

HOW MANY HOURS
HAVE I BEEN ASLEEP...?
OH... MY *HEAD!*

"LET'S SEE...
DRANK FORMULA...
CHANGED PHYSICAL
STRUCTURE... TORE
DEAN LIMB FROM
LIMB...! IT'S ALL
GOOD. I'M A *GENIUS!*"

"URGH... PRIMITIVE
URGES SURFACING...
WHERE'S THAT *GIRL*
ANYWAY?"

"SO, WOULD YOU
LIKE TO GO TO
THE *DANCE?*"

"TEE HEE! OH,
I'D LIKE THAT,
MITCHIE!"

"SO! A *BOYFRIEND,*
EH? TRAITOROUS
WRETCH! WE'LL
JUST *SEE*
ABOUT THAT.

"PERHAPS JUST A
TEENY BIT *STRONGER*
DOSE THIS TIME..."

"AAAARGH! I MUST BE
MORE SENSITIVE NOW! THE
RETROGRESSION IS WORKING
FASTER!"

ROOOAR!

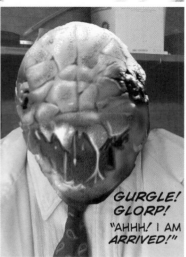

GURGLE!
GLORP!
"AHHH! I AM
ARRIVED!"

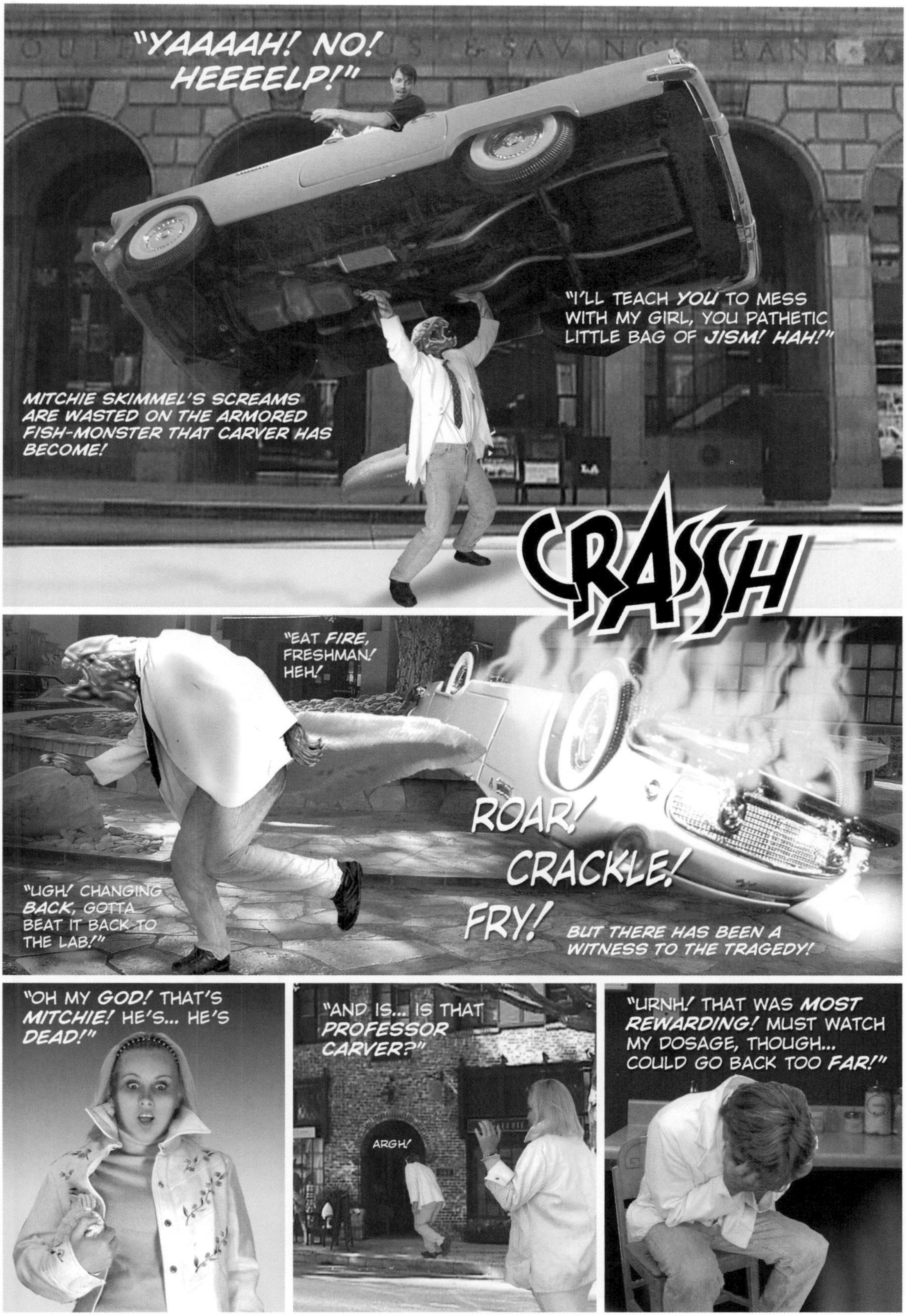
"YAAAAH! NO! HEEEELP!"
"I'LL TEACH YOU TO MESS WITH MY GIRL, YOU PATHETIC LITTLE BAG OF JISM! HAH!"
MITCHIE SKIMMEL'S SCREAMS ARE WASTED ON THE ARMORED FISH-MONSTER THAT CARVER HAS BECOME!
CRASH
"EAT FIRE, FRESHMAN! HEH!
ROAR! CRACKLE! FRY!
"UGH! CHANGING BACK, GOTTA BEAT IT BACK TO THE LAB!"
BUT THERE HAS BEEN A WITNESS TO THE TRAGEDY!
"OH MY GOD! THAT'S MITCHIE! HE'S... HE'S DEAD!"
"AND IS... IS THAT PROFESSOR CARVER?"
ARGH!
"URNH! THAT WAS MOST REWARDING! MUST WATCH MY DOSAGE, THOUGH... COULD GO BACK TOO FAR!"

DAYS LATER, MARY MEDLEY ACCOSTS CARVER AT THE CEMETERY...

"HI, PROFESSOR! SAY, MAYBE YOU COULD USE MY *HELP* WITH SOME OF YOUR GREAT EXPERIMENTS?"

"I COULD *USE* SOME ACTIVITY TO HELP GET OVER ALL THESE *KILLINGS!*"

"WHY, CERTAINLY, MY DEAR MISS MEDLEY."

"AN INTELLIGENT AND ATTRACTIVE YOUNG LADY LIKE YOU WOULD BE A GREAT PLEASURE TO HAVE AROUND! AND YOU'RE ALSO MY TOP *BIOLOGY* STUDENT!"

"STEP RIGHT IN HERE..."

"WHAT? A *GUN!* WHAT ARE YOU..."

"SHUT UP AND DRINK THIS NOW!"

"I WANT TO TEST THIS MORE *POTENT* BATCH ON SOMEONE *ELSE!*"

"YOU MEAN YOU WANT TO TURN *ANOTHER* PERSON INTO A *MONSTER TOO!*"

"SO... YOU *KNOW?*"

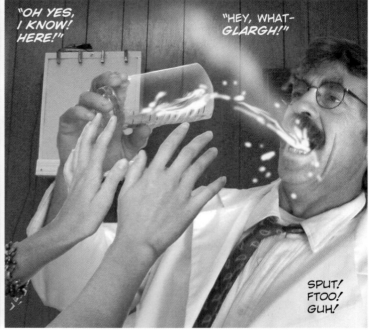

"OH YES, I KNOW! HERE!"

"HEY, WHAT— GLARGH!"

SPUT! FTOO! GUH!

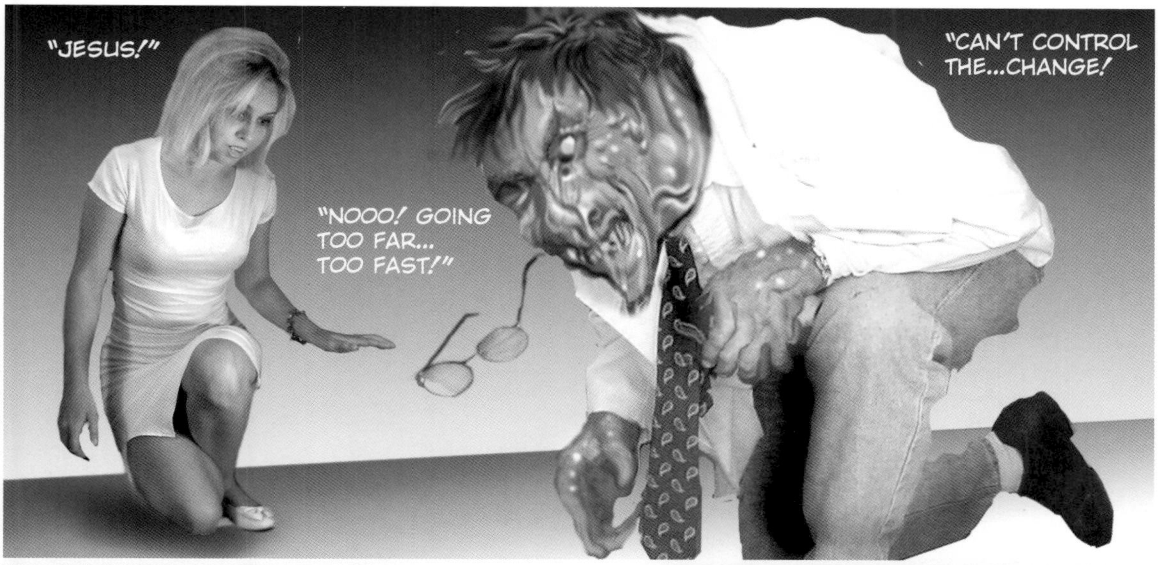
"JESUS!"
"CAN'T CONTROL THE...CHANGE!
"NOOO! GOING TOO FAR... TOO FAST!"

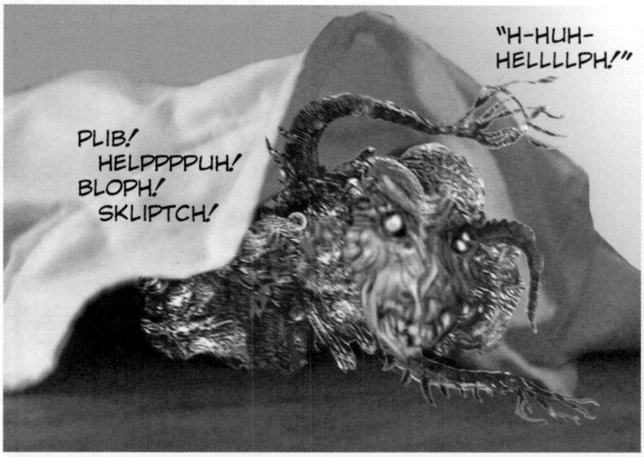
"H-HUH-HELLLLPH!"
PLIB! HELPPPPUH! BLOPH! SKLIPTCH!

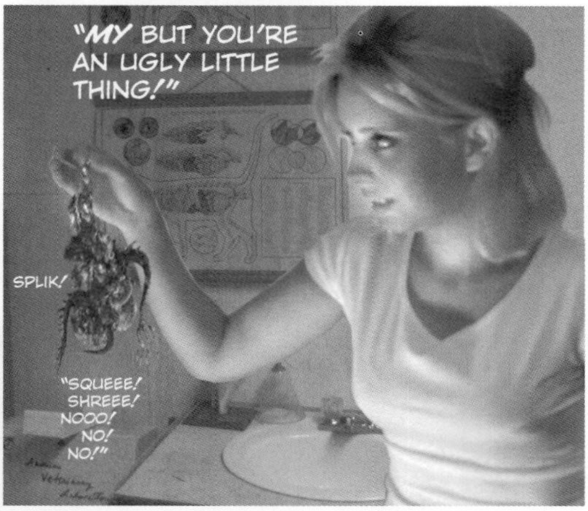
"MY BUT YOU'RE AN UGLY LITTLE THING!"
SPLIK!
"SQUEEE! SHREEE! NOOO! NO! NO!"

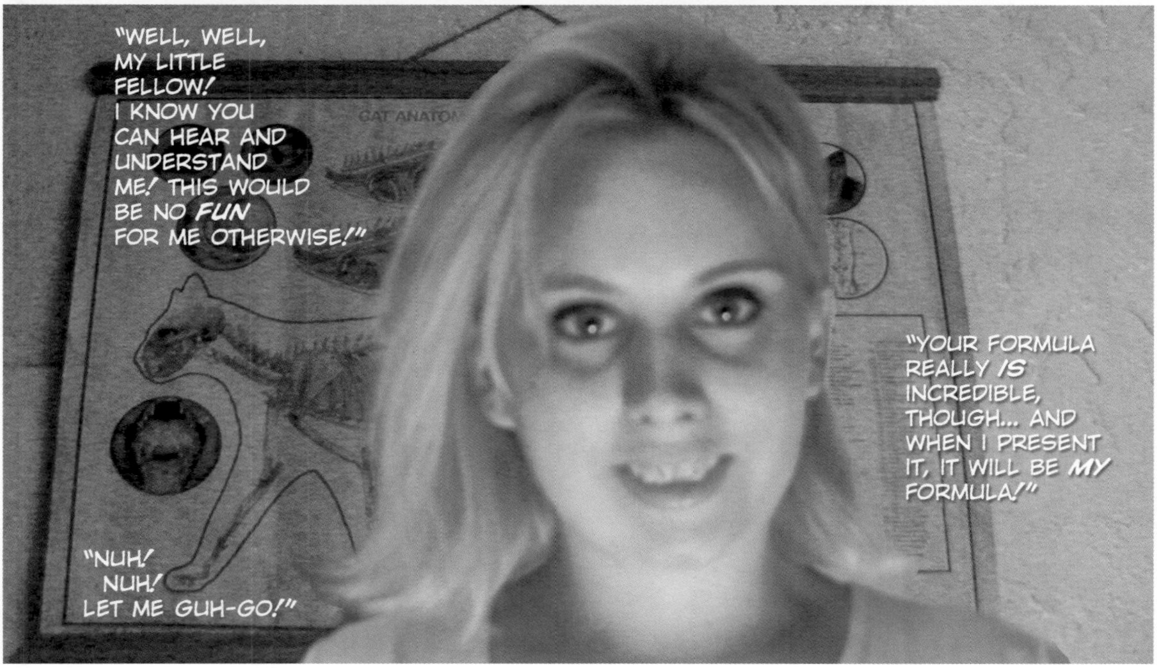
"WELL, WELL, MY LITTLE FELLOW! I KNOW YOU CAN HEAR AND UNDERSTAND ME! THIS WOULD BE NO FUN FOR ME OTHERWISE!"
"YOUR FORMULA REALLY IS INCREDIBLE, THOUGH... AND WHEN I PRESENT IT, IT WILL BE MY FORMULA!"
"NUH! NUH! LET ME GUH-GO!"

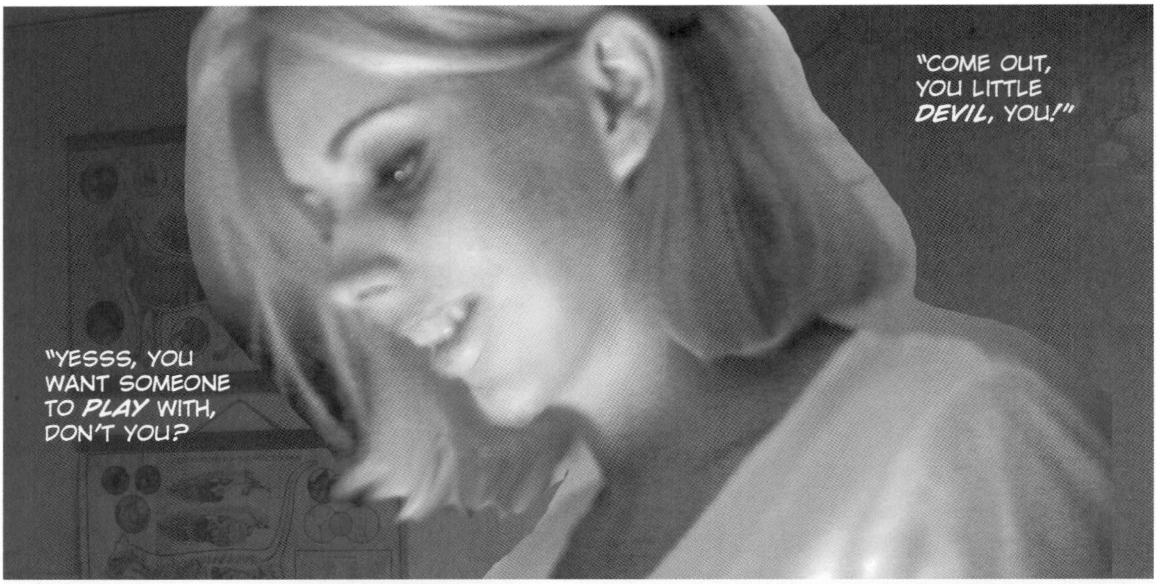
"COME OUT, YOU LITTLE DEVIL, YOU!"
"YESSS, YOU WANT SOMEONE TO PLAY WITH, DON'T YOU?

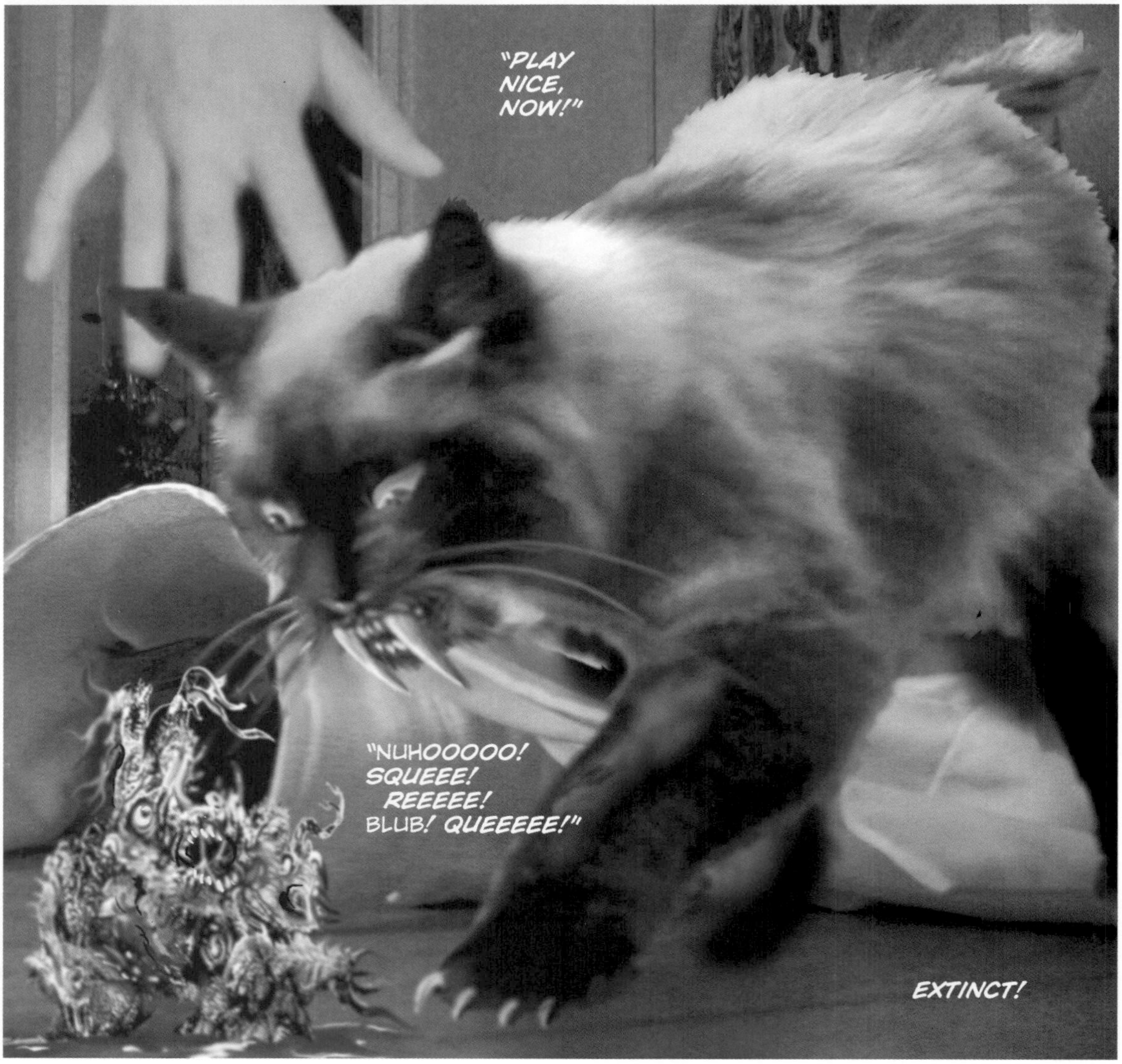
"PLAY NICE, NOW!"
"NUHOOOOO! SQUEEE! REEEEE! BLUB! QUEEEEE!"
EXTINCT!

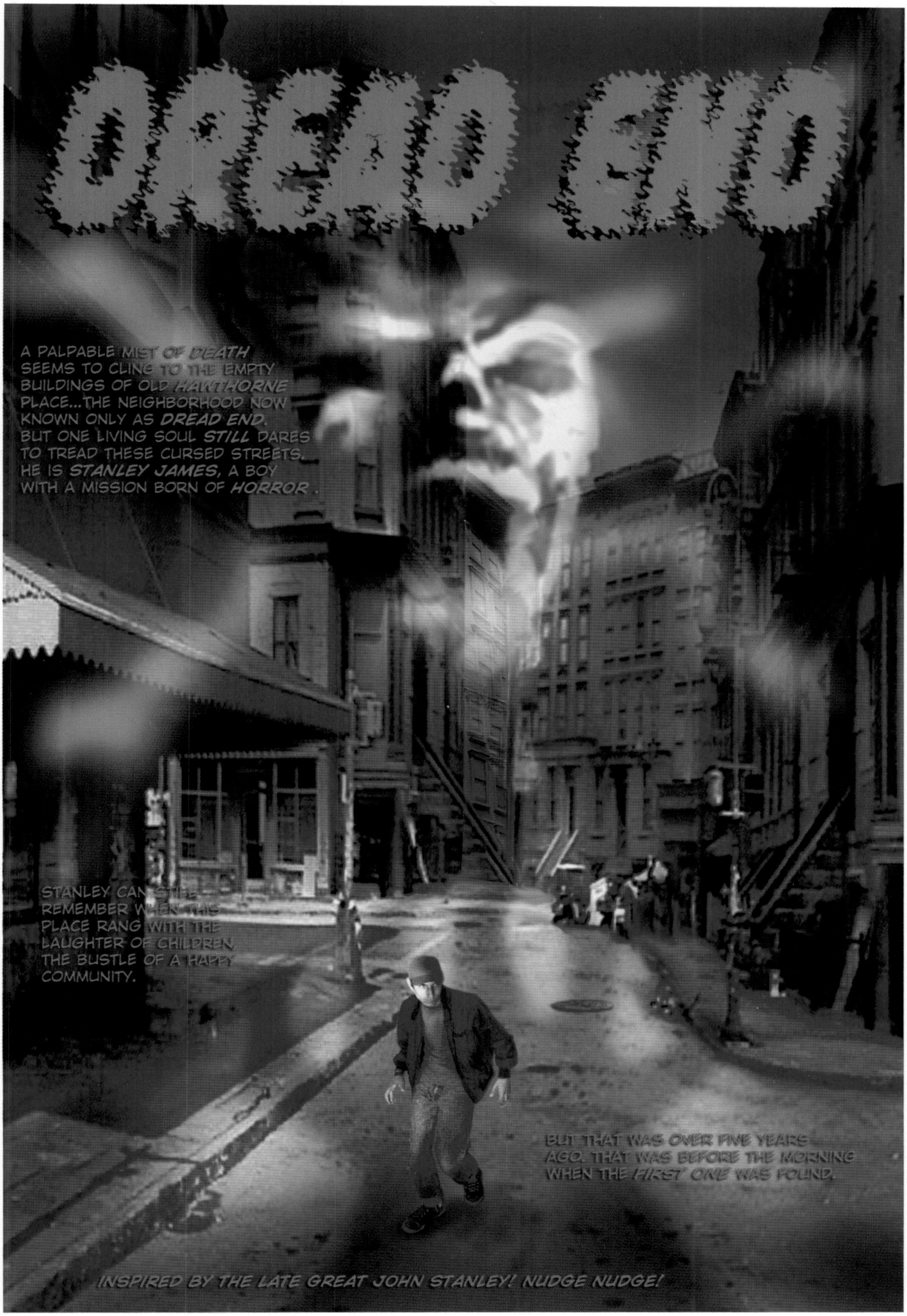
DREAD END
A PALPABLE MIST OF DEATH SEEMS TO CLING TO THE EMPTY BUILDINGS OF OLD HAWTHORNE PLACE...THE NEIGHBORHOOD NOW KNOWN ONLY AS DREAD END. BUT ONE LIVING SOUL STILL DARES TO TREAD THESE CURSED STREETS. HE IS STANLEY JAMES, A BOY WITH A MISSION BORN OF HORROR.
STANLEY CAN STILL REMEMBER WHEN THIS PLACE RANG WITH THE LAUGHTER OF CHILDREN, THE BUSTLE OF A HAPPY COMMUNITY.
BUT THAT WAS OVER FIVE YEARS AGO. THAT WAS BEFORE THE MORNING WHEN THE FIRST ONE WAS FOUND.
INSPIRED BY THE LATE GREAT JOHN STANLEY! NUDGE NUDGE!

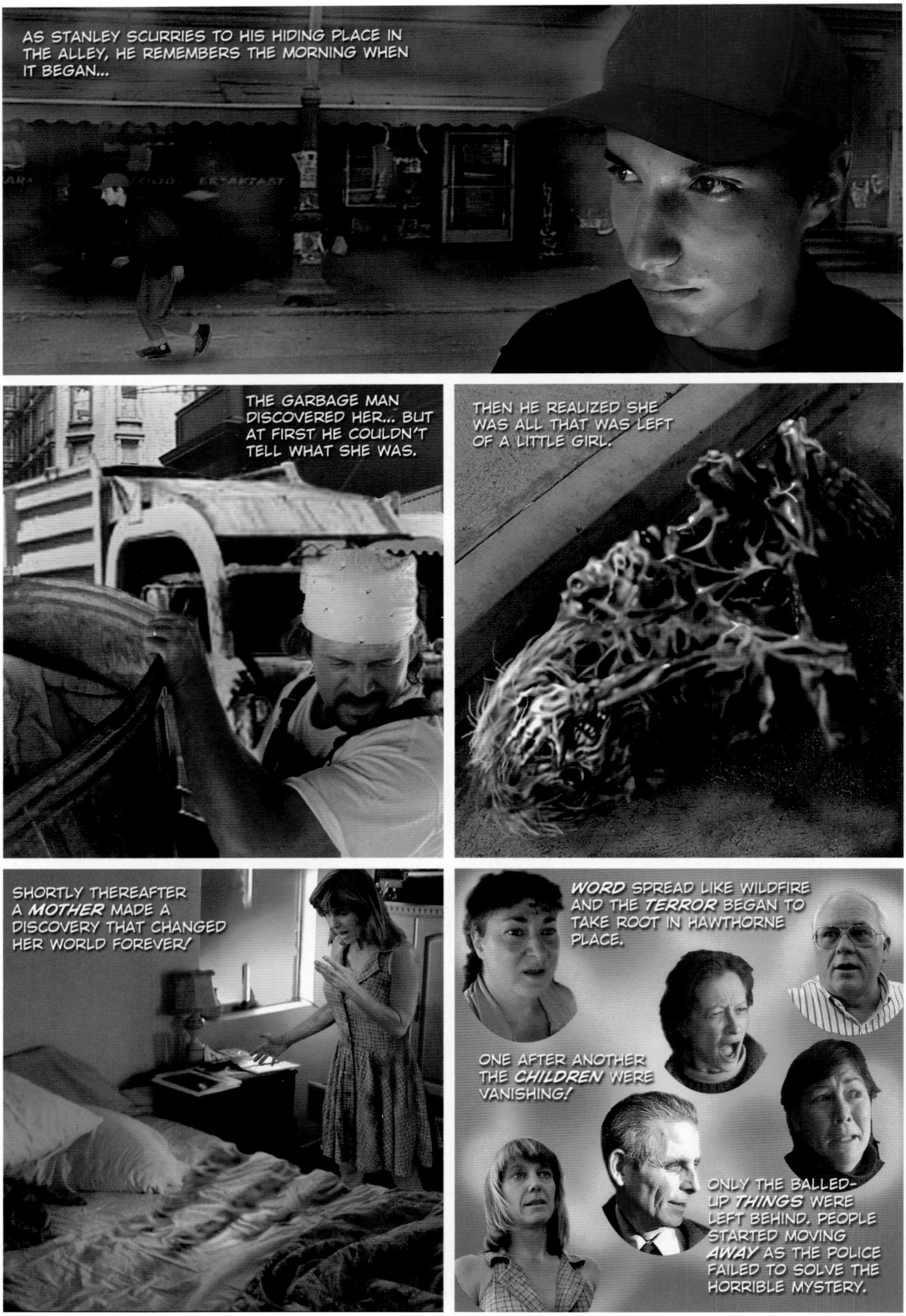
AS STANLEY SCURRIES TO HIS HIDING PLACE IN THE ALLEY, HE REMEMBERS THE MORNING WHEN IT BEGAN...
THE GARBAGE MAN DISCOVERED HER... BUT AT FIRST HE COULDN'T TELL WHAT SHE WAS.
THEN HE REALIZED SHE WAS ALL THAT WAS LEFT OF A LITTLE GIRL.
SHORTLY THEREAFTER A *MOTHER* MADE A DISCOVERY THAT CHANGED HER WORLD FOREVER!
WORD SPREAD LIKE WILDFIRE AND THE *TERROR* BEGAN TO TAKE ROOT IN HAWTHORNE PLACE.
ONE AFTER ANOTHER THE *CHILDREN* WERE VANISHING!
ONLY THE BALLED-UP *THINGS* WERE LEFT BEHIND. PEOPLE STARTED MOVING *AWAY* AS THE POLICE FAILED TO SOLVE THE HORRIBLE MYSTERY.

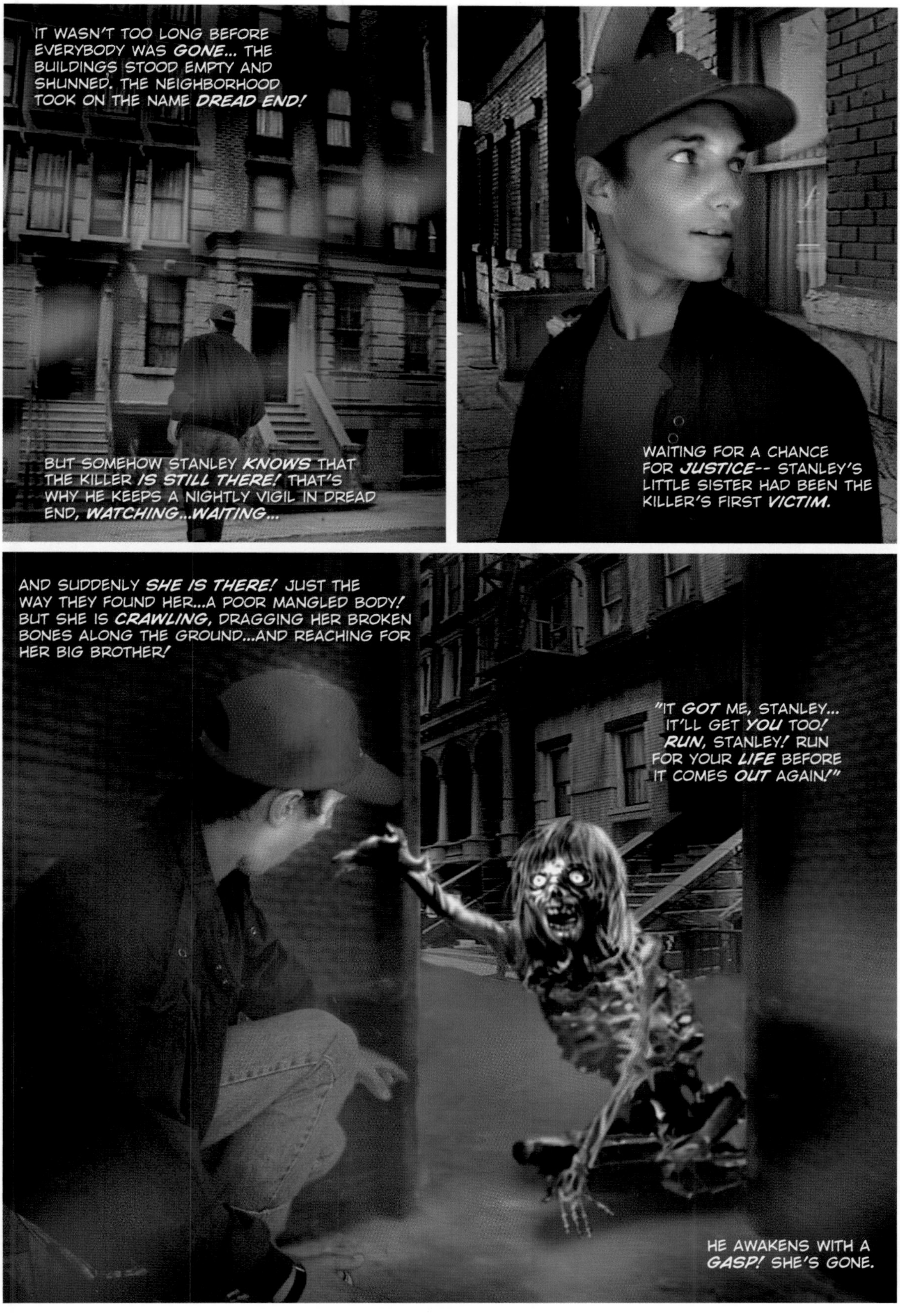
IT WASN'T TOO LONG BEFORE EVERYBODY WAS GONE... THE BUILDINGS STOOD EMPTY AND SHUNNED. THE NEIGHBORHOOD TOOK ON THE NAME DREAD END!
BUT SOMEHOW STANLEY KNOWS THAT THE KILLER IS STILL THERE! THAT'S WHY HE KEEPS A NIGHTLY VIGIL IN DREAD END, WATCHING...WAITING...
WAITING FOR A CHANCE FOR JUSTICE-- STANLEY'S LITTLE SISTER HAD BEEN THE KILLER'S FIRST VICTIM.
AND SUDDENLY SHE IS THERE! JUST THE WAY THEY FOUND HER...A POOR MANGLED BODY! BUT SHE IS CRAWLING, DRAGGING HER BROKEN BONES ALONG THE GROUND...AND REACHING FOR HER BIG BROTHER!
"IT GOT ME, STANLEY... IT'LL GET YOU TOO! RUN, STANLEY! RUN FOR YOUR LIFE BEFORE IT COMES OUT AGAIN!"
HE AWAKENS WITH A GASP! SHE'S GONE.

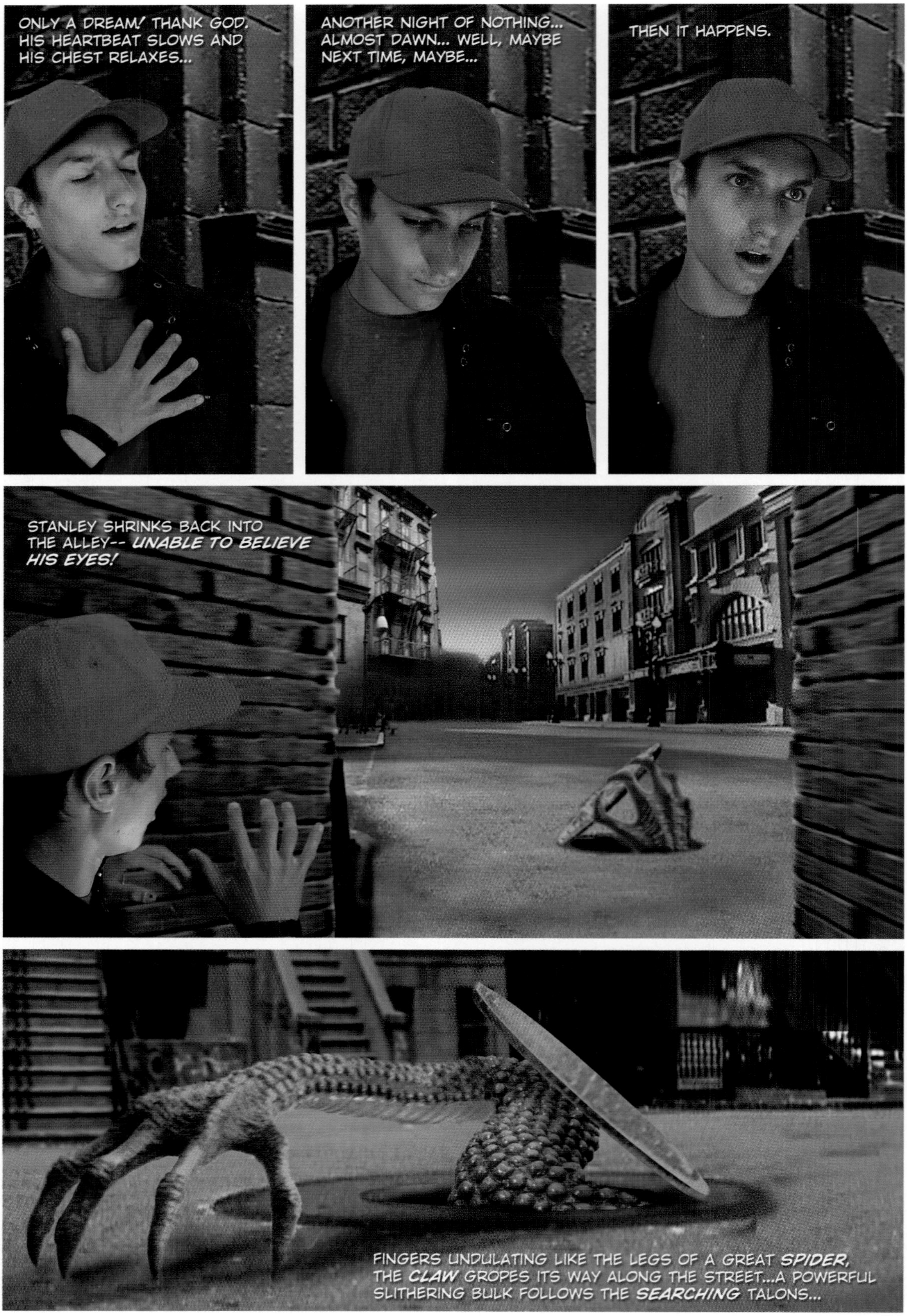
ONLY A DREAM! THANK GOD. HIS HEARTBEAT SLOWS AND HIS CHEST RELAXES...
ANOTHER NIGHT OF NOTHING... ALMOST DAWN... WELL, MAYBE NEXT TIME, MAYBE...
THEN IT HAPPENS.
STANLEY SHRINKS BACK INTO THE ALLEY-- *UNABLE TO BELIEVE HIS EYES!*
FINGERS UNDULATING LIKE THE LEGS OF A GREAT *SPIDER*, THE *CLAW* GROPES ITS WAY ALONG THE STREET...A POWERFUL SLITHERING BULK FOLLOWS THE *SEARCHING* TALONS...

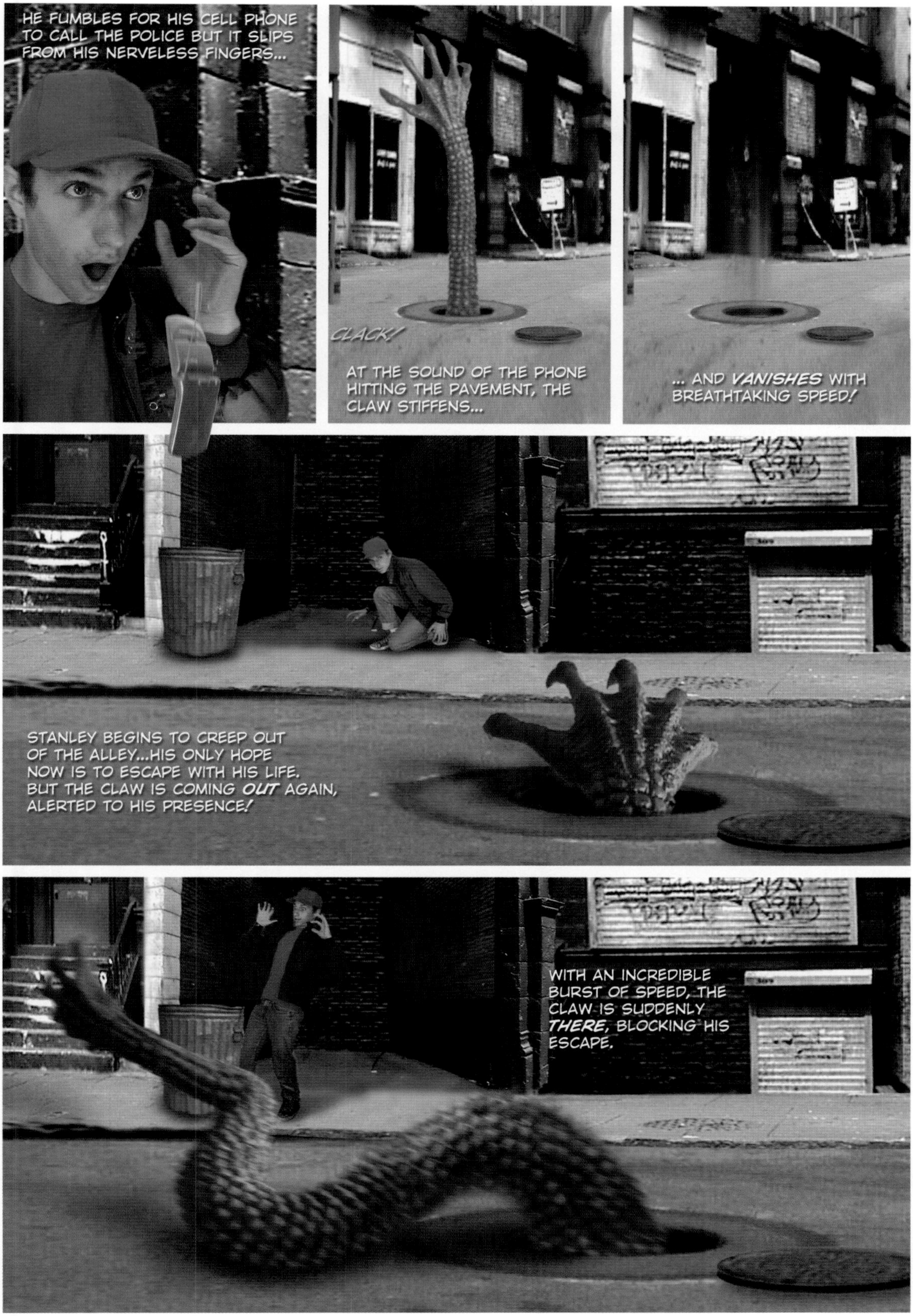
HE FUMBLES FOR HIS CELL PHONE TO CALL THE POLICE BUT IT SLIPS FROM HIS NERVELESS FINGERS...
CLACK!
AT THE SOUND OF THE PHONE HITTING THE PAVEMENT, THE CLAW STIFFENS...
... AND VANISHES WITH BREATHTAKING SPEED!
STANLEY BEGINS TO CREEP OUT OF THE ALLEY...HIS ONLY HOPE NOW IS TO ESCAPE WITH HIS LIFE. BUT THE CLAW IS COMING OUT AGAIN, ALERTED TO HIS PRESENCE!
WITH AN INCREDIBLE BURST OF SPEED, THE CLAW IS SUDDENLY THERE, BLOCKING HIS ESCAPE.

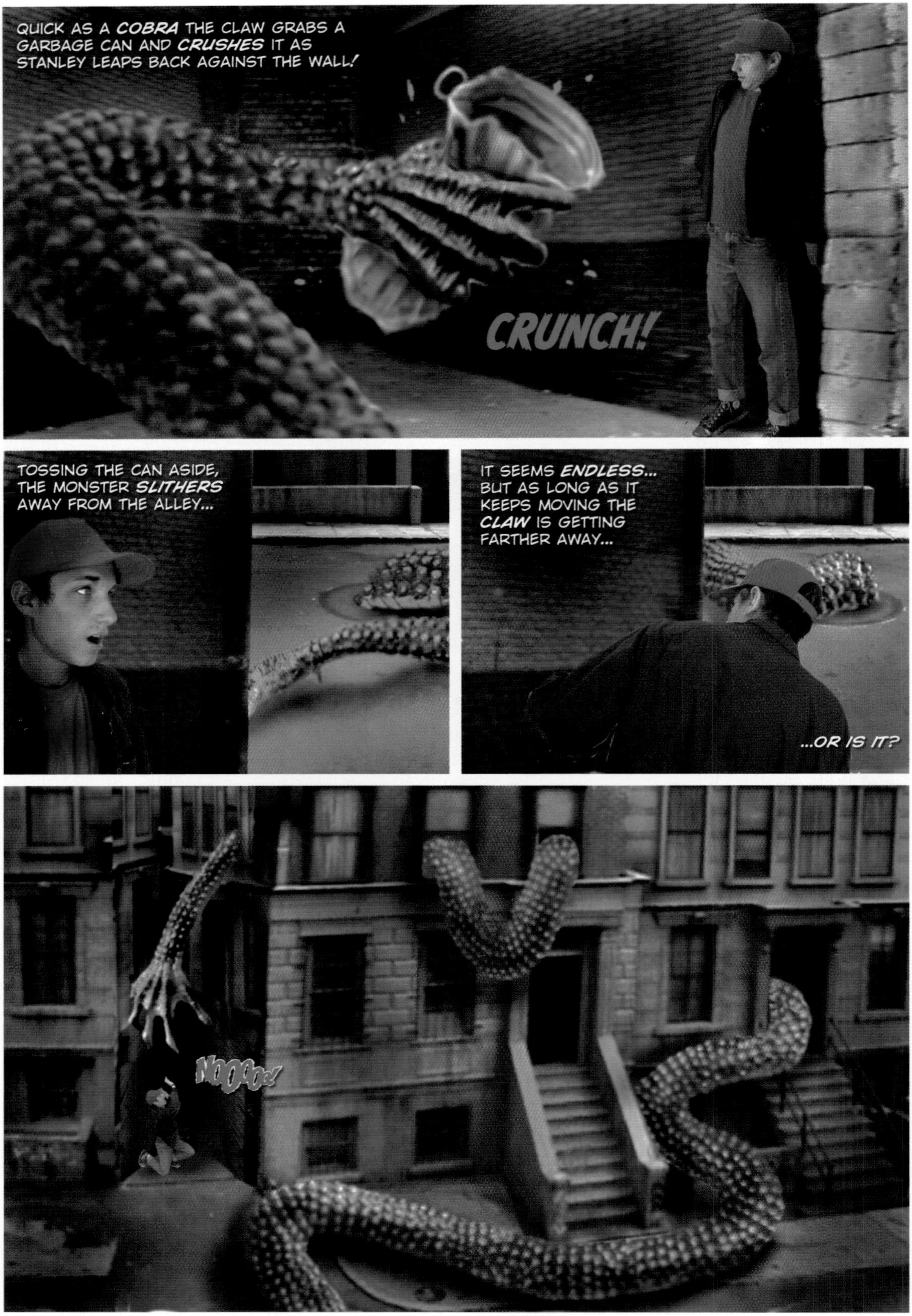
QUICK AS A *COBRA* THE CLAW GRABS A GARBAGE CAN AND *CRUSHES* IT AS STANLEY LEAPS BACK AGAINST THE WALL!
CRUNCH!
TOSSING THE CAN ASIDE, THE MONSTER *SLITHERS* AWAY FROM THE ALLEY...
IT SEEMS *ENDLESS*... BUT AS LONG AS IT KEEPS MOVING THE *CLAW* IS GETTING FARTHER AWAY...
...OR IS IT?
NOOOOO!

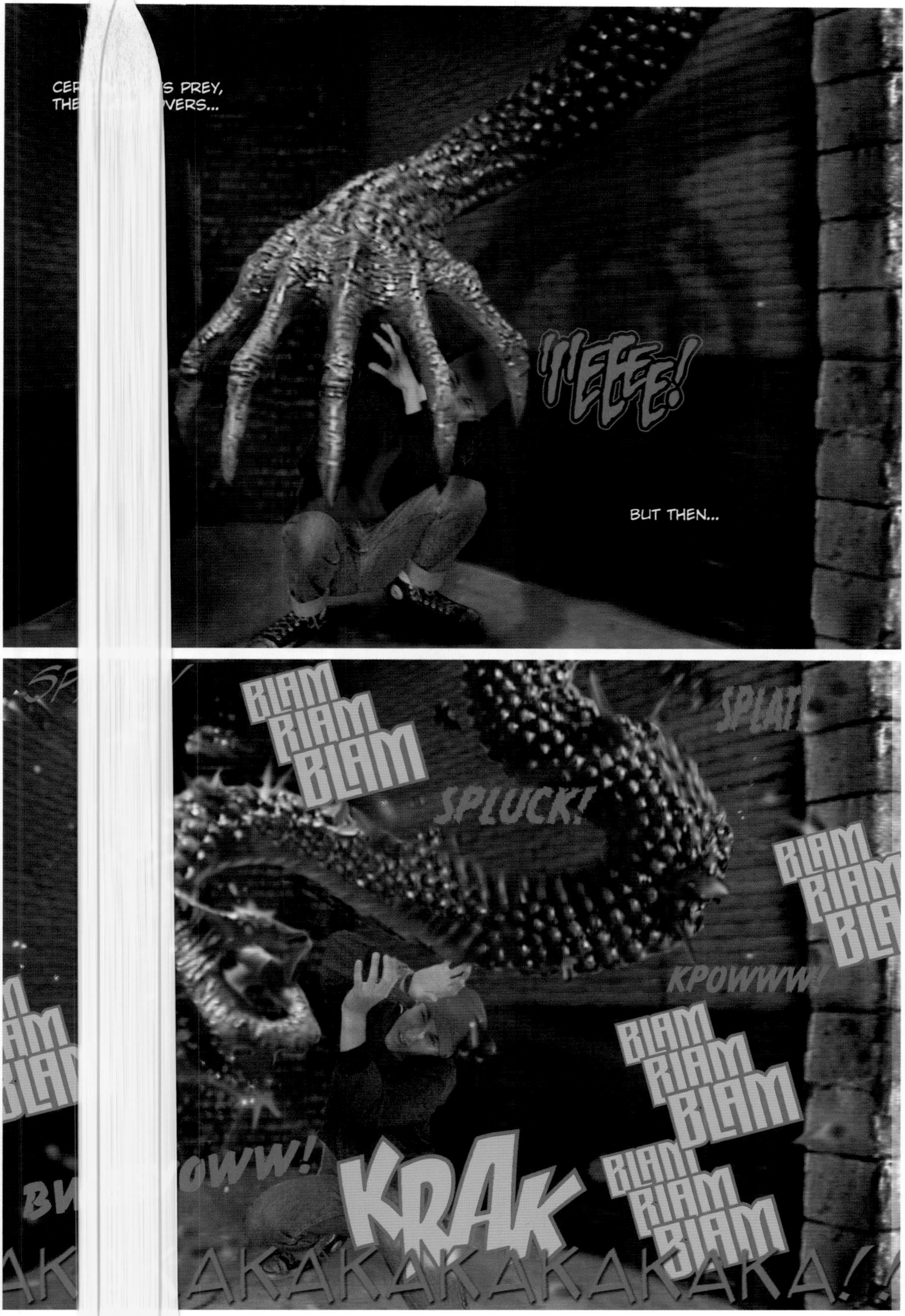
S PREY,
VERS...
BUT THEN...
BLAM
BLAM
BLAM
SPLUCK!
SPLAT!
BLAM
BLAM
KPOWWW!
BLAM
BLAM
BLAM
KRAK
BLAM
BLAM
BLAM
KAKAKAKAKAKAKAKA!!

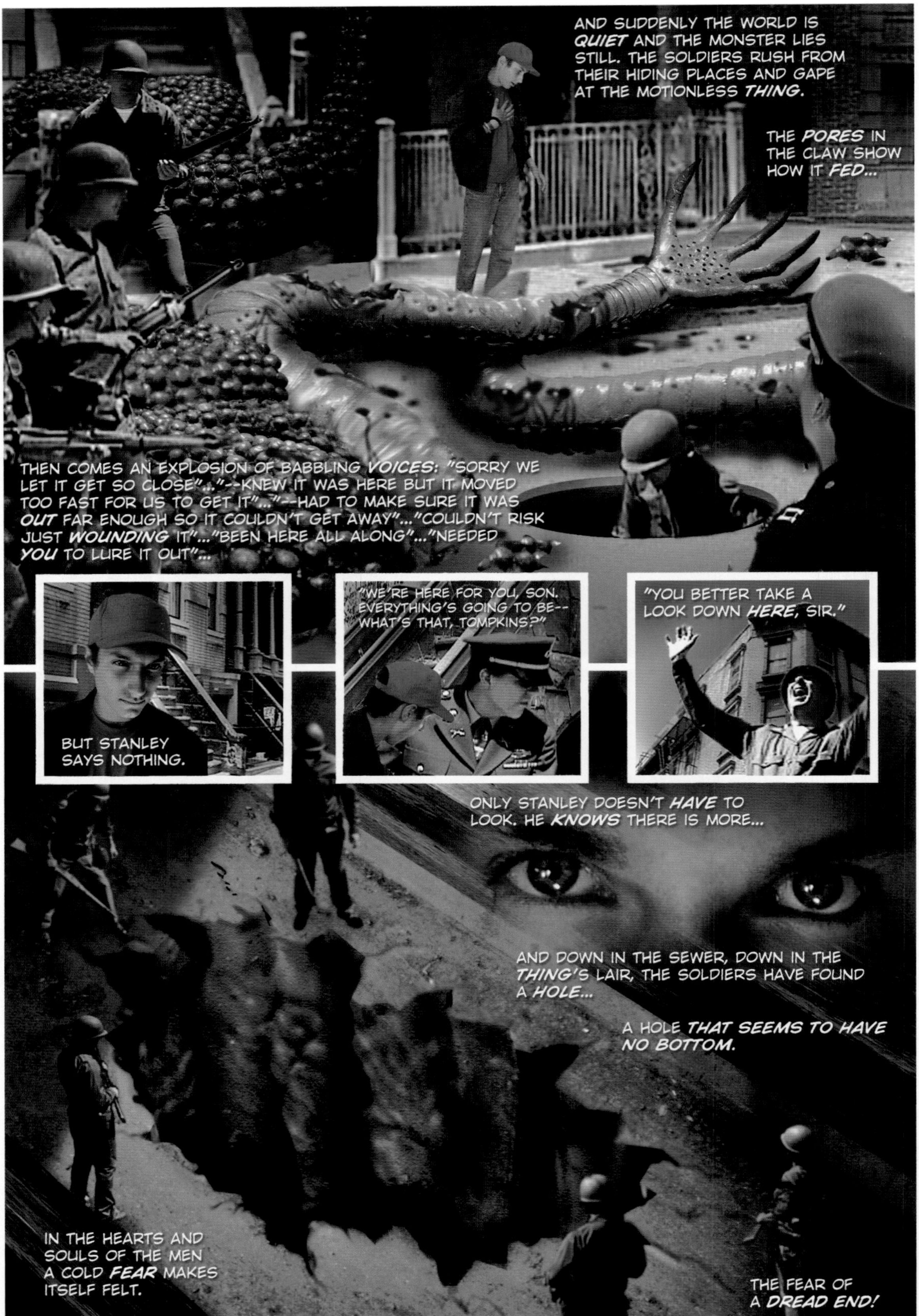

AND SUDDENLY THE WORLD IS QUIET AND THE MONSTER LIES STILL. THE SOLDIERS RUSH FROM THEIR HIDING PLACES AND GAPE AT THE MOTIONLESS THING.
THE PORES IN THE CLAW SHOW HOW IT FED...
THEN COMES AN EXPLOSION OF BABBLING VOICES: "SORRY WE LET IT GET SO CLOSE"..."--KNEW IT WAS HERE BUT IT MOVED TOO FAST FOR US TO GET IT"..."--HAD TO MAKE SURE IT WAS OUT FAR ENOUGH SO IT COULDN'T GET AWAY"..."COULDN'T RISK JUST WOUNDING IT"..."BEEN HERE ALL ALONG"..."NEEDED YOU TO LURE IT OUT"...
BUT STANLEY SAYS NOTHING.
"WE'RE HERE FOR YOU, SON. EVERYTHING'S GOING TO BE--WHAT'S THAT, TOMPKINS?"
"YOU BETTER TAKE A LOOK DOWN HERE, SIR."
ONLY STANLEY DOESN'T HAVE TO LOOK. HE KNOWS THERE IS MORE...
AND DOWN IN THE SEWER, DOWN IN THE THING'S LAIR, THE SOLDIERS HAVE FOUND A HOLE...
A HOLE THAT SEEMS TO HAVE NO BOTTOM.
IN THE HEARTS AND SOULS OF THE MEN A COLD FEAR MAKES ITSELF FELT.
THE FEAR OF A DREAD END!

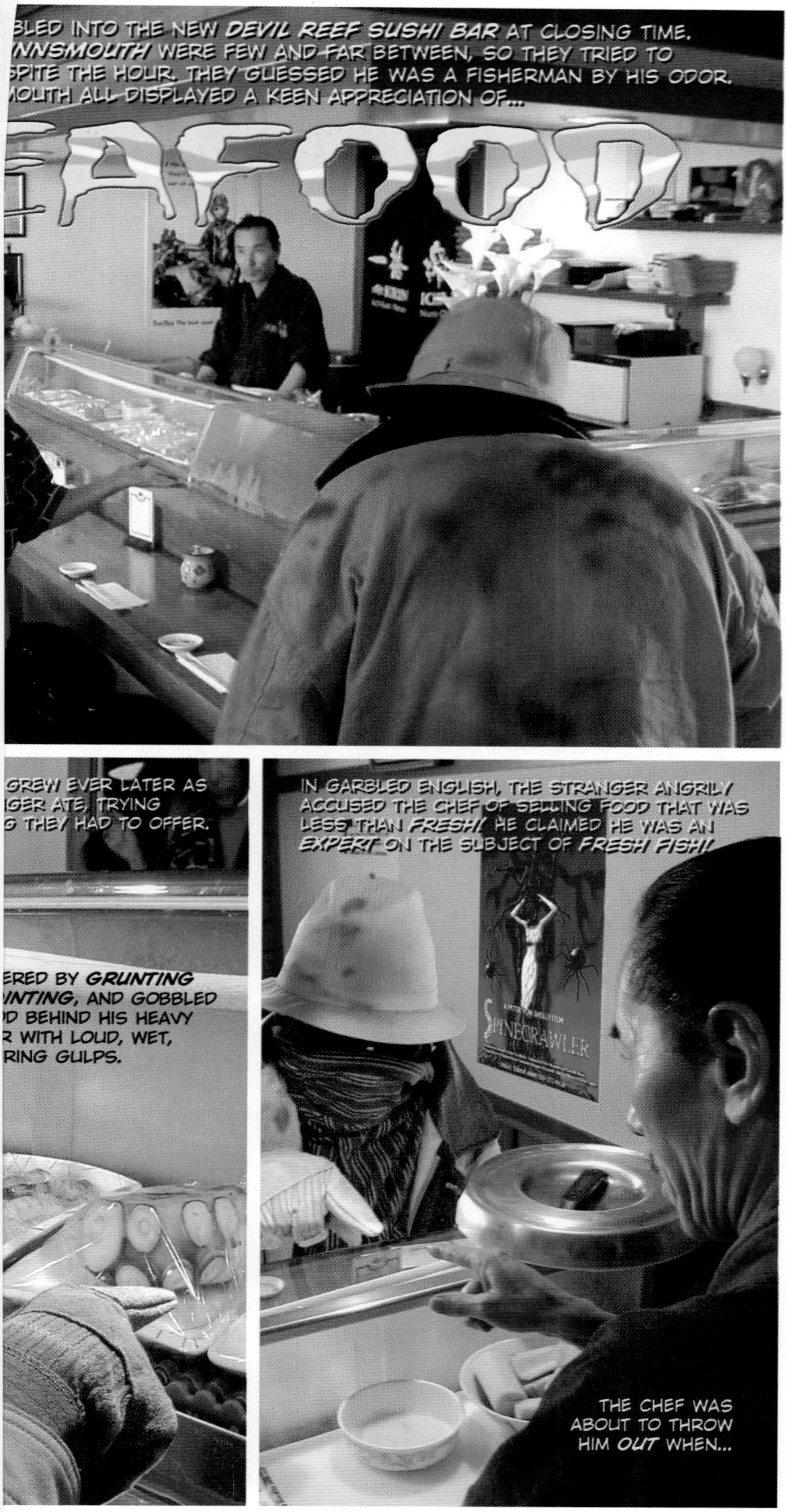
BLED INTO THE NEW *DEVIL REEF SUSHI BAR* AT CLOSING TIME.
INNSMOUTH WERE FEW AND FAR BETWEEN, SO THEY TRIED TO
SPITE THE HOUR. THEY GUESSED HE WAS A FISHERMAN BY HIS ODOR.
MOUTH ALL DISPLAYED A KEEN APPRECIATION OF...
AFOOD
GREW EVER LATER AS
NGER ATE, TRYING
G THEY HAD TO OFFER.
ERED BY **GRUNTING**
UNTING, AND GOBBLED
OD BEHIND HIS HEAVY
R WITH LOUD, WET,
RING GULPS.
IN GARBLED ENGLISH, THE STRANGER ANGRILY ACCUSED THE CHEF OF SELLING FOOD THAT WAS LESS THAN *FRESH!* HE CLAIMED HE WAS AN *EXPERT* ON THE SUBJECT OF *FRESH FISH!*
SPINECRAWLER
THE CHEF WAS ABOUT TO THROW HIM *OUT* WHEN...

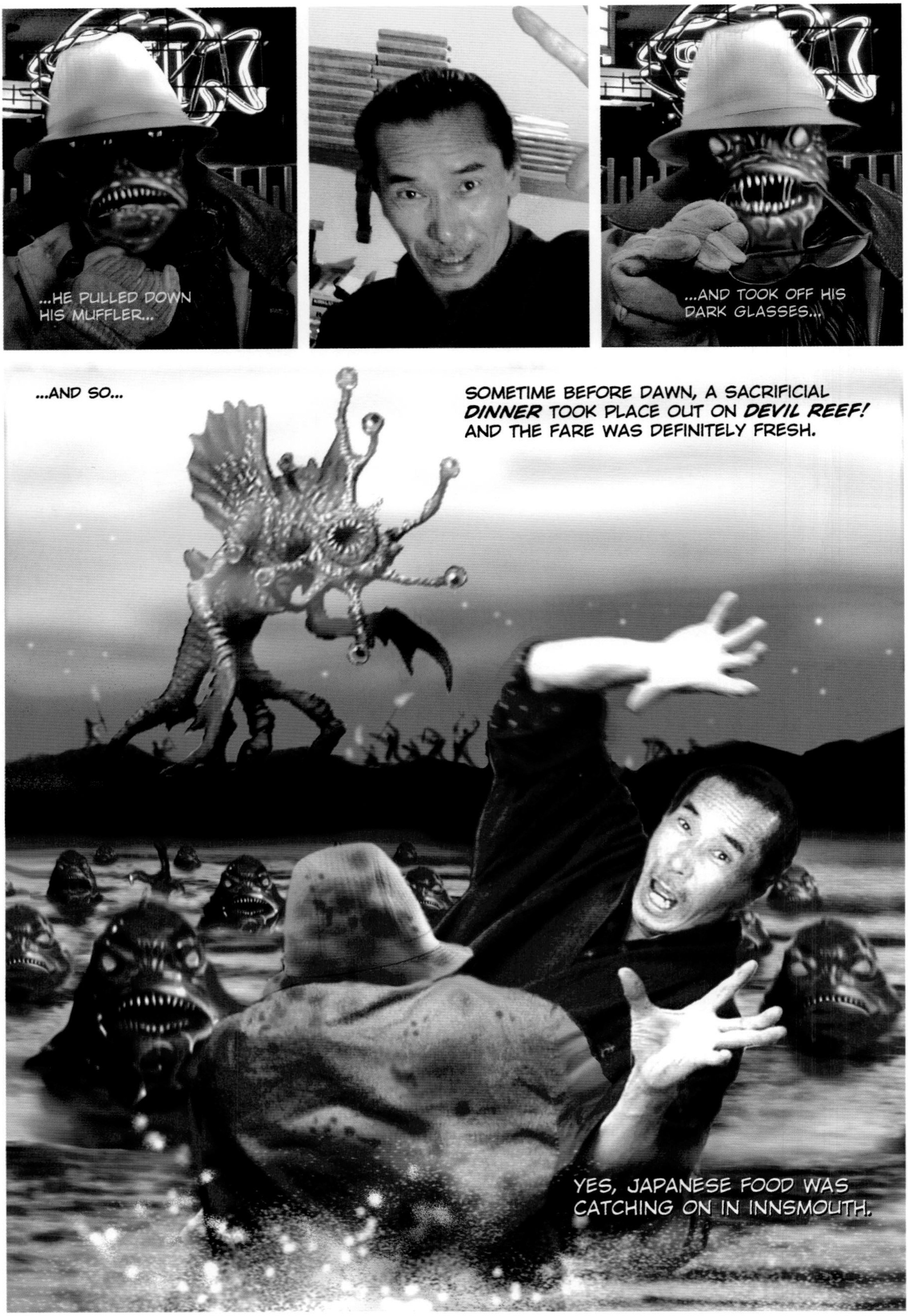
...HE PULLED DOWN HIS MUFFLER...
...AND TOOK OFF HIS DARK GLASSES...
...AND SO...
SOMETIME BEFORE DAWN, A SACRIFICIAL *DINNER* TOOK PLACE OUT ON *DEVIL REEF!* AND THE FARE WAS DEFINITELY FRESH.
YES, JAPANESE FOOD WAS CATCHING ON IN INNSMOUTH.

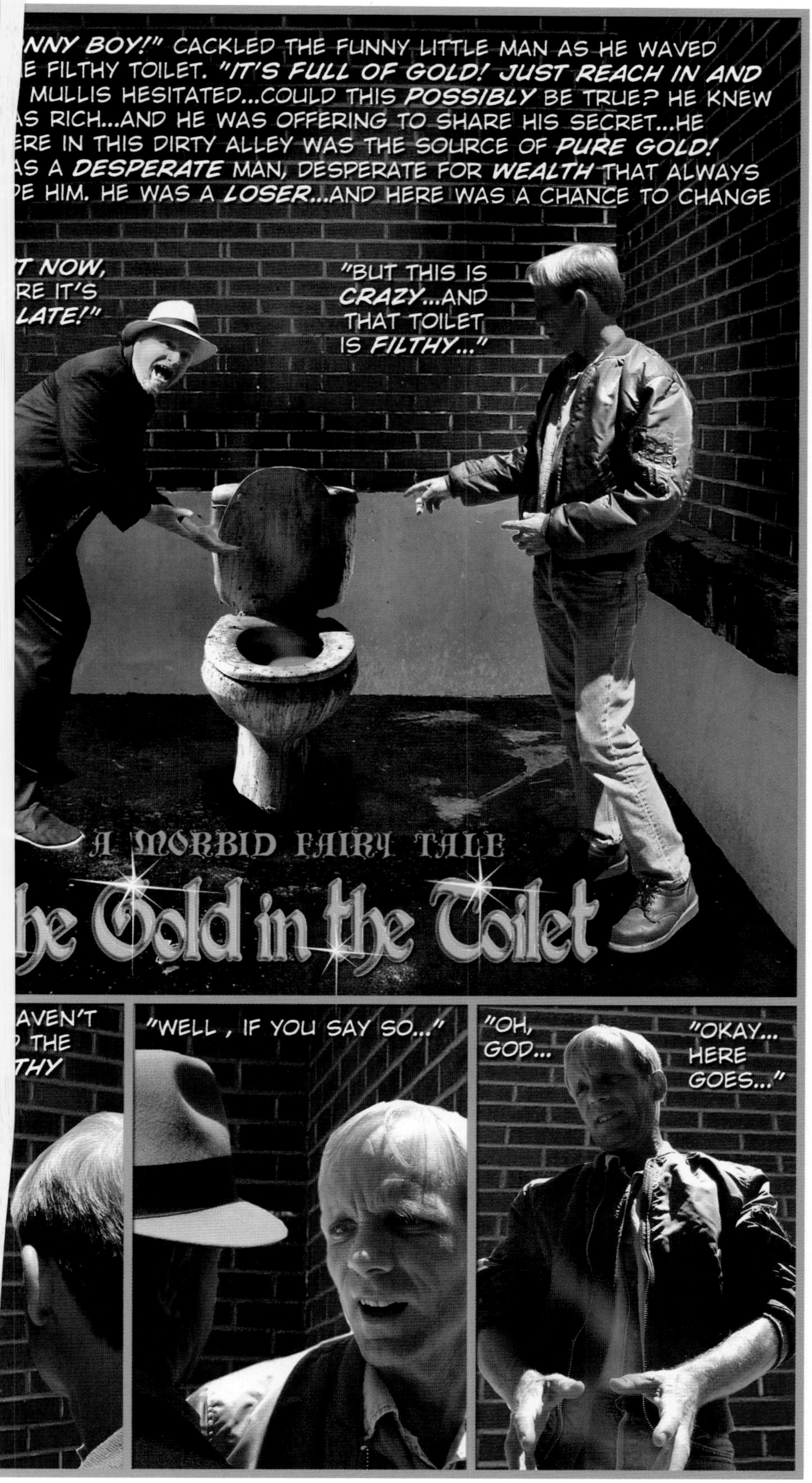
NNY BOY!" CACKLED THE FUNNY LITTLE MAN AS HE WAVED
E FILTHY TOILET. "IT'S FULL OF GOLD! JUST REACH IN AND
MULLIS HESITATED...COULD THIS POSSIBLY BE TRUE? HE KNEW
AS RICH...AND HE WAS OFFERING TO SHARE HIS SECRET...HE
ERE IN THIS DIRTY ALLEY WAS THE SOURCE OF PURE GOLD!
AS A DESPERATE MAN, DESPERATE FOR WEALTH THAT ALWAYS
DE HIM. HE WAS A LOSER...AND HERE WAS A CHANCE TO CHANGE
T NOW, RE IT'S LATE!"
"BUT THIS IS CRAZY...AND THAT TOILET IS FILTHY..."
A MORBID FAIRY TALE
he Gold in the Toilet
AVEN'T THE THY
"WELL , IF YOU SAY SO..."
"OH, GOD...
"OKAY... HERE GOES..."

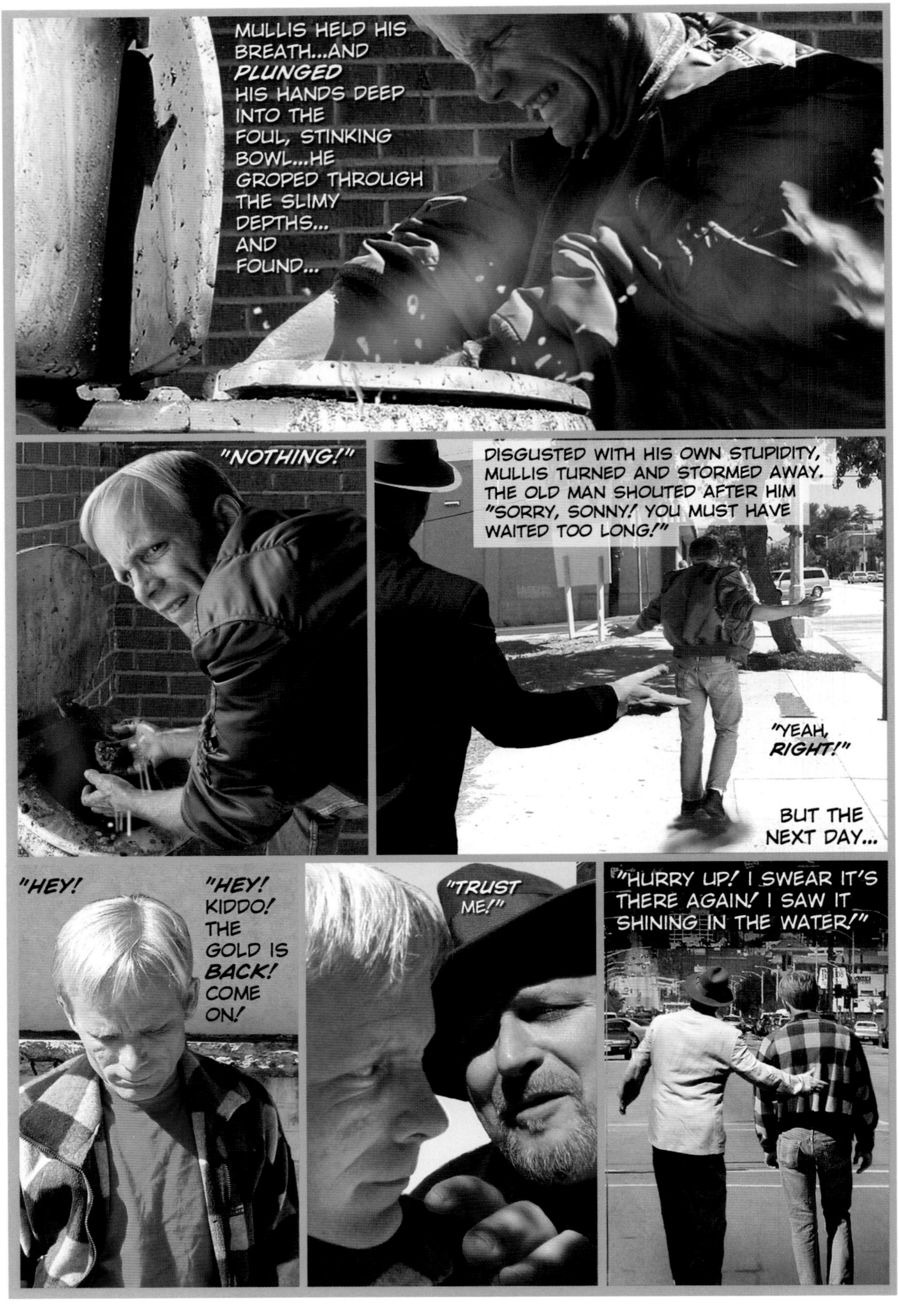
MULLIS HELD HIS BREATH...AND PLUNGED HIS HANDS DEEP INTO THE FOUL, STINKING BOWL...HE GROPED THROUGH THE SLIMY DEPTHS... AND FOUND...
"NOTHING!"
DISGUSTED WITH HIS OWN STUPIDITY, MULLIS TURNED AND STORMED AWAY. THE OLD MAN SHOUTED AFTER HIM "SORRY, SONNY! YOU MUST HAVE WAITED TOO LONG!"
"YEAH, RIGHT!"
BUT THE NEXT DAY...
"HEY!
"HEY! KIDDO! THE GOLD IS BACK! COME ON!
"TRUST ME!"
"HURRY UP! I SWEAR IT'S THERE AGAIN! I SAW IT SHINING IN THE WATER!"

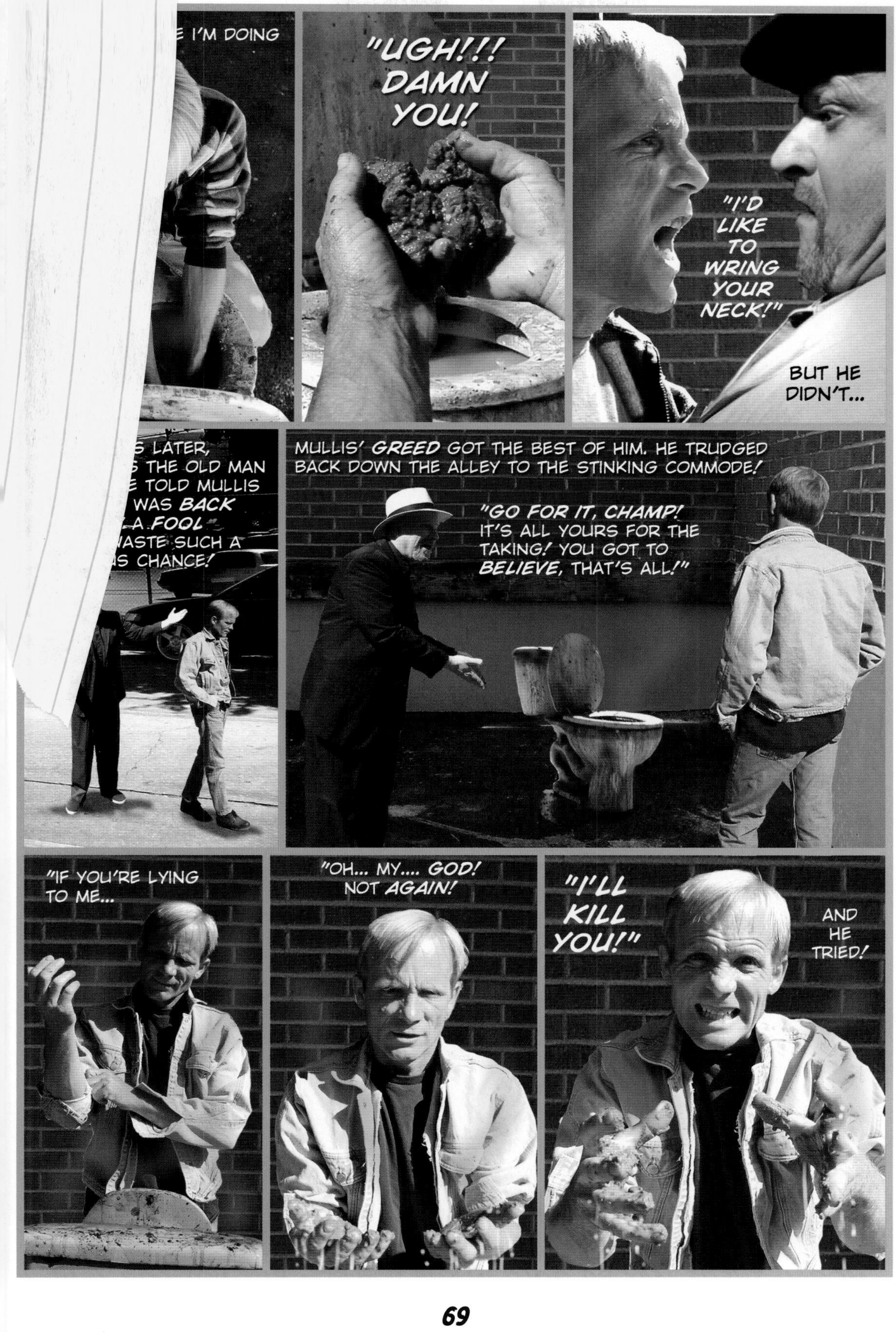
I'M DOING
"UGH!!! DAMN YOU!
"I'D LIKE TO WRING YOUR NECK!"
BUT HE DIDN'T...
LATER,
THE OLD MAN
TOLD MULLIS
WAS BACK
A FOOL
WASTE SUCH A
CHANCE!
MULLIS' GREED GOT THE BEST OF HIM. HE TRUDGED BACK DOWN THE ALLEY TO THE STINKING COMMODE!
"GO FOR IT, CHAMP! IT'S ALL YOURS FOR THE TAKING! YOU GOT TO BELIEVE, THAT'S ALL!"
"IF YOU'RE LYING TO ME...
"OH... MY.... GOD! NOT AGAIN!
"I'LL KILL YOU!"
AND HE TRIED!

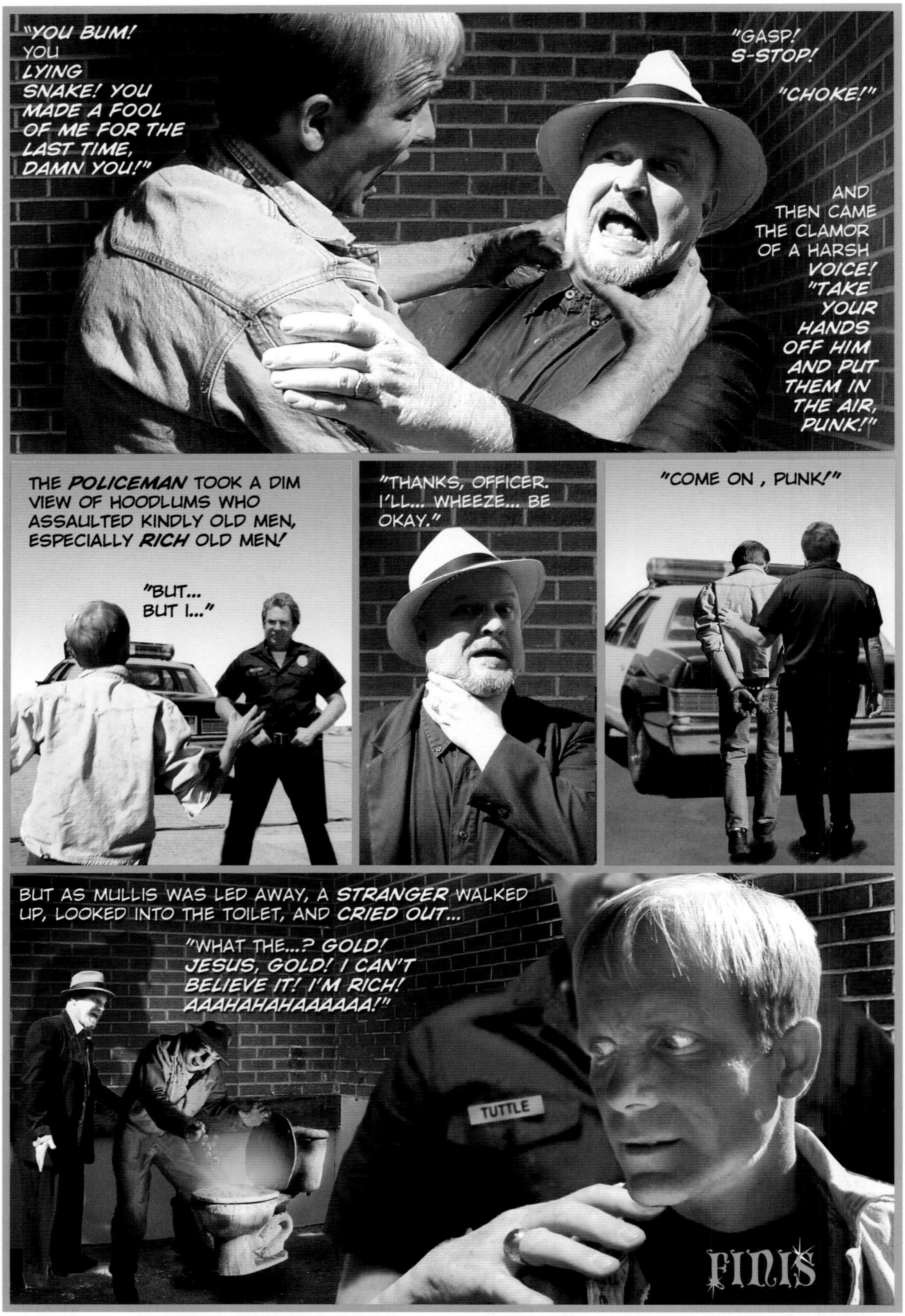
"YOU BUM! YOU LYING SNAKE! YOU MADE A FOOL OF ME FOR THE LAST TIME, DAMN YOU!"
"GASP! S-STOP!
"CHOKE!"
AND THEN CAME THE CLAMOR OF A HARSH VOICE! "TAKE YOUR HANDS OFF HIM AND PUT THEM IN THE AIR, PUNK!"
THE POLICEMAN TOOK A DIM VIEW OF HOODLUMS WHO ASSAULTED KINDLY OLD MEN, ESPECIALLY RICH OLD MEN!
"BUT... BUT I..."
"THANKS, OFFICER. I'LL... WHEEZE... BE OKAY."
"COME ON , PUNK!"
BUT AS MULLIS WAS LED AWAY, A STRANGER WALKED UP, LOOKED INTO THE TOILET, AND CRIED OUT...
"WHAT THE...? GOLD! JESUS, GOLD! I CAN'T BELIEVE IT! I'M RICH! AAAHAHAHAAAAAA!"
TUTTLE
FINIS

MORAL: THERE MAY BE GOLD IN THE TOILET-- BUT NOT FOR YOU!

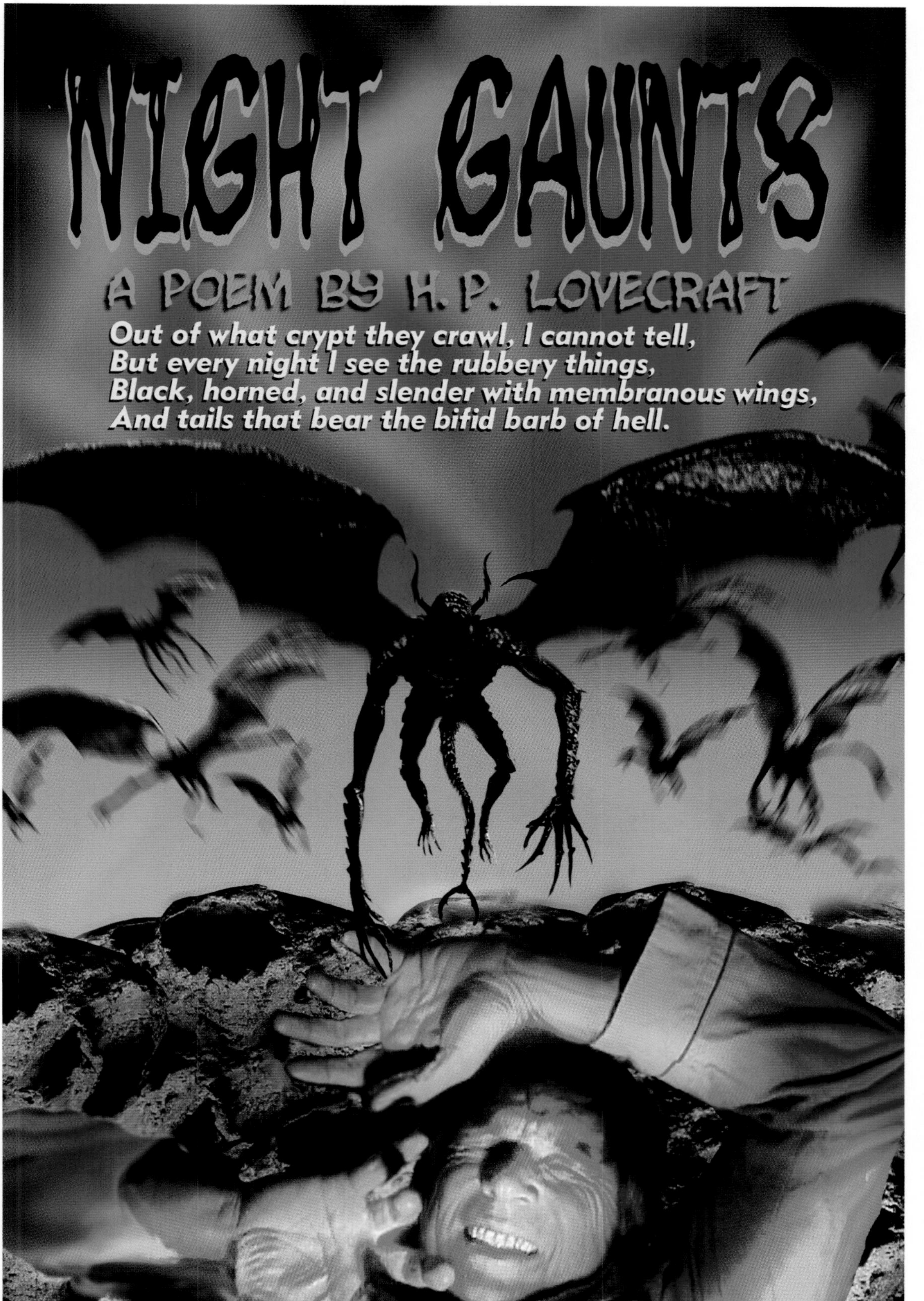
NIGHT GAUNTS
A POEM BY H. P. LOVECRAFT
Out of what crypt they crawl, I cannot tell,
But every night I see the rubbery things,
Black, horned, and slender with membranous wings,
And tails that bear the bifid barb of hell.

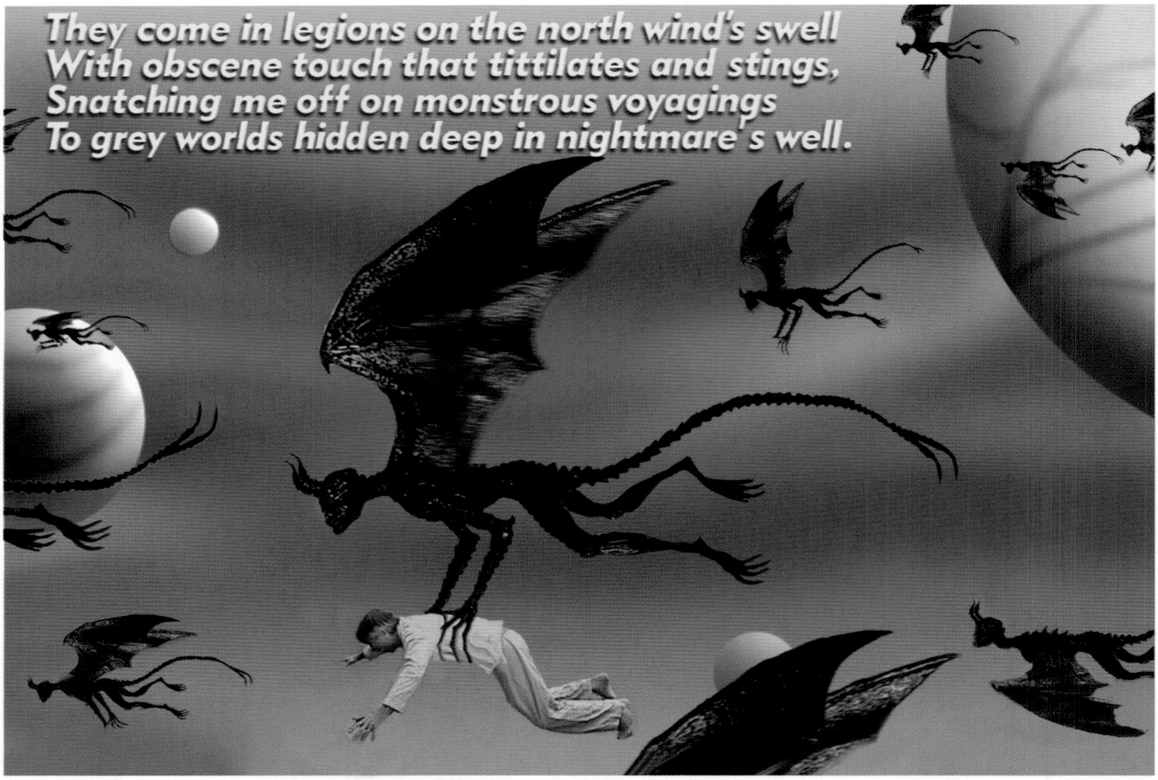
They come in legions on the north wind's swell
With obscene touch that tittilates and stings,
Snatching me off on monstrous voyagings
To grey worlds hidden deep in nightmare's well.

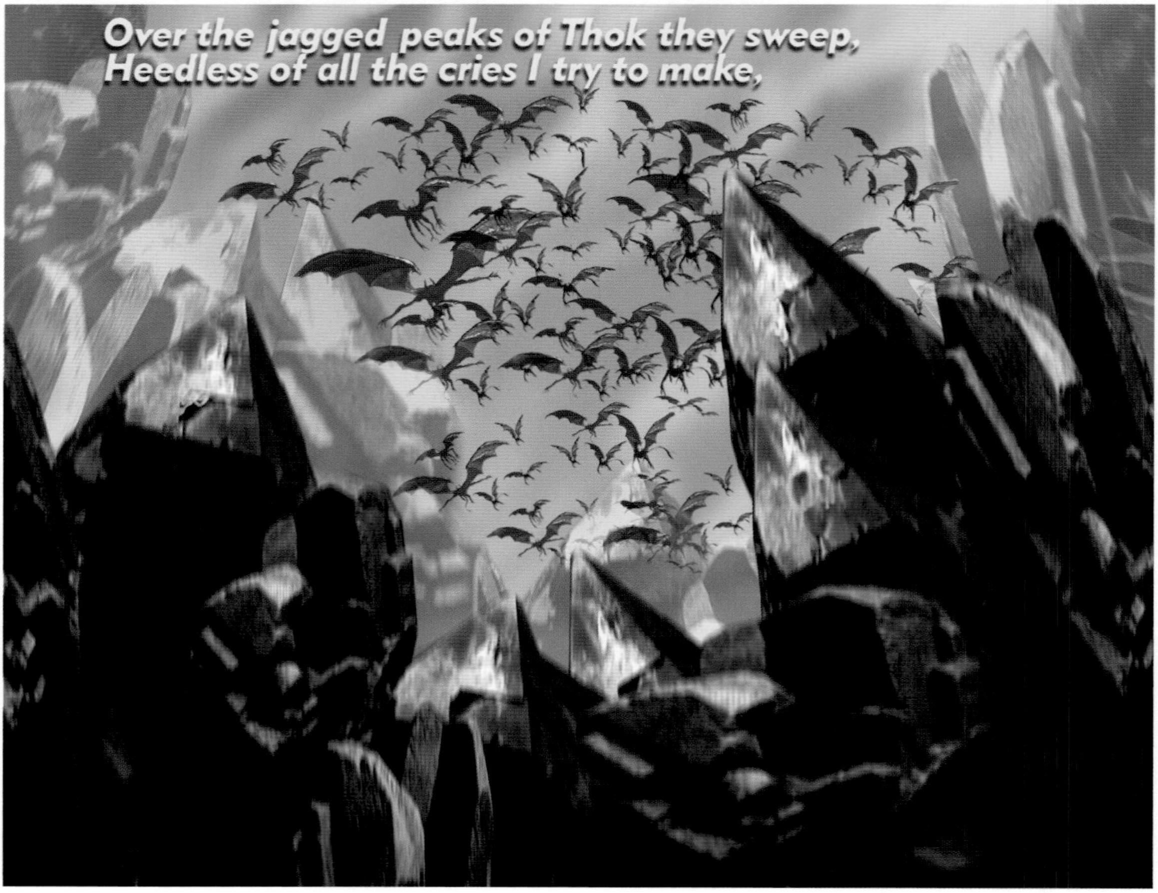
Over the jagged peaks of Thok they sweep,
Heedless of all the cries I try to make,

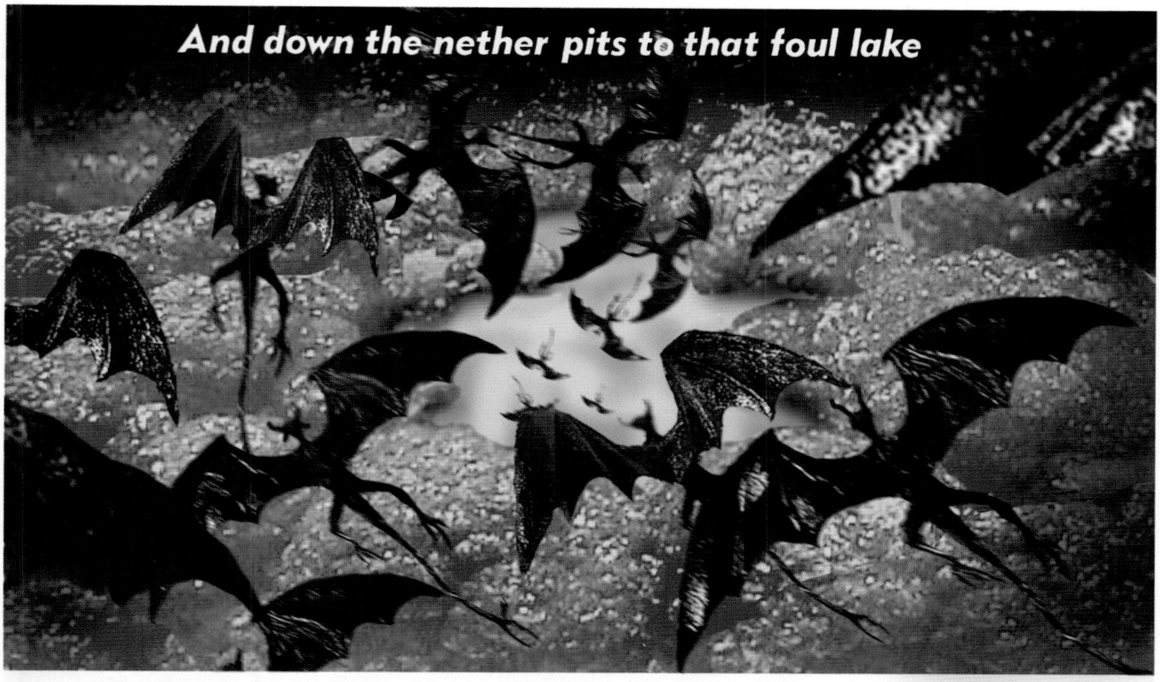
And down the nether pits to that foul lake

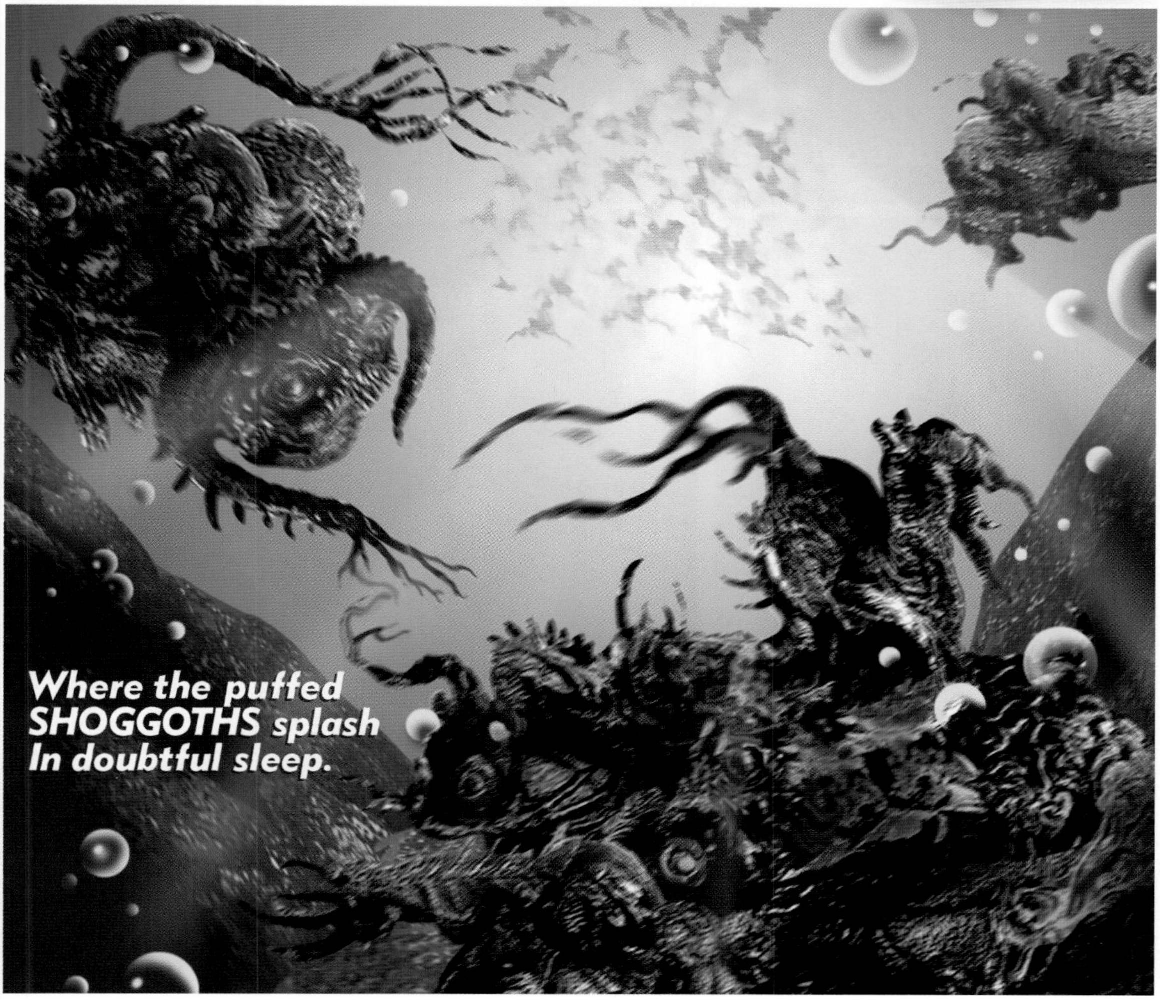
Where the puffed
SHOGGOTHS splash
In doubtful sleep.

But oh! If only they would make some sound,

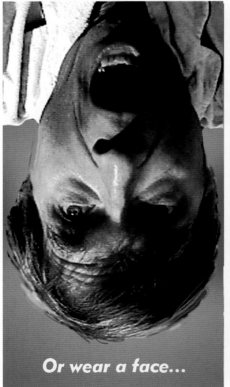

Or wear a face...

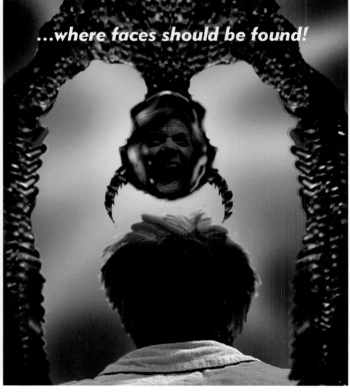

...where faces should be found!

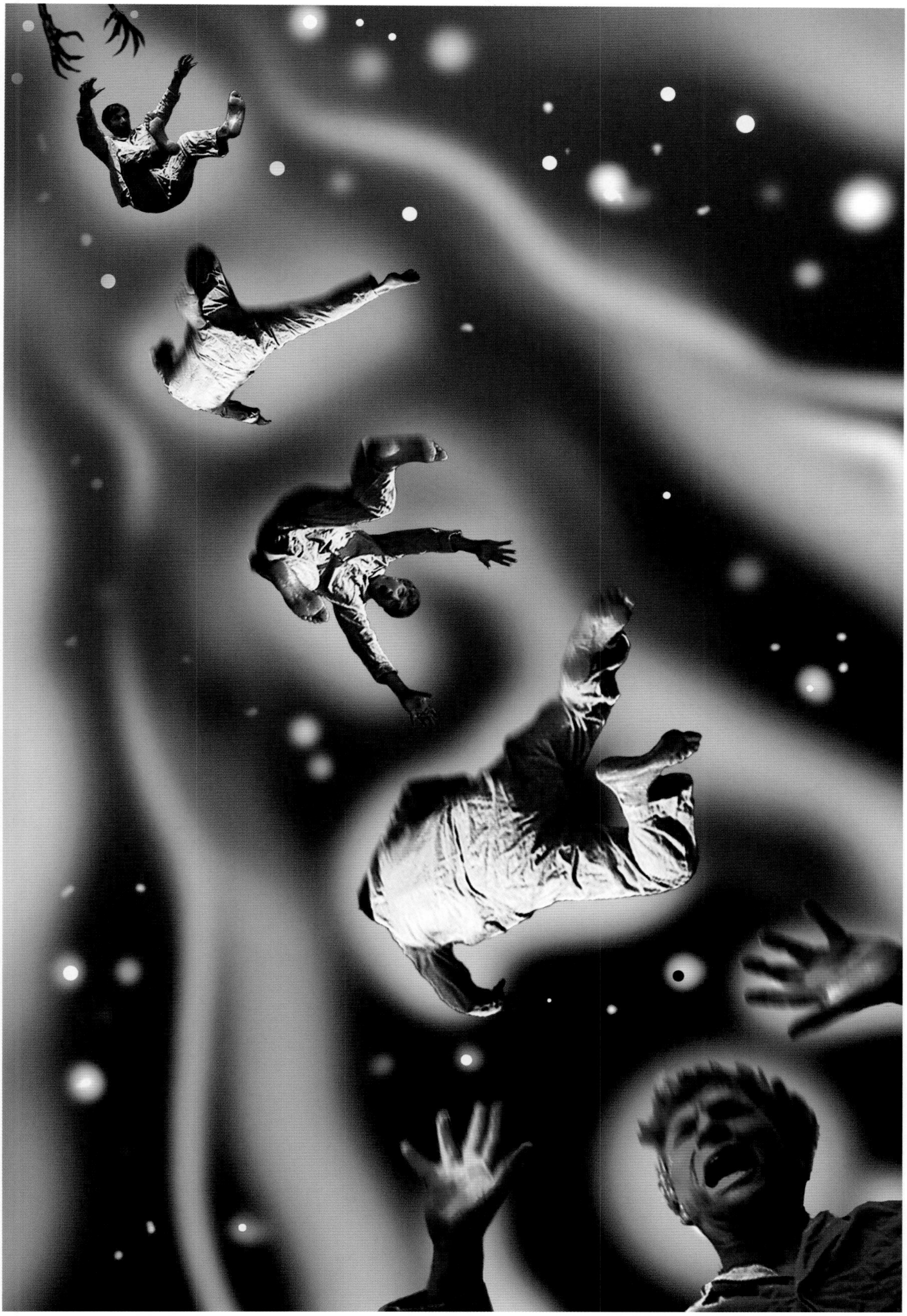

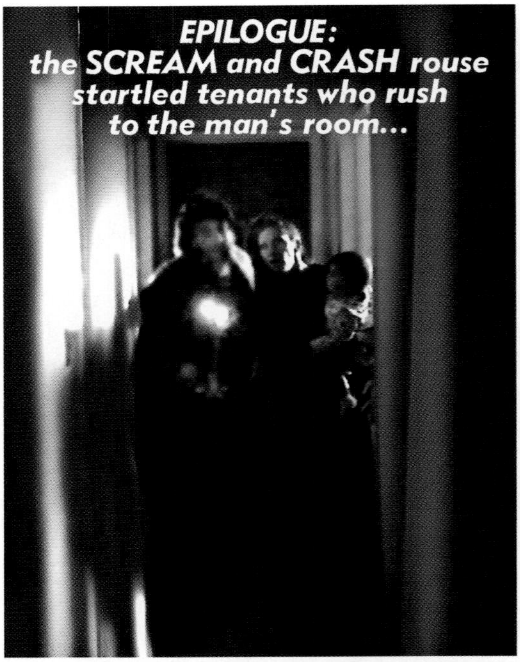
EPILOGUE:
the SCREAM and CRASH rouse startled tenants who rush to the man's room...

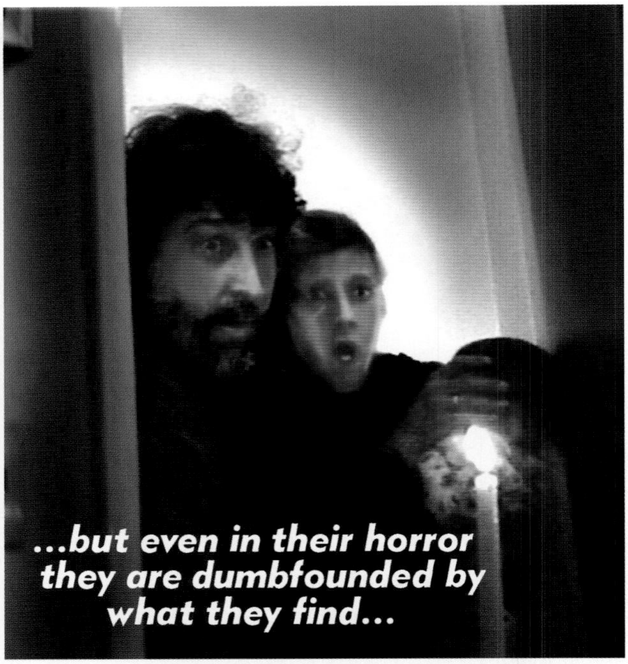
...but even in their horror they are dumbfounded by what they find...

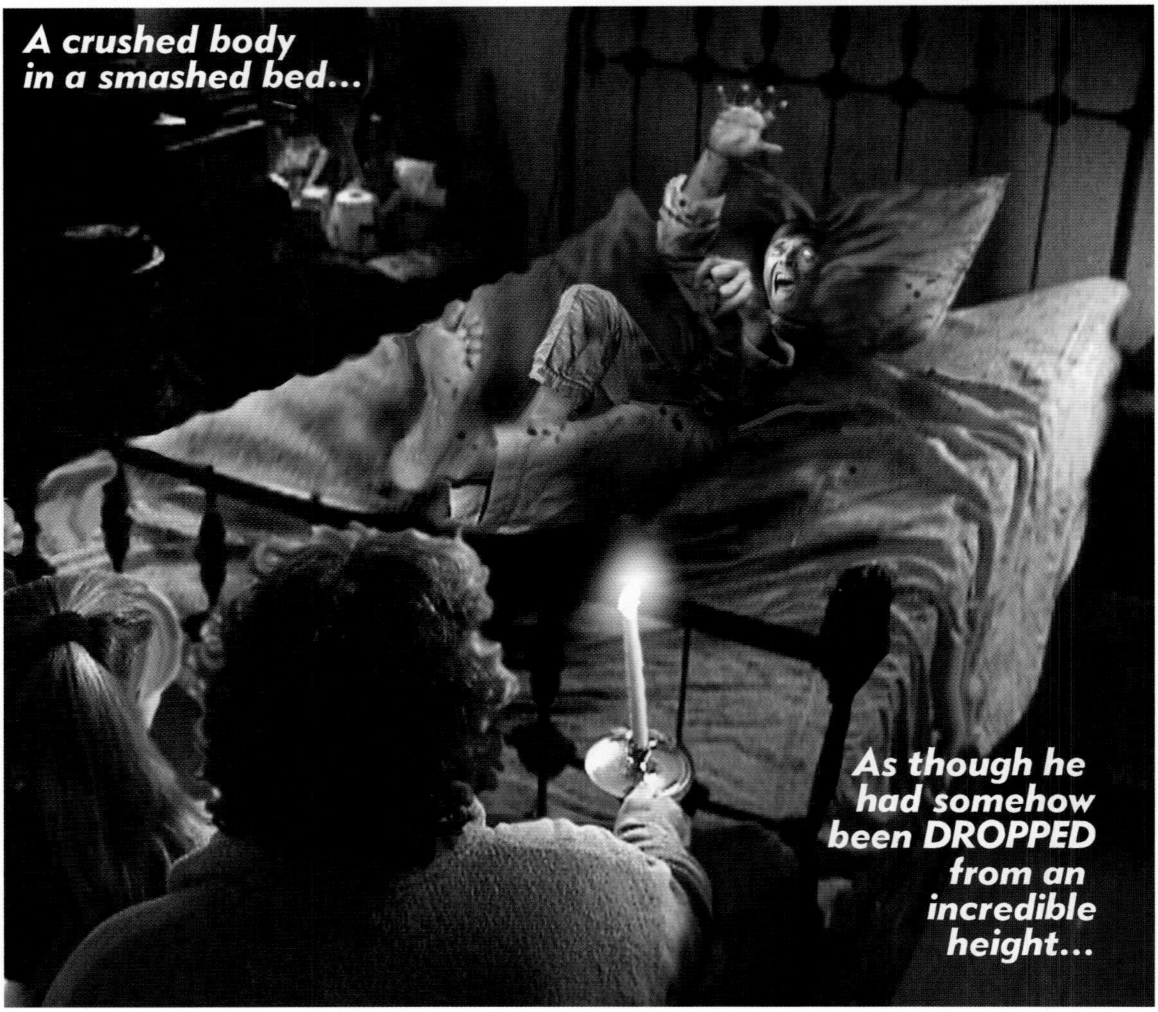
A crushed body in a smashed bed...
As though he had somehow been DROPPED from an incredible height...

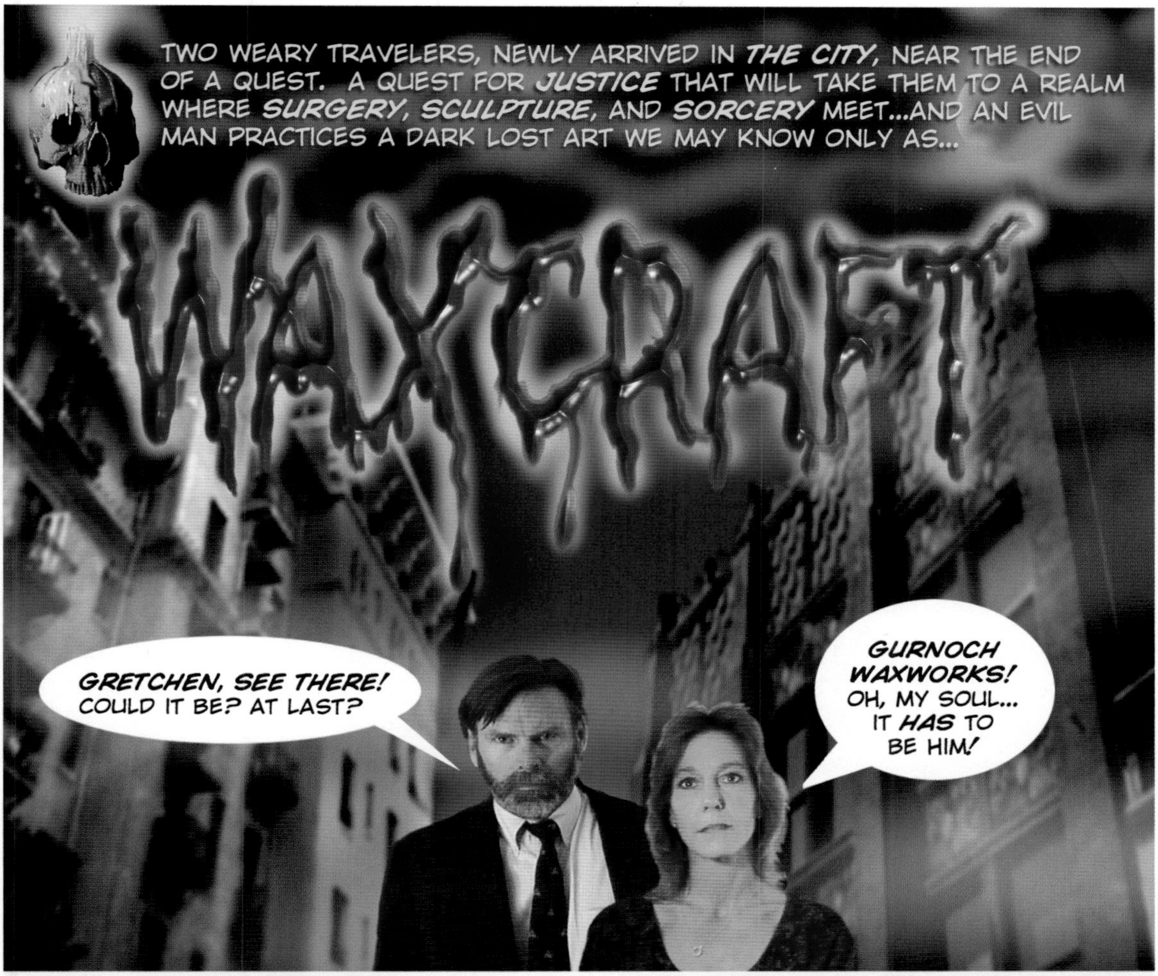
TWO WEARY TRAVELERS, NEWLY ARRIVED IN THE CITY, NEAR THE END OF A QUEST. A QUEST FOR JUSTICE THAT WILL TAKE THEM TO A REALM WHERE SURGERY, SCULPTURE, AND SORCERY MEET...AND AN EVIL MAN PRACTICES A DARK LOST ART WE MAY KNOW ONLY AS...
WAXCRAFT
GRETCHEN, SEE THERE! COULD IT BE? AT LAST?
GURNOCH WAXWORKS! OH, MY SOUL... IT HAS TO BE HIM!

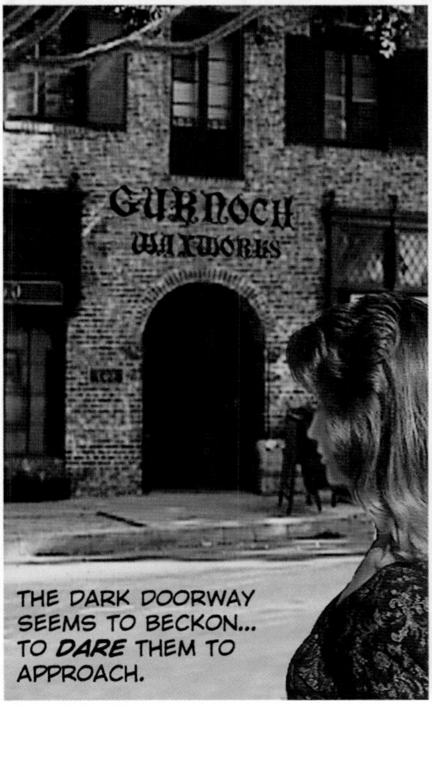
GURNOCH
WAXWORKS
THE DARK DOORWAY SEEMS TO BECKON... TO DARE THEM TO APPROACH.

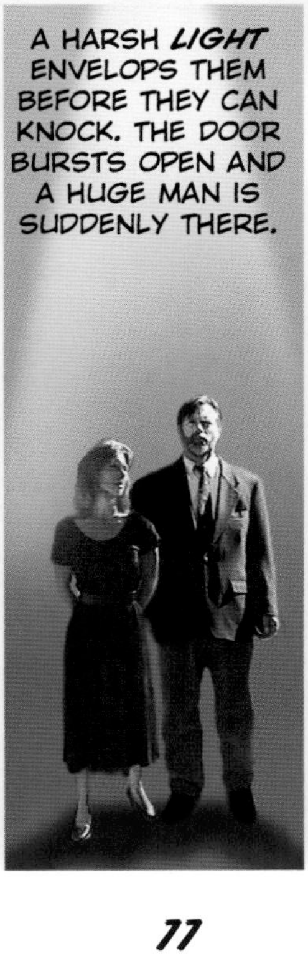
A HARSH LIGHT ENVELOPS THEM BEFORE THEY CAN KNOCK. THE DOOR BURSTS OPEN AND A HUGE MAN IS SUDDENLY THERE.

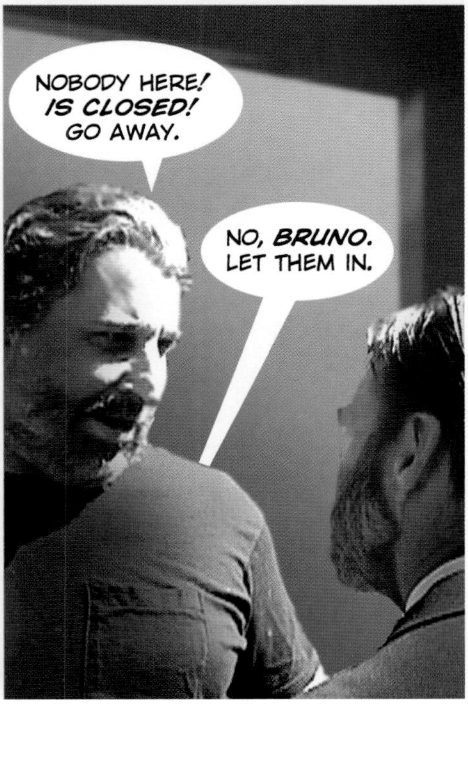
NOBODY HERE! IS CLOSED! GO AWAY.
NO, BRUNO. LET THEM IN.

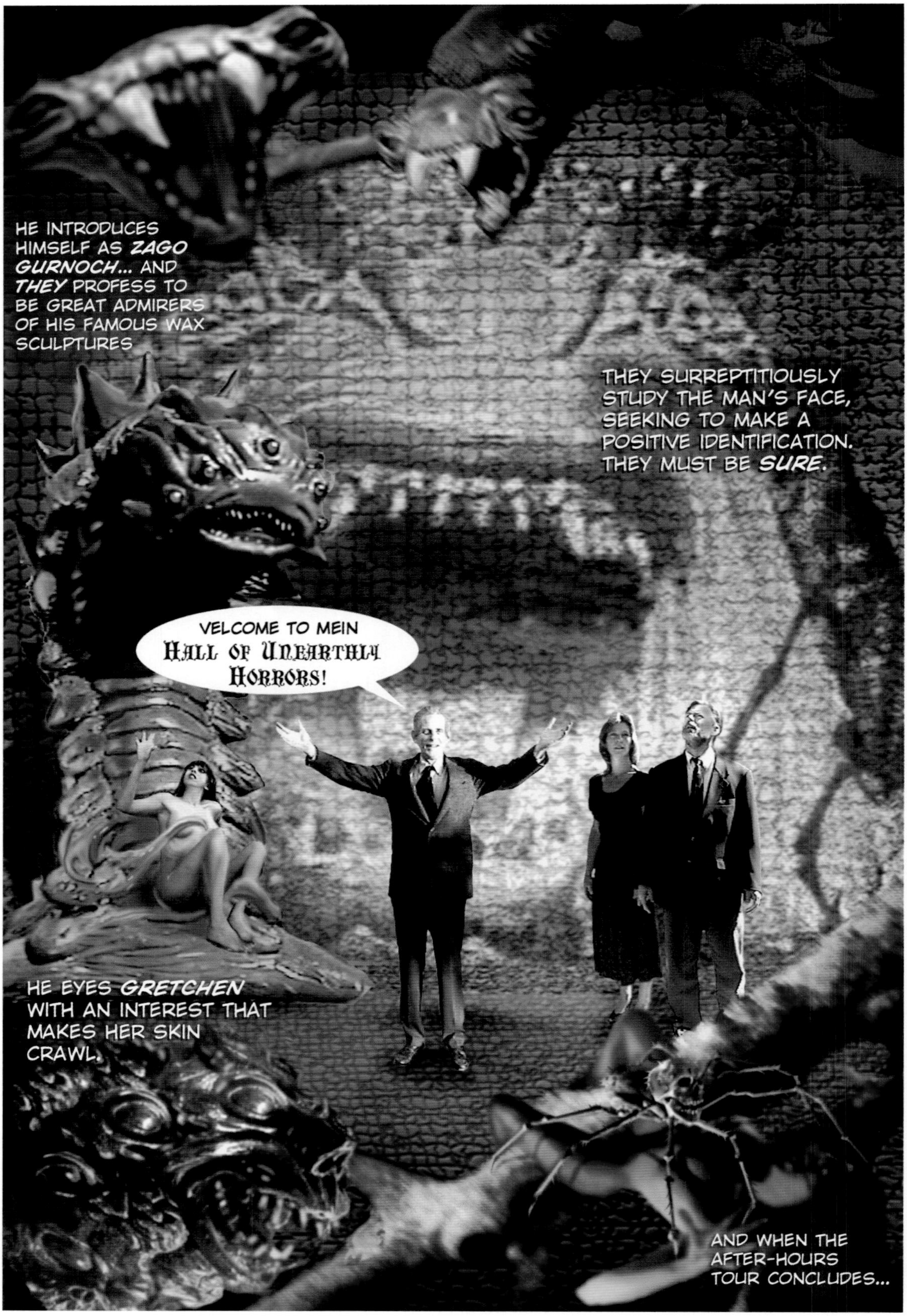
HE INTRODUCES HIMSELF AS ZAGO GURNOCH... AND THEY PROFESS TO BE GREAT ADMIRERS OF HIS FAMOUS WAX SCULPTURES
THEY SURREPTITIOUSLY STUDY THE MAN'S FACE, SEEKING TO MAKE A POSITIVE IDENTIFICATION. THEY MUST BE SURE.
VELCOME TO MEIN HALL OF UNEARTHLY HORRORS!
HE EYES GRETCHEN WITH AN INTEREST THAT MAKES HER SKIN CRAWL.
AND WHEN THE AFTER-HOURS TOUR CONCLUDES...

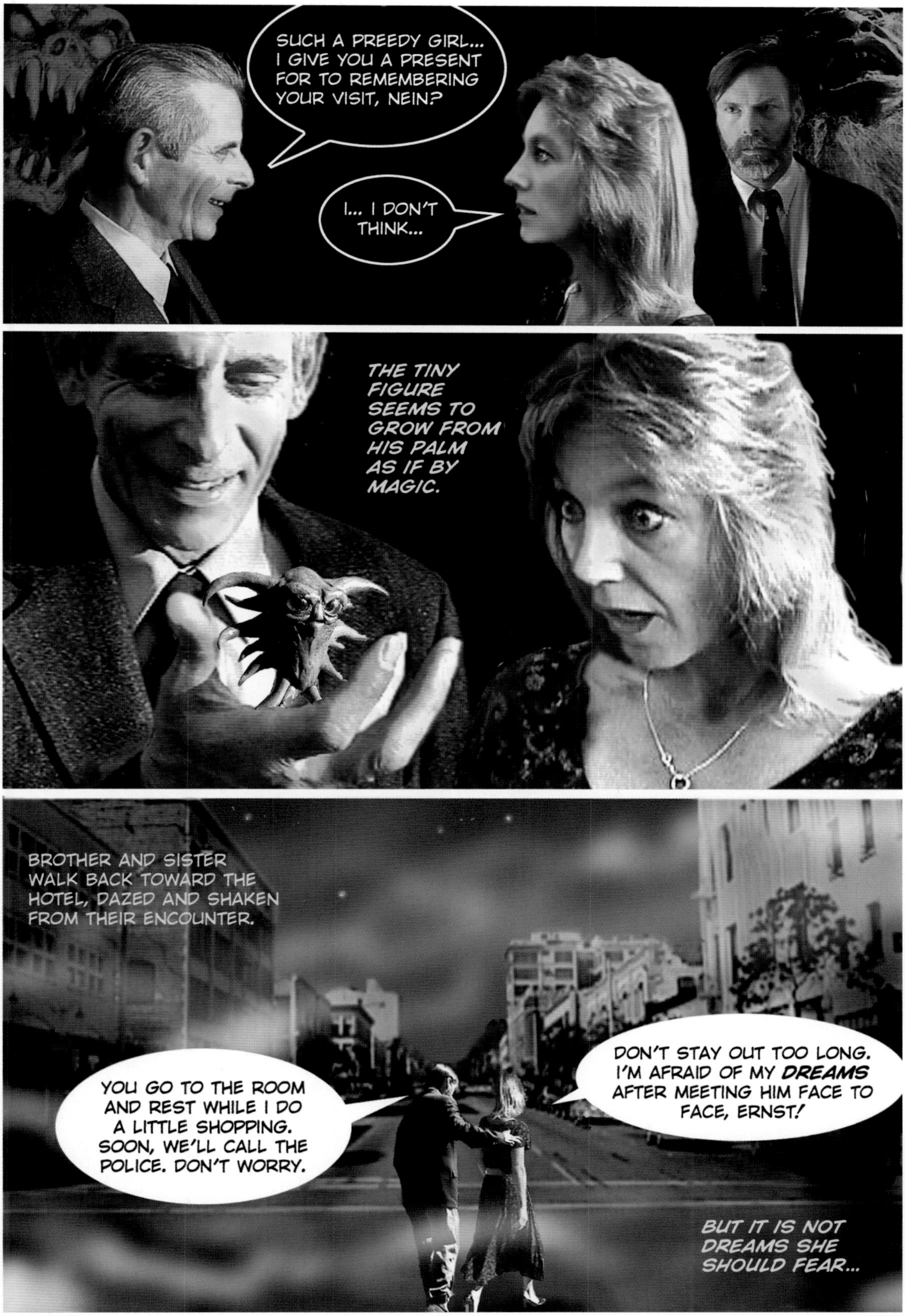
SUCH A PREEDY GIRL... I GIVE YOU A PRESENT FOR TO REMEMBERING YOUR VISIT, NEIN?
I... I DON'T THINK...
THE TINY FIGURE SEEMS TO GROW FROM HIS PALM AS IF BY MAGIC.
BROTHER AND SISTER WALK BACK TOWARD THE HOTEL, DAZED AND SHAKEN FROM THEIR ENCOUNTER.
YOU GO TO THE ROOM AND REST WHILE I DO A LITTLE SHOPPING. SOON, WE'LL CALL THE POLICE. DON'T WORRY.
DON'T STAY OUT TOO LONG. I'M AFRAID OF MY *DREAMS* AFTER MEETING HIM FACE TO FACE, ERNST!
BUT IT IS NOT DREAMS SHE SHOULD FEAR...

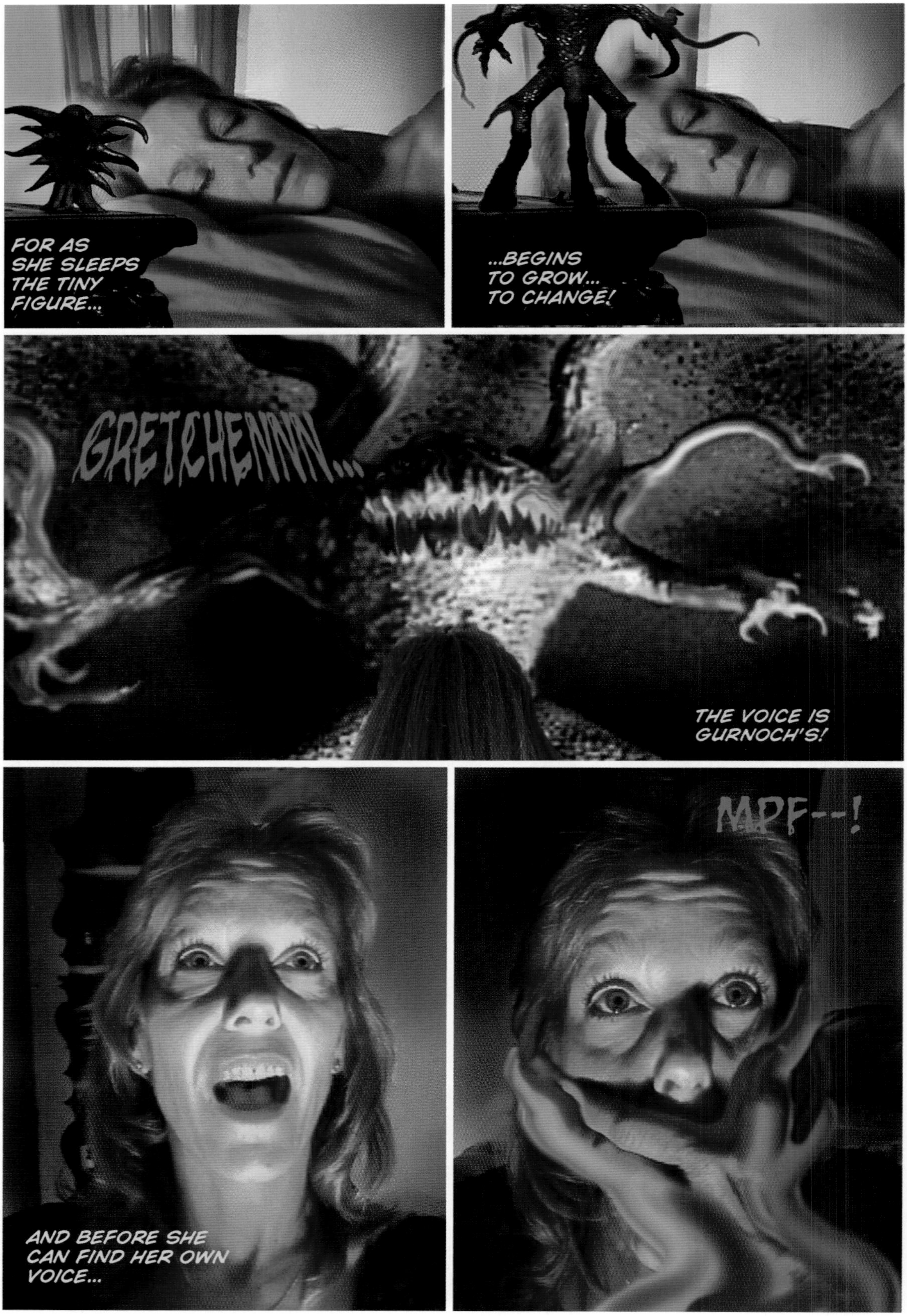
FOR AS SHE SLEEPS THE TINY FIGURE...
...BEGINS TO GROW... TO CHANGE!
GRETCHENNN...
THE VOICE IS GURNOCH'S!
AND BEFORE SHE CAN FIND HER OWN VOICE...
MPF--!

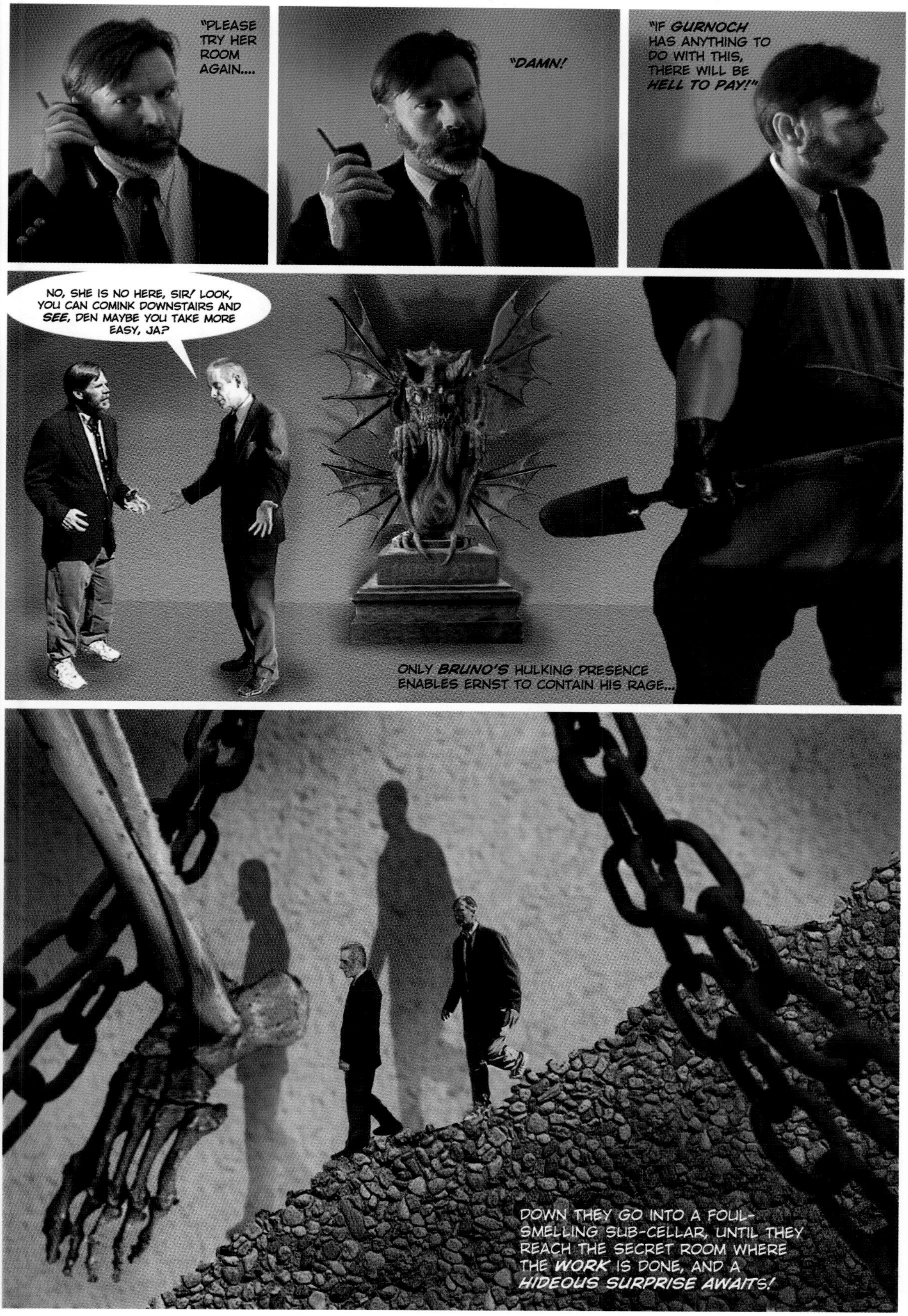
"PLEASE TRY HER ROOM AGAIN....
"DAMN!
"IF GURNOCH HAS ANYTHING TO DO WITH THIS, THERE WILL BE HELL TO PAY!"
NO, SHE IS NO HERE, SIR! LOOK, YOU CAN COMINK DOWNSTAIRS AND SEE, DEN MAYBE YOU TAKE MORE EASY, JA?
ONLY BRUNO'S HULKING PRESENCE ENABLES ERNST TO CONTAIN HIS RAGE...
DOWN THEY GO INTO A FOUL-SMELLING SUB-CELLAR, UNTIL THEY REACH THE SECRET ROOM WHERE THE WORK IS DONE, AND A HIDEOUS SURPRISE AWAITS!

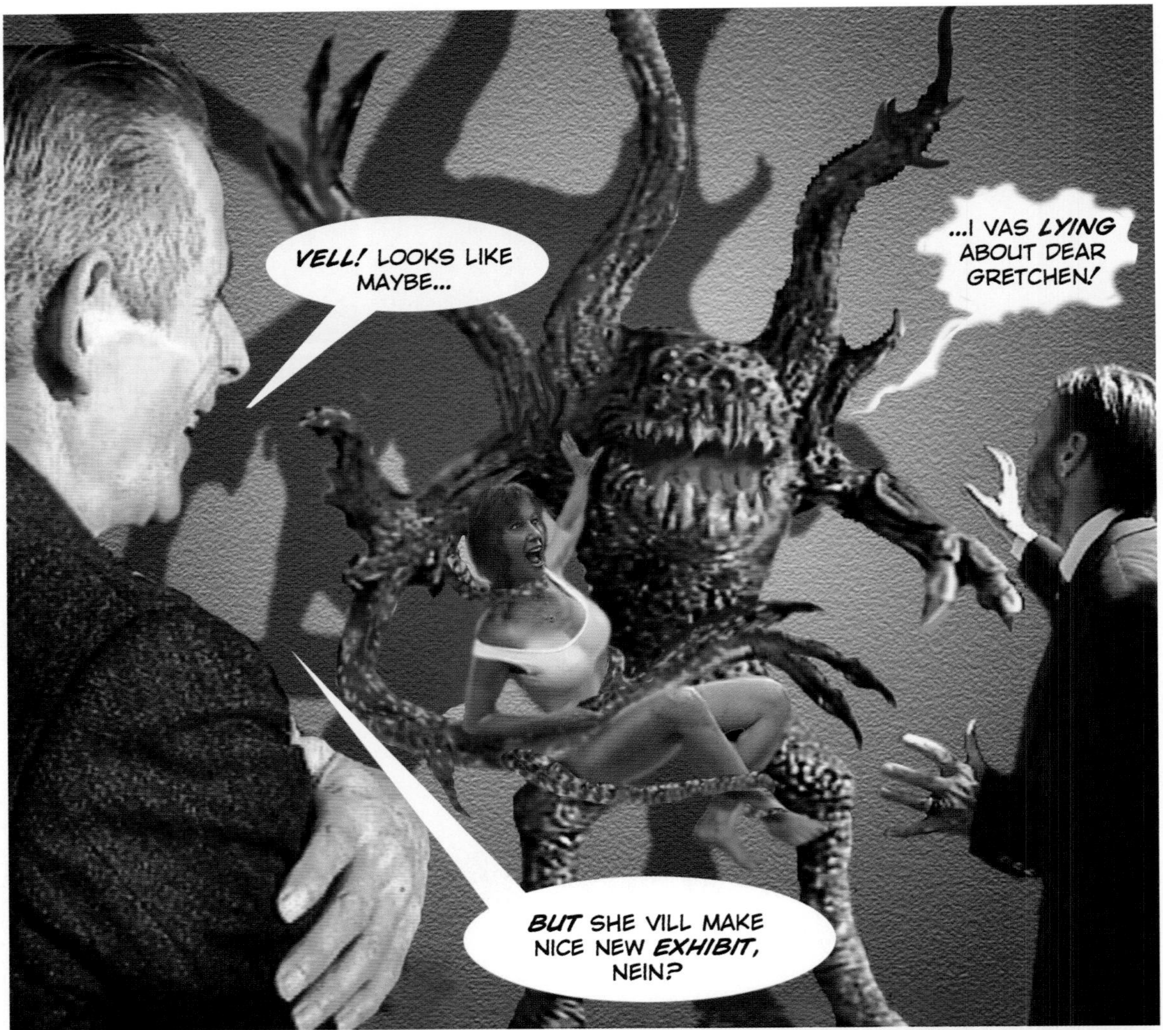
VELL! LOOKS LIKE MAYBE...
...I VAS LYING ABOUT DEAR GRETCHEN!
BUT SHE VILL MAKE NICE NEW EXHIBIT, NEIN?
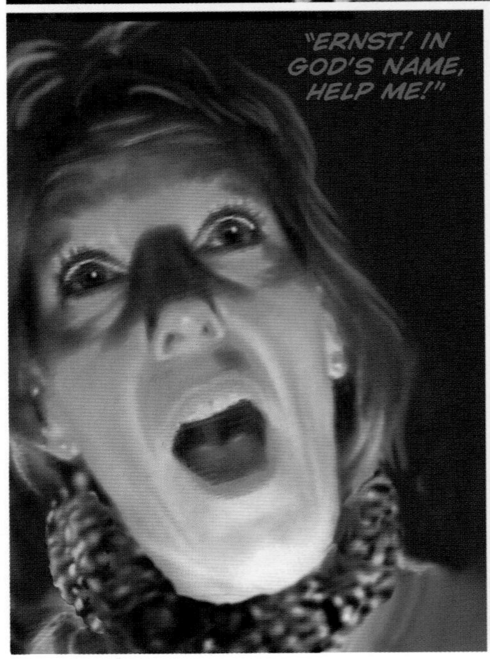
"ERNST! IN GOD'S NAME, HELP ME!"
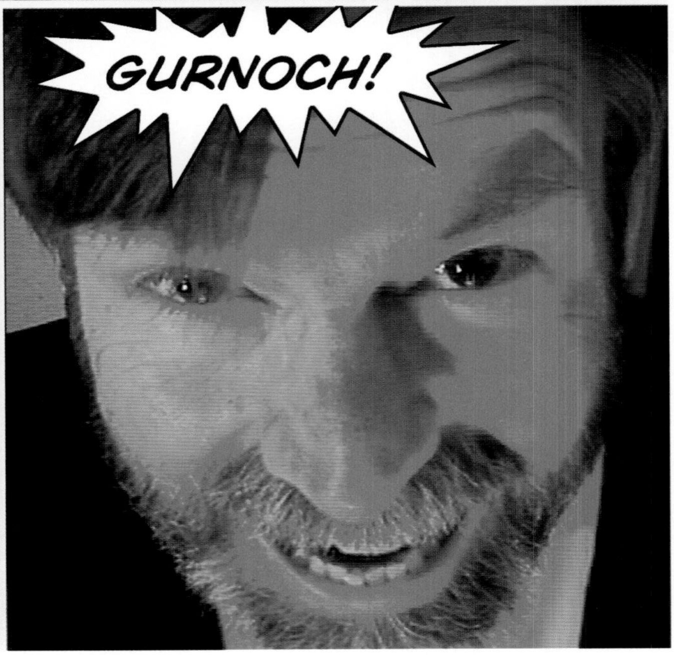
GURNOCH!

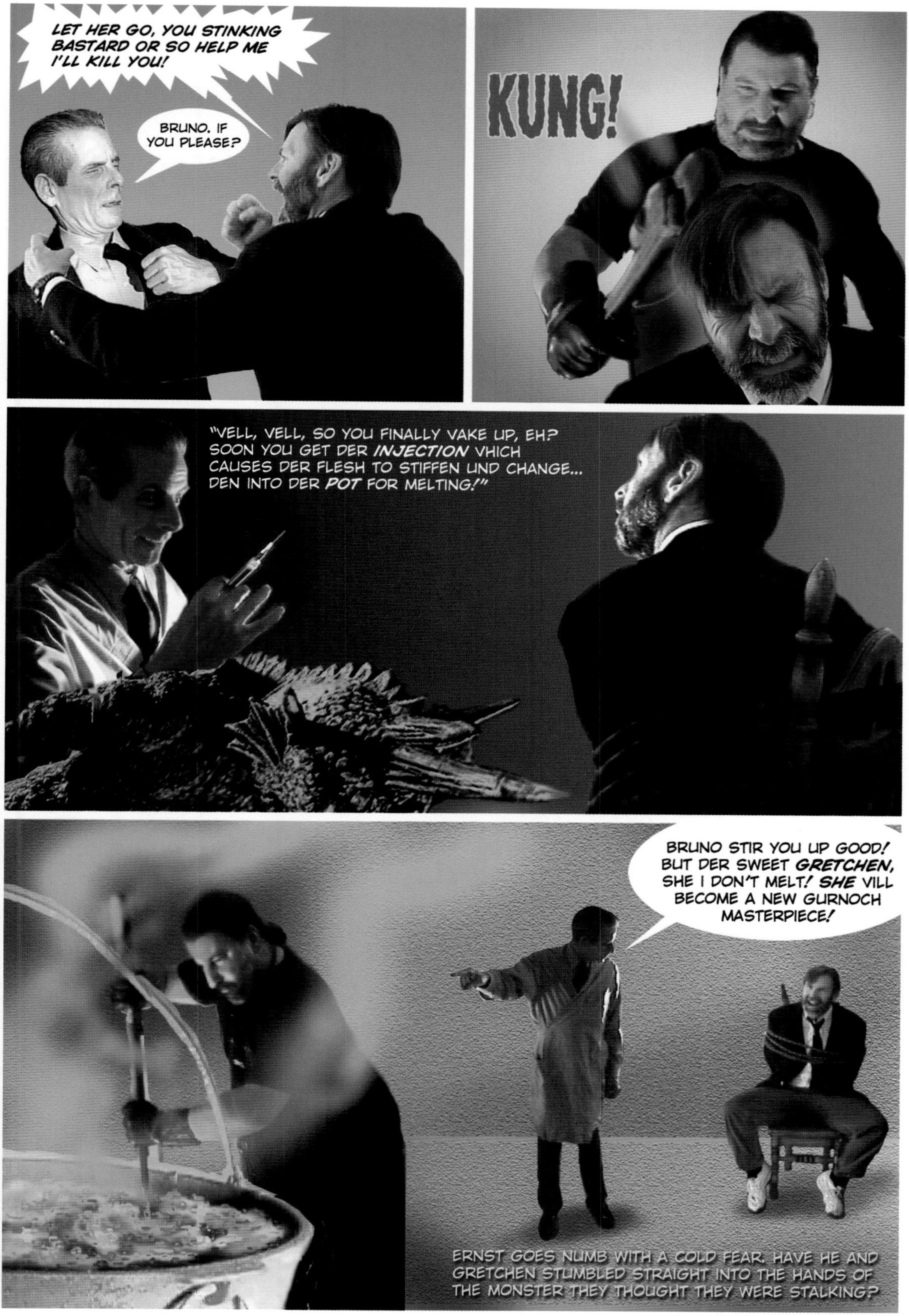
LET HER GO, YOU STINKING BASTARD OR SO HELP ME I'LL KILL YOU!
BRUNO. IF YOU PLEASE?
KUNG!
"VELL, VELL, SO YOU FINALLY VAKE UP, EH? SOON YOU GET DER INJECTION VHICH CAUSES DER FLESH TO STIFFEN UND CHANGE... DEN INTO DER POT FOR MELTING!"
BRUNO STIR YOU UP GOOD! BUT DER SWEET GRETCHEN, SHE I DON'T MELT! SHE VILL BECOME A NEW GURNOCH MASTERPIECE!
ERNST GOES NUMB WITH A COLD FEAR. HAVE HE AND GRETCHEN STUMBLED STRAIGHT INTO THE HANDS OF THE MONSTER THEY THOUGHT THEY WERE STALKING?

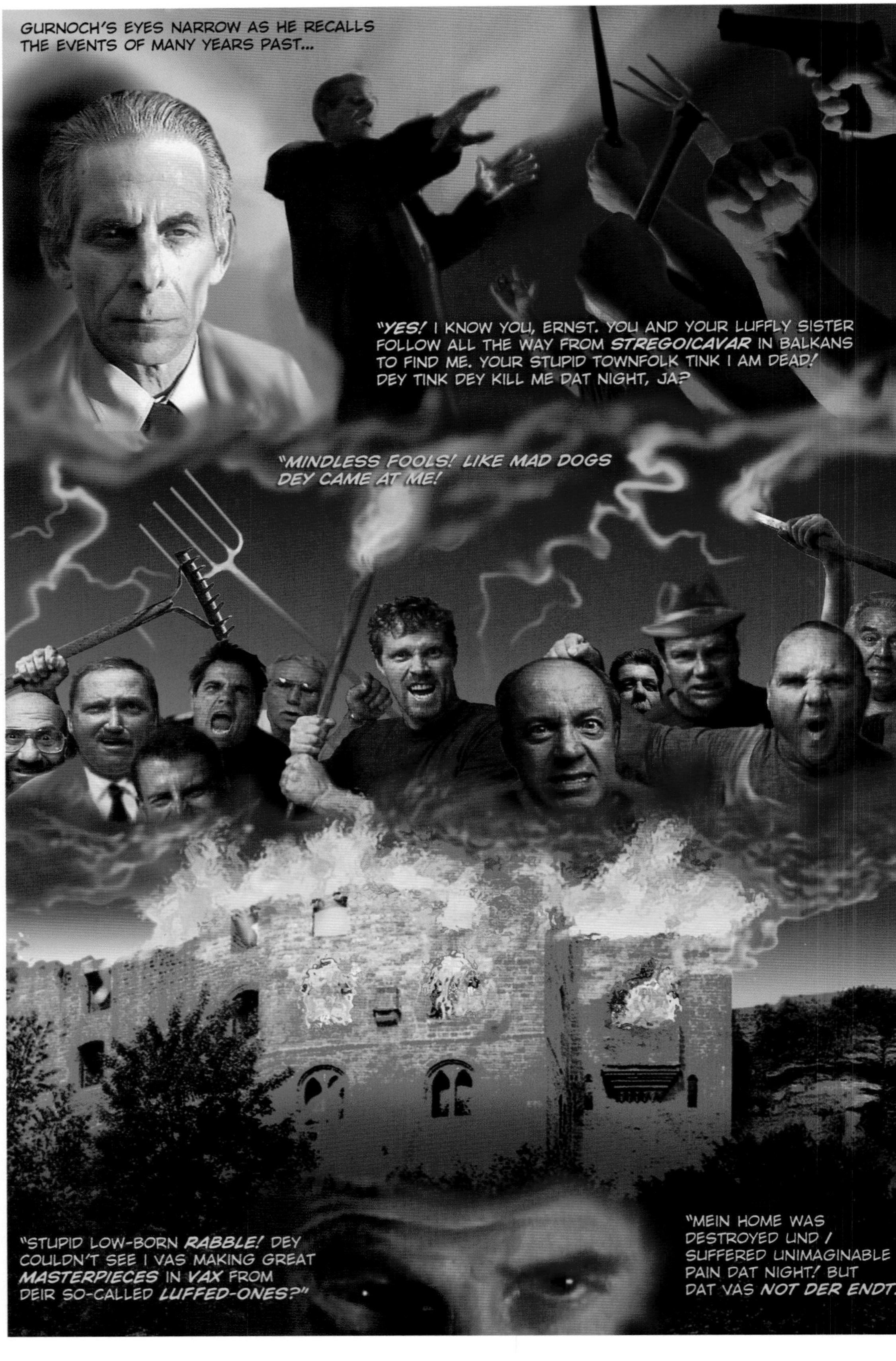
GURNOCH'S EYES NARROW AS HE RECALLS THE EVENTS OF MANY YEARS PAST...
"YES! I KNOW YOU, ERNST. YOU AND YOUR LUFFLY SISTER FOLLOW ALL THE WAY FROM STREGOICAVAR IN BALKANS TO FIND ME. YOUR STUPID TOWNFOLK TINK I AM DEAD! DEY TINK DEY KILL ME DAT NIGHT, JA?
"MINDLESS FOOLS! LIKE MAD DOGS DEY CAME AT ME!
"STUPID LOW-BORN RABBLE! DEY COULDN'T SEE I VAS MAKING GREAT MASTERPIECES IN VAX FROM DEIR SO-CALLED LUFFED-ONES?"
"MEIN HOME WAS DESTROYED UND I SUFFERED UNIMAGINABLE PAIN DAT NIGHT! BUT DAT VAS NOT DER ENDT!"

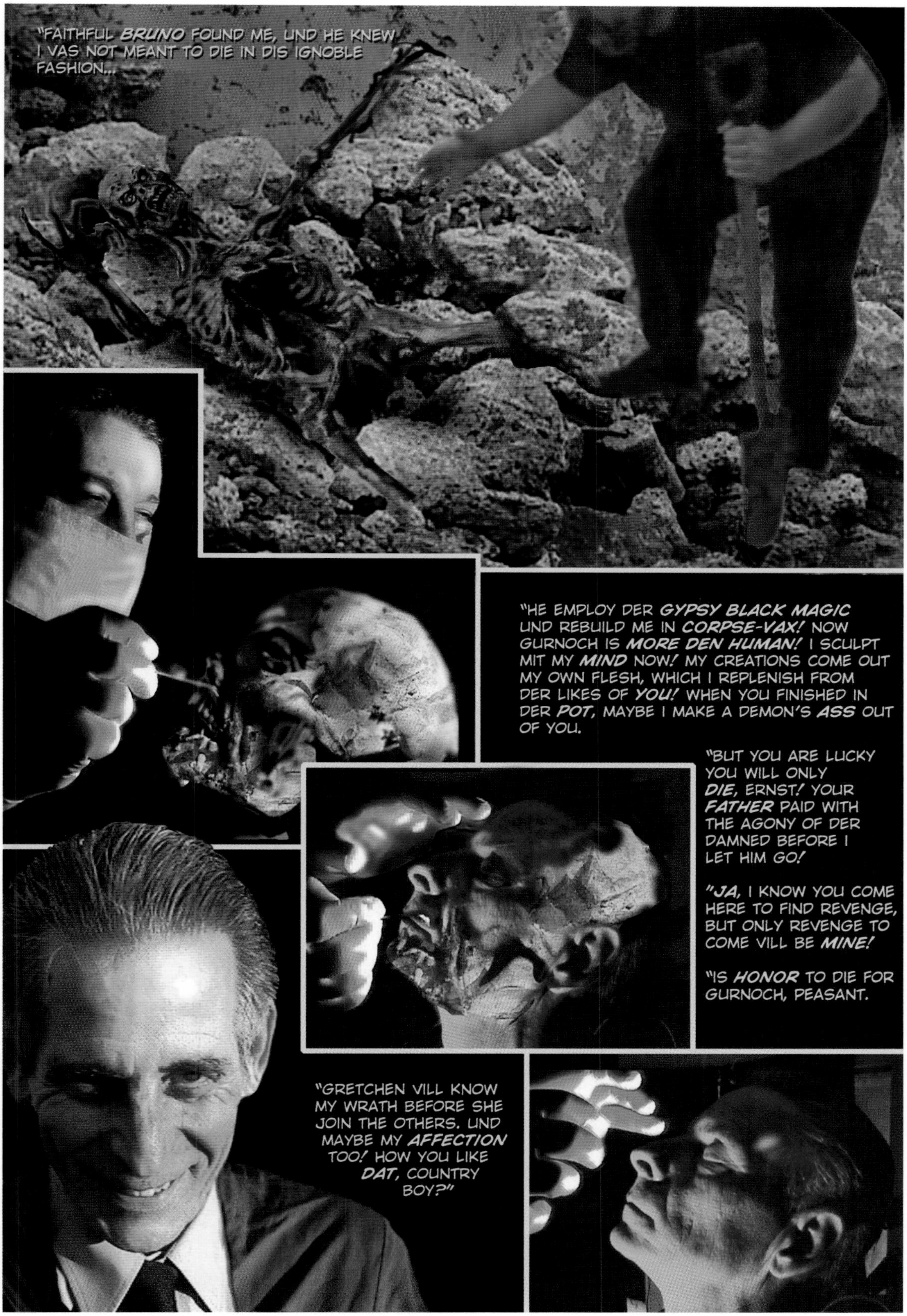
"FAITHFUL BRUNO FOUND ME, UND HE KNEW I VAS NOT MEANT TO DIE IN DIS IGNOBLE FASHION...
"HE EMPLOY DER GYPSY BLACK MAGIC UND REBUILD ME IN CORPSE-VAX! NOW GURNOCH IS MORE DEN HUMAN! I SCULPT MIT MY MIND NOW! MY CREATIONS COME OUT MY OWN FLESH, WHICH I REPLENISH FROM DER LIKES OF YOU! WHEN YOU FINISHED IN DER POT, MAYBE I MAKE A DEMON'S ASS OUT OF YOU.
"BUT YOU ARE LUCKY YOU WILL ONLY DIE, ERNST! YOUR FATHER PAID WITH THE AGONY OF DER DAMNED BEFORE I LET HIM GO!
"JA, I KNOW YOU COME HERE TO FIND REVENGE, BUT ONLY REVENGE TO COME VILL BE MINE!
"IS HONOR TO DIE FOR GURNOCH, PEASANT.
"GRETCHEN VILL KNOW MY WRATH BEFORE SHE JOIN THE OTHERS. UND MAYBE MY AFFECTION TOO! HOW YOU LIKE DAT, COUNTRY BOY?"

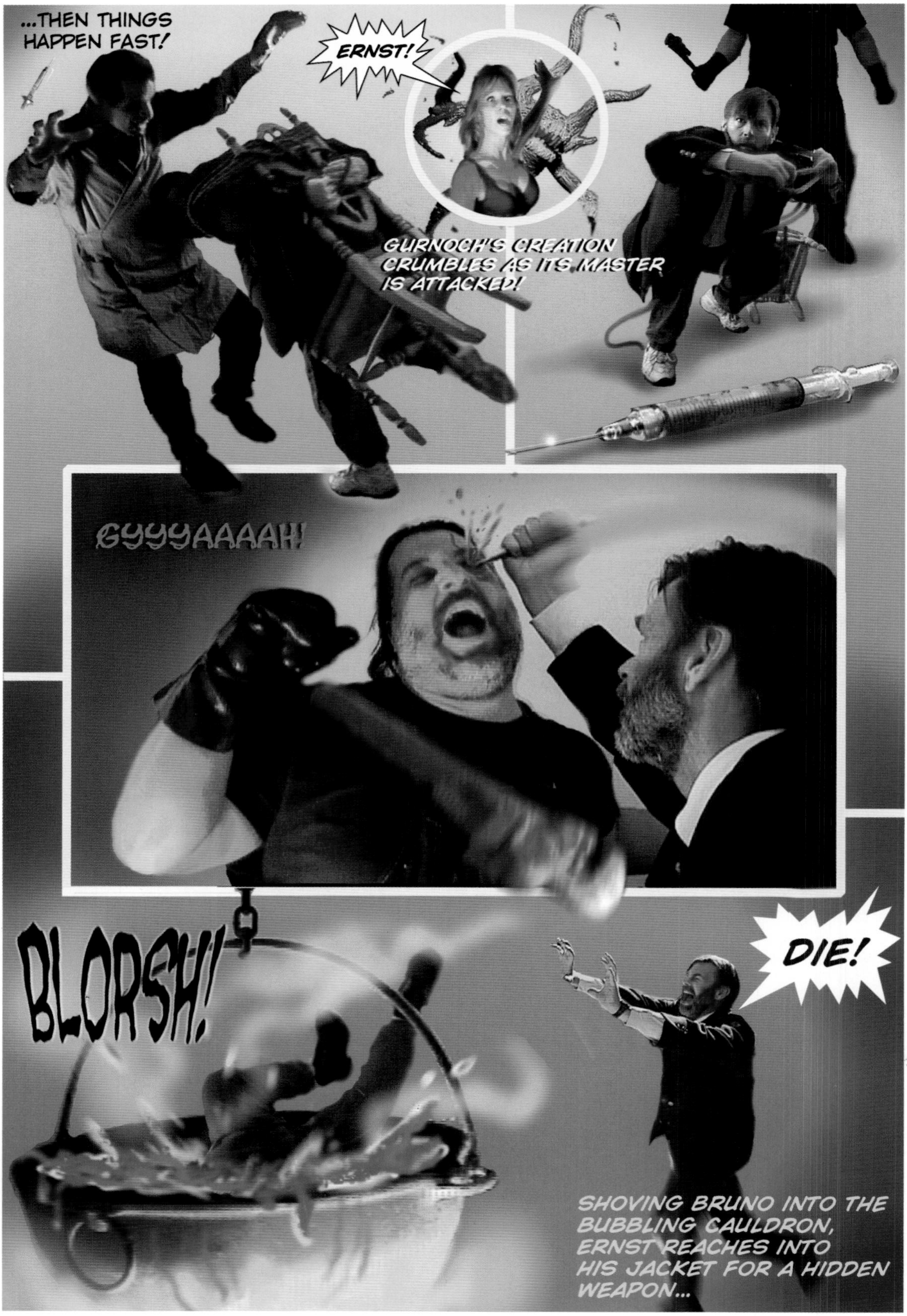
...THEN THINGS HAPPEN FAST!
ERNST!
GURNOCH'S CREATION CRUMBLES AS ITS MASTER IS ATTACKED!
GYYYAAAAH!
BLORSH!
DIE!
SHOVING BRUNO INTO THE BUBBLING CAULDRON, ERNST REACHES INTO HIS JACKET FOR A HIDDEN WEAPON...

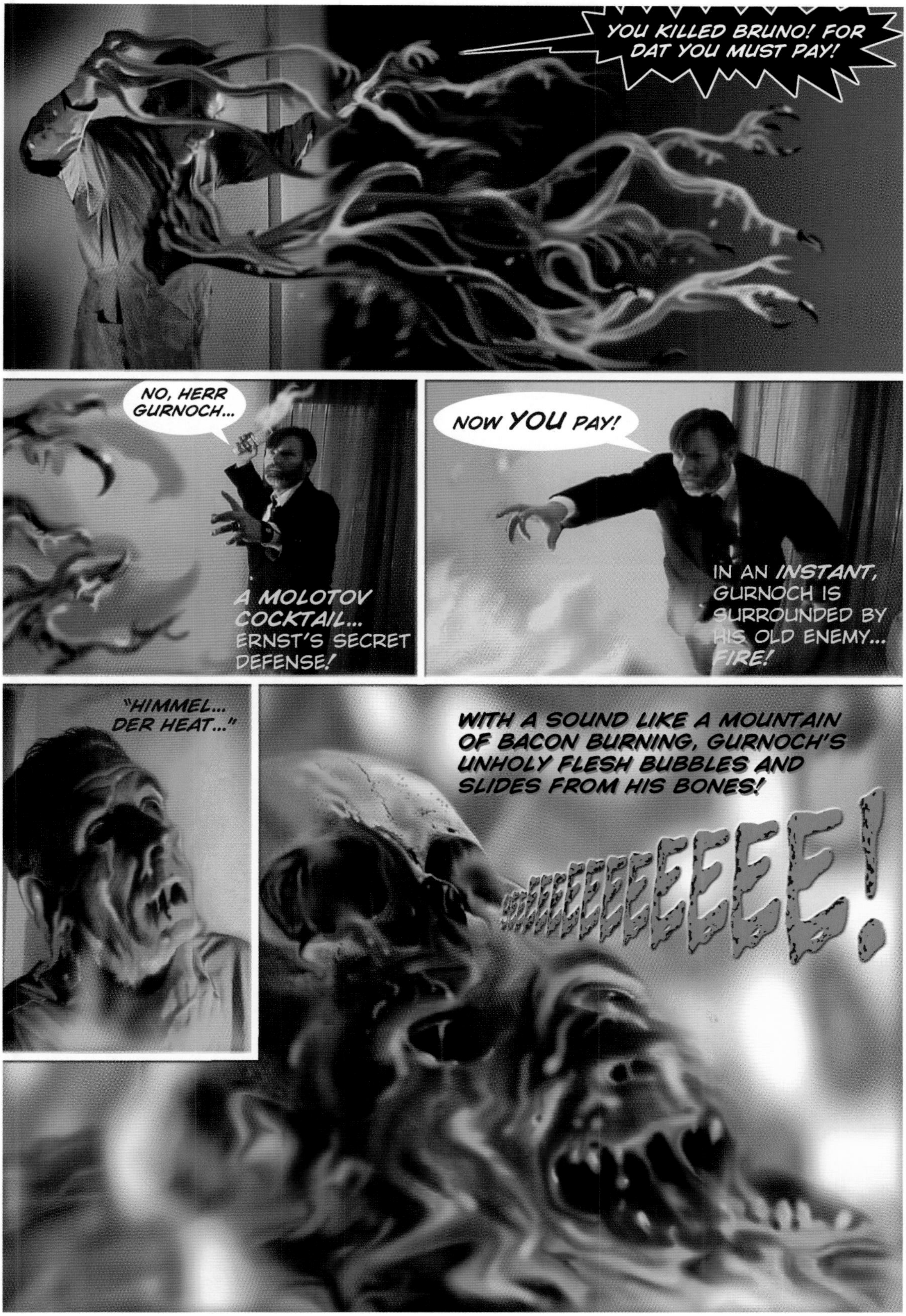
YOU KILLED BRUNO! FOR DAT YOU MUST PAY!
NO, HERR GURNOCH...
A MOLOTOV COCKTAIL... ERNST'S SECRET DEFENSE!
NOW YOU PAY!
IN AN INSTANT, GURNOCH IS SURROUNDED BY HIS OLD ENEMY... FIRE!
"HIMMEL... DER HEAT..."
WITH A SOUND LIKE A MOUNTAIN OF BACON BURNING, GURNOCH'S UNHOLY FLESH BUBBLES AND SLIDES FROM HIS BONES!
EEEEEEEEEE!

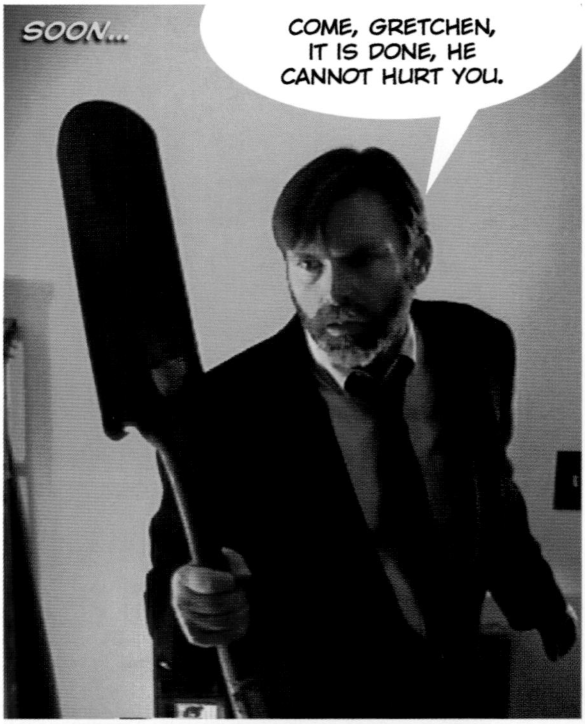
SOON...
COME, GRETCHEN, IT IS DONE, HE CANNOT HURT YOU.

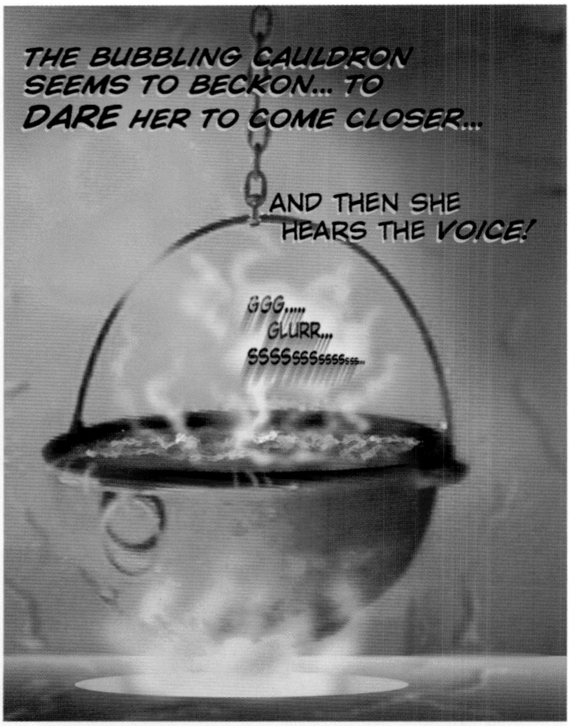
THE BUBBLING CAULDRON SEEMS TO BECKON... TO DARE HER TO COME CLOSER...
AND THEN SHE HEARS THE VOICE!
GGG..... GLURR... SSSSSSSSSSSsss...

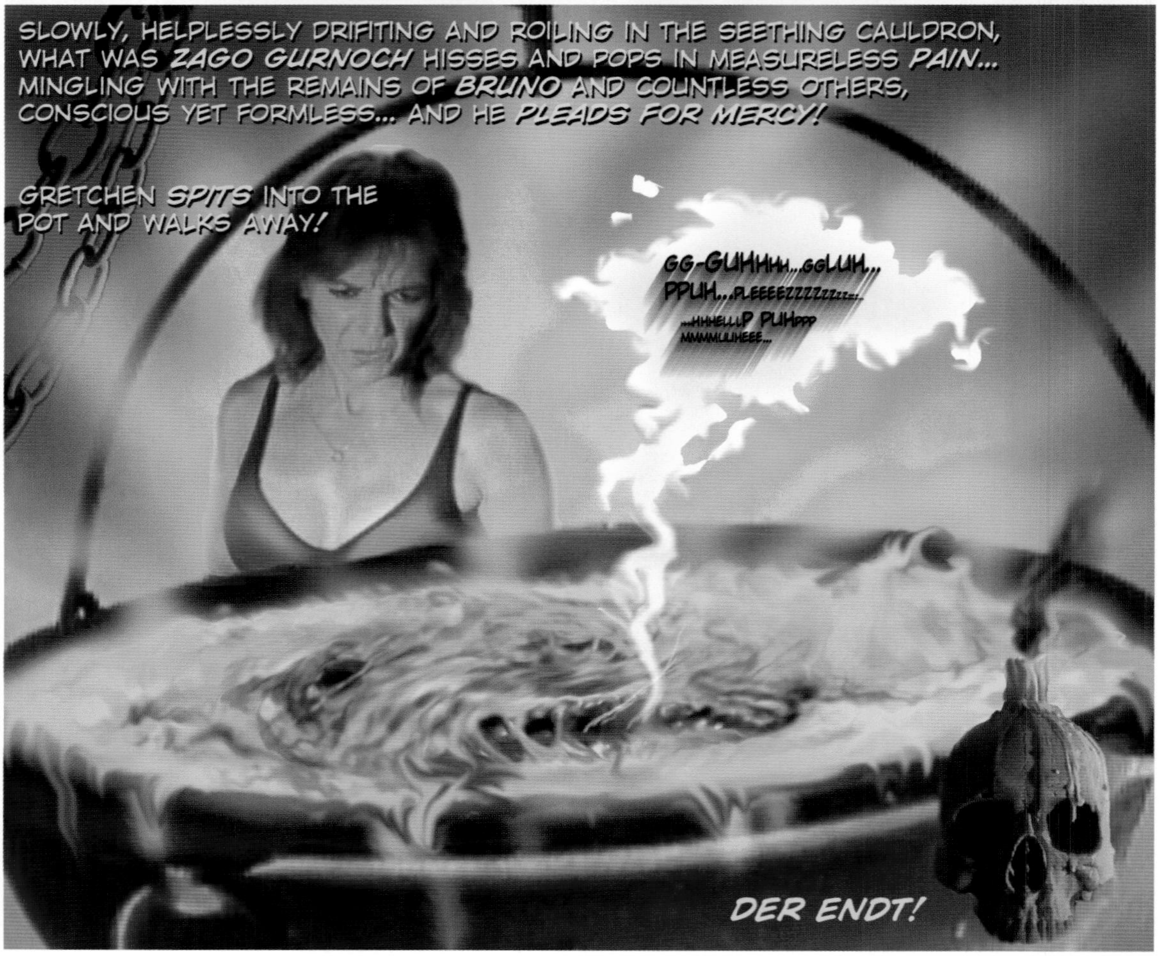
SLOWLY, HELPLESSLY DRIFITING AND ROILING IN THE SEETHING CAULDRON, WHAT WAS ZAGO GURNOCH HISSES AND POPS IN MEASURELESS PAIN... MINGLING WITH THE REMAINS OF BRUNO AND COUNTLESS OTHERS, CONSCIOUS YET FORMLESS... AND HE PLEADS FOR MERCY!
GRETCHEN SPITS INTO THE POT AND WALKS AWAY!
GG-GUHHHH...GGLUH... PPUH...PLEEEEZZZZZzzzz... ...HHHELLLP PUHPPP MMMMULHEEE...
DER ENDT!

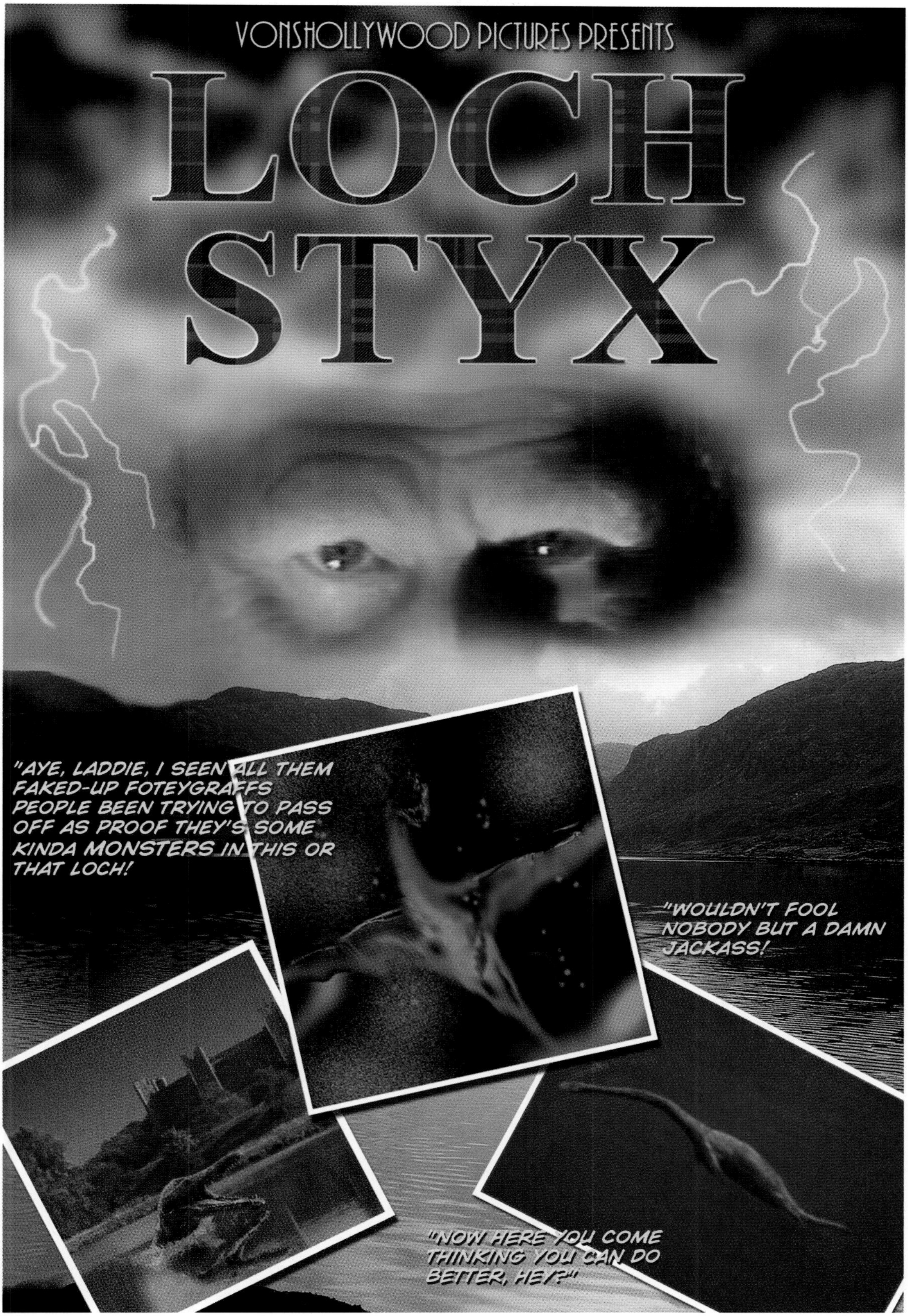
VONSHOLLYWOOD PICTURES PRESENTS
LOCH STYX
"AYE, LADDIE, I SEEN ALL THEM FAKED-UP FOTEYGRAFFS PEOPLE BEEN TRYING TO PASS OFF AS PROOF THEY'S SOME KINDA MONSTERS IN THIS OR THAT LOCH!
"WOULDN'T FOOL NOBODY BUT A DAMN JACKASS!
"NOW HERE YOU COME THINKING YOU CAN DO BETTER, HEY?"

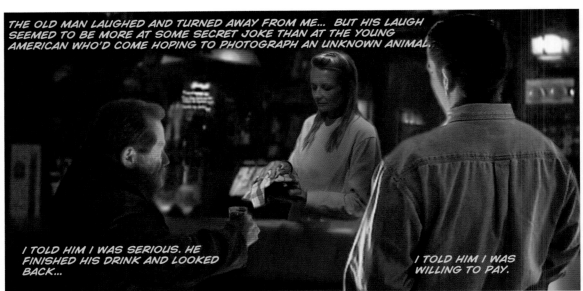

THE OLD MAN LAUGHED AND TURNED AWAY FROM ME... BUT HIS LAUGH SEEMED TO BE MORE AT SOME SECRET JOKE THAN AT THE YOUNG AMERICAN WHO'D COME HOPING TO PHOTOGRAPH AN UNKNOWN ANIMAL.

I TOLD HIM I WAS SERIOUS. HE FINISHED HIS DRINK AND LOOKED BACK...

I TOLD HIM I WAS WILLING TO PAY.

"SERIOUS, ARE YE? AND WILLING TO PAY?"

"DAMN RIGHT."

"THEN BRING YER CAMERA... AND YER BALLS."

AS WE DROVE OFF INTO THE GLOOMY HILLS HE TOLD ME THERE *WAS* SOMETHING LIVING IN ONE OF THE LOCHS, BUT NOT LIKE WHAT PEOPLE THOUGHT. THE DESIRE FOR DISCOVERY BURNED HOTTER WITHIN ME, KEEPING THE CHILL SCOTTISH NIGHT AT BAY.

FINALLY WE ARRIVED AT WHAT HE CALLED "LOCH STYX." HE SAID THE BOOKS DIDN'T SHOW IT AND VERY FEW LOCALS KNEW HOW TO FIND IT.

"HELP ME LAUNCH THE BOAT, LADDIE, AND WE'LL DO US A LITTLE FISHIN'."

AS WE ROWED OUT INTO THE GRAY DAWN, HE PULLED SOMETHING OUT FROM UNDER THE SEAT...

"WHAT'S THAT?"

"BAIT."

"JESUS CHRIST!"

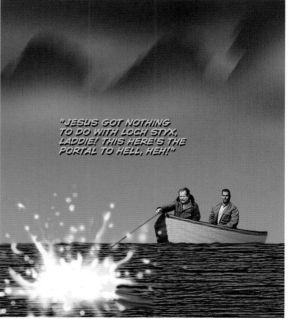

"JESUS GOT NOTHING TO DO WITH LOCH STYX, LADDIE! THIS HERE'S THE PORTAL TO HELL, HEH!"

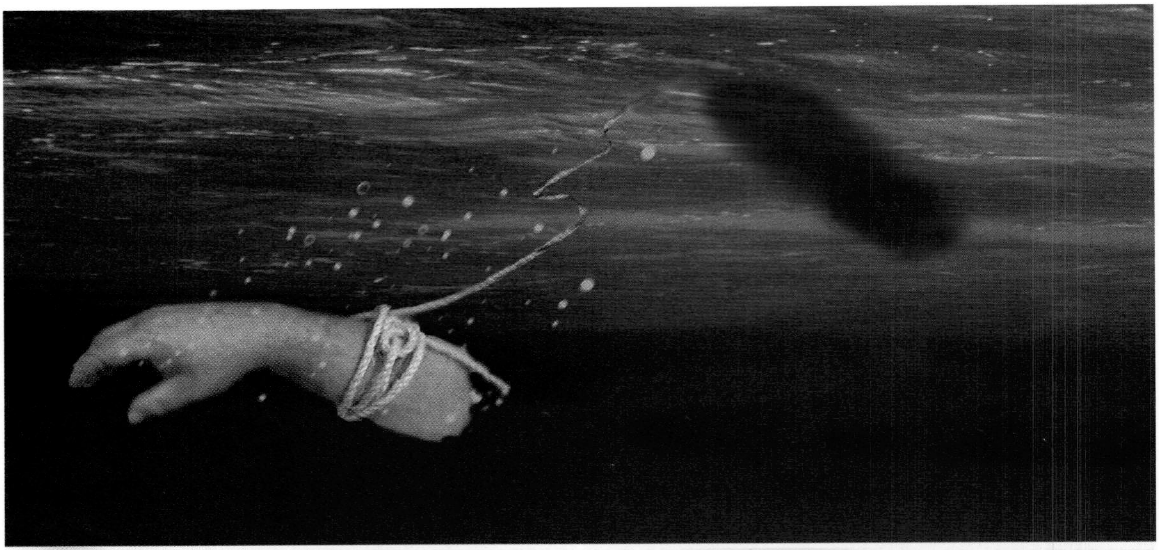

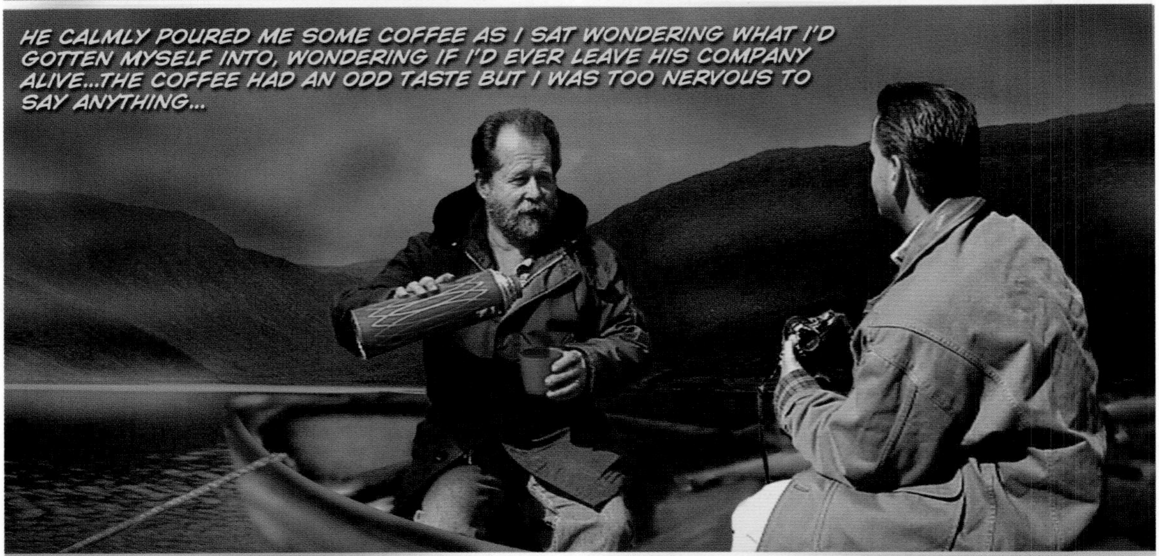
HE CALMLY POURED ME SOME COFFEE AS I SAT WONDERING WHAT I'D GOTTEN MYSELF INTO, WONDERING IF I'D EVER LEAVE HIS COMPANY ALIVE...THE COFFEE HAD AN ODD TASTE BUT I WAS TOO NERVOUS TO SAY ANYTHING...

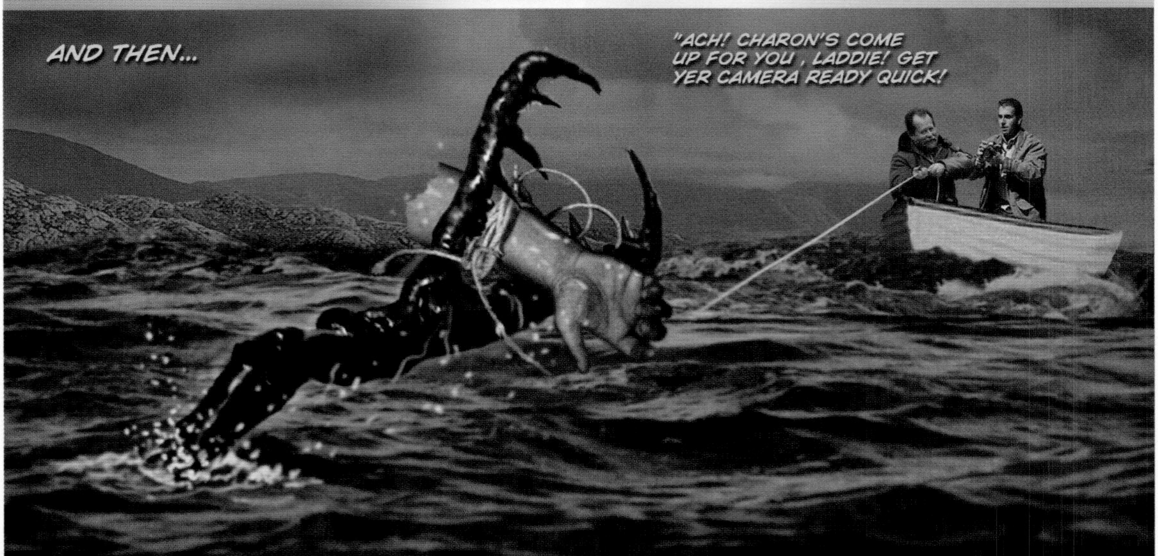
AND THEN...
"ACH! CHARON'S COME UP FOR YOU , LADDIE! GET YER CAMERA READY QUICK!

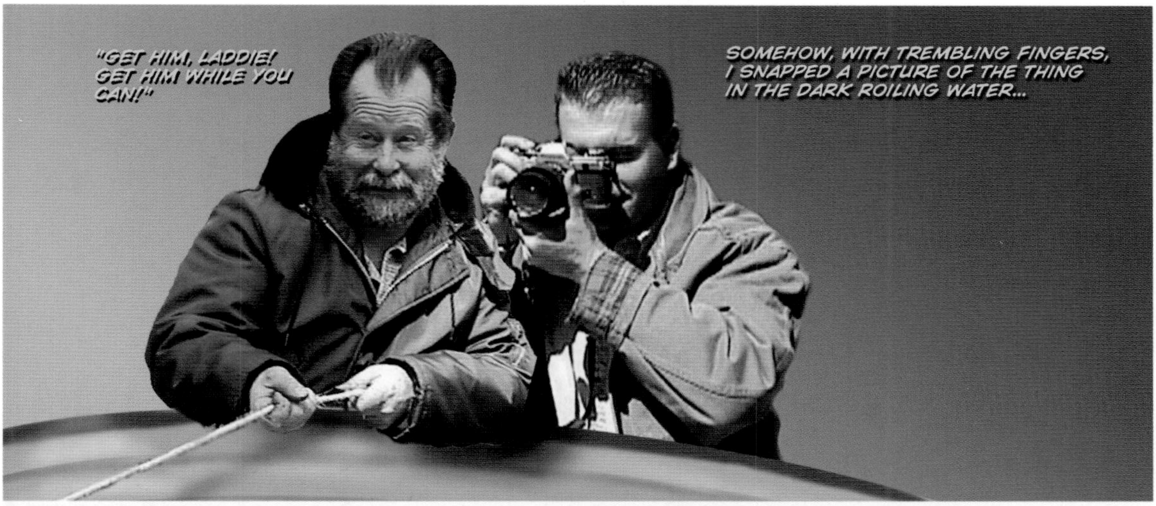
"GET HIM, LADDIE! GET HIM WHILE YOU CAN!"
SOMEHOW, WITH TREMBLING FINGERS, I SNAPPED A PICTURE OF THE THING IN THE DARK ROILING WATER...

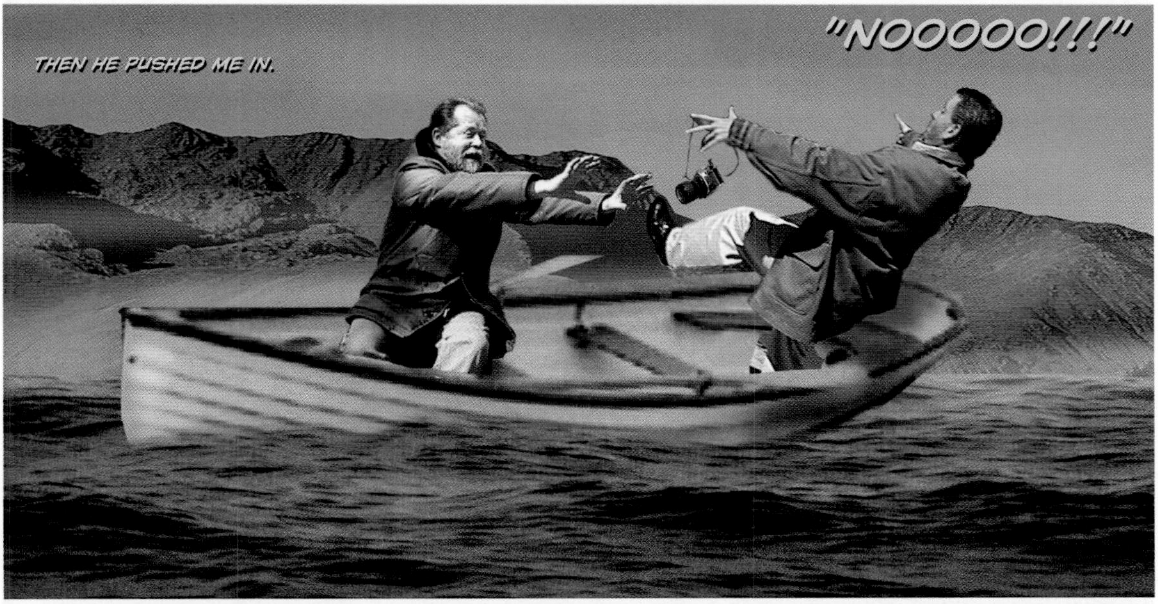
THEN HE PUSHED ME IN.
"NOOOOOO!!!"

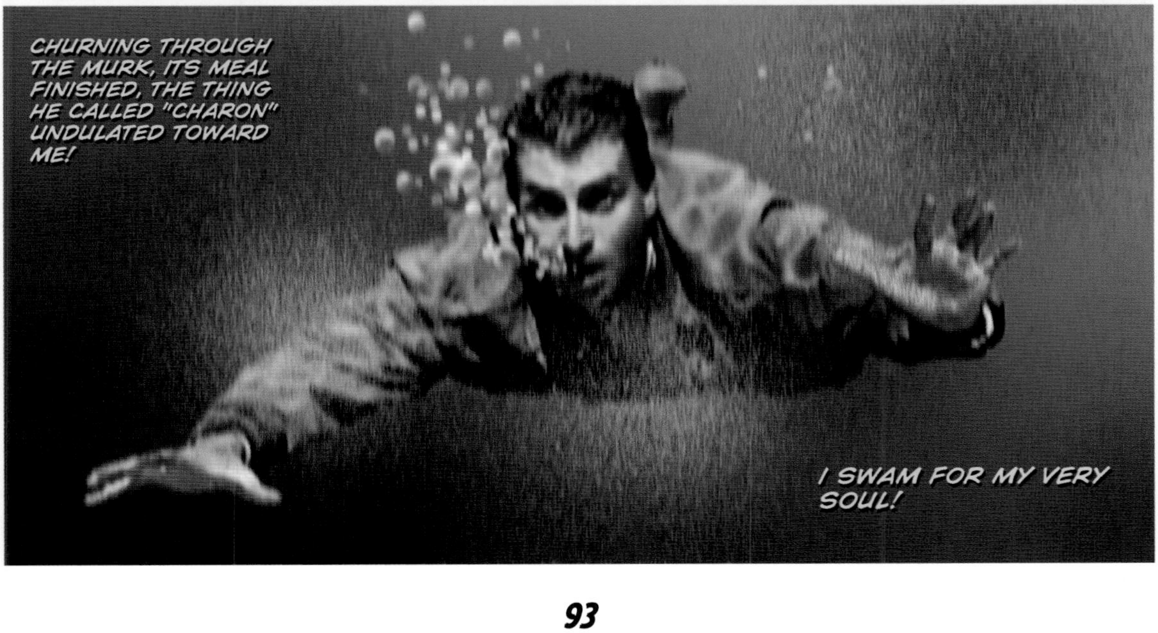
CHURNING THROUGH THE MURK, ITS MEAL FINISHED, THE THING HE CALLED "CHARON" UNDULATED TOWARD ME!
I SWAM FOR MY VERY SOUL!

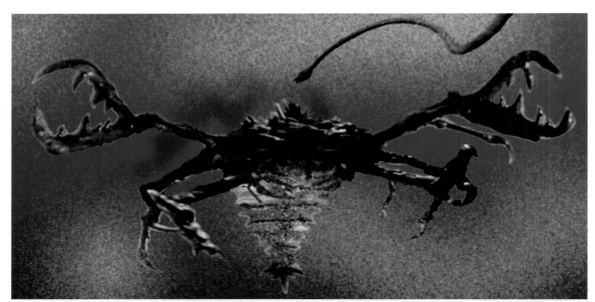

LAUGHING LIKE A MANIAC, HE PULLED ME BACK INTO THE BOAT AS THE THING'S CLAWS CLACKED ANXIOUSLY AT MY HEELS.

"WHAT'S WRONG, LADDIE? THOUGHT YOU WANTED TO SEE SOMETHIN'?"

WEEPING, I TRIED TO STAMMER OUT SOME INCOHERENT QUESTIONS AS THE BITTER TANG OF THE COFFEE OVERCAME THE FOUL TASTE OF LOCH STYX....THEN I BEGAN TO FEEL DIZZY...

"CHARON FERRIES YOU ACROSS THE STYX INTO HELL. THAT'S WHAT HE DOES. BUT YOU GOT TO PAY FOR THE RIDE, LADDIE.

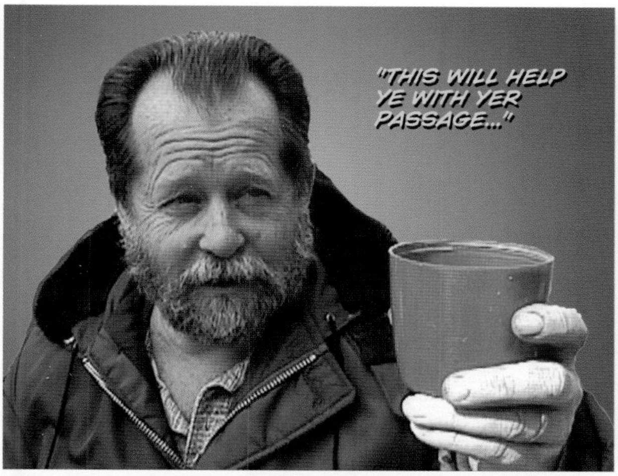
"THIS WILL HELP YE WITH YER PASSAGE..."

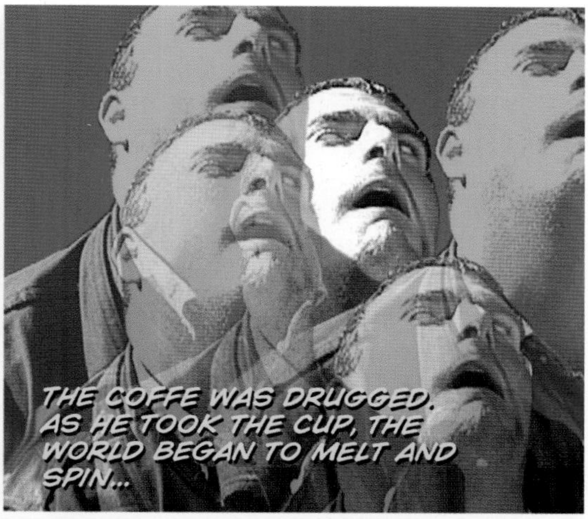
THE COFFE WAS DRUGGED. AS HE TOOK THE CUP, THE WORLD BEGAN TO MELT AND SPIN...

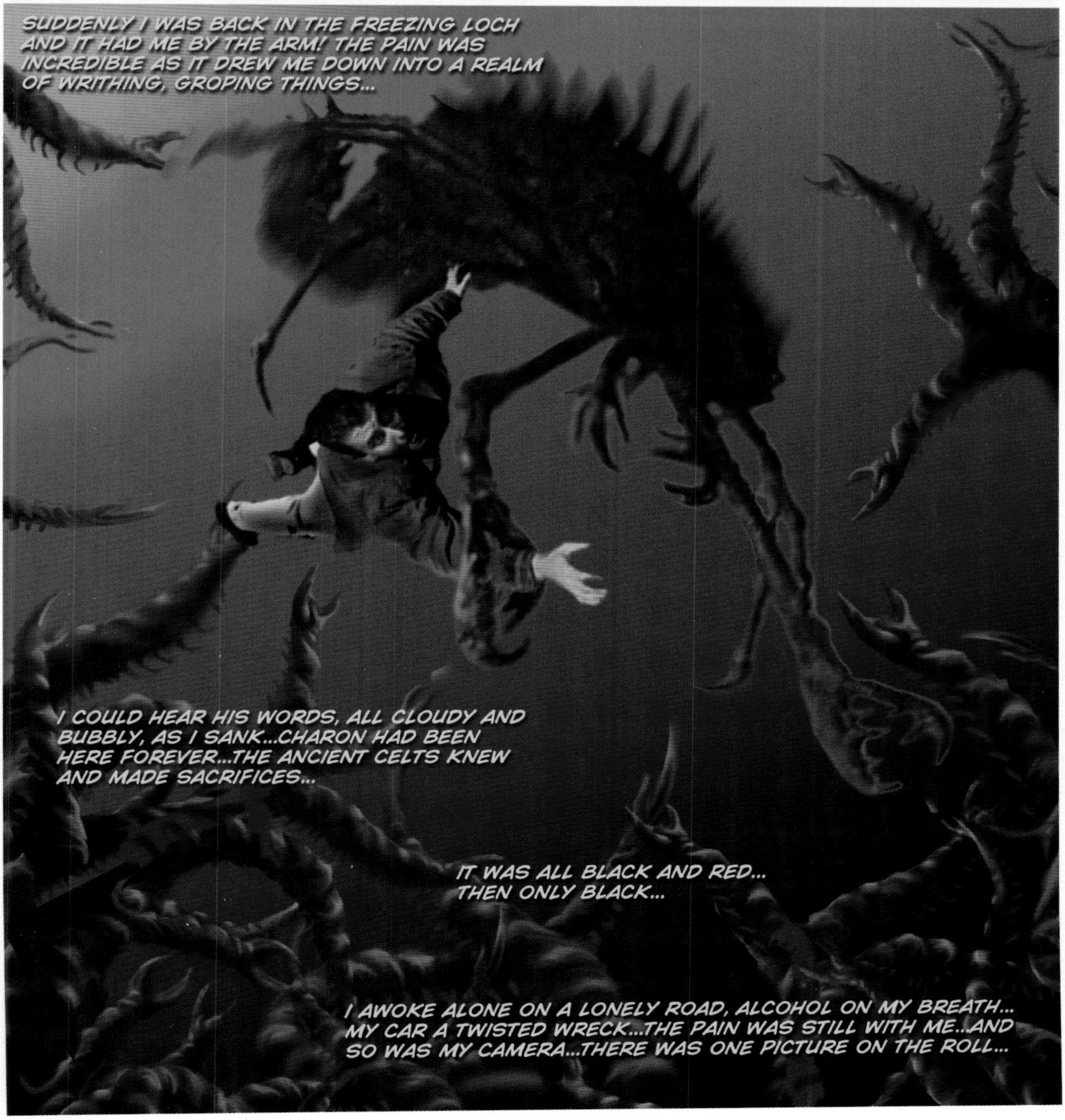
SUDDENLY I WAS BACK IN THE FREEZING LOCH AND IT HAD ME BY THE ARM! THE PAIN WAS INCREDIBLE AS IT DREW ME DOWN INTO A REALM OF WRITHING, GROPING THINGS...
I COULD HEAR HIS WORDS, ALL CLOUDY AND BUBBLY, AS I SANK...CHARON HAD BEEN HERE FOREVER...THE ANCIENT CELTS KNEW AND MADE SACRIFICES...
IT WAS ALL BLACK AND RED... THEN ONLY BLACK...
I AWOKE ALONE ON A LONELY ROAD, ALCOHOL ON MY BREATH... MY CAR A TWISTED WRECK...THE PAIN WAS STILL WITH ME...AND SO WAS MY CAMERA...THERE WAS ONE PICTURE ON THE ROLL...

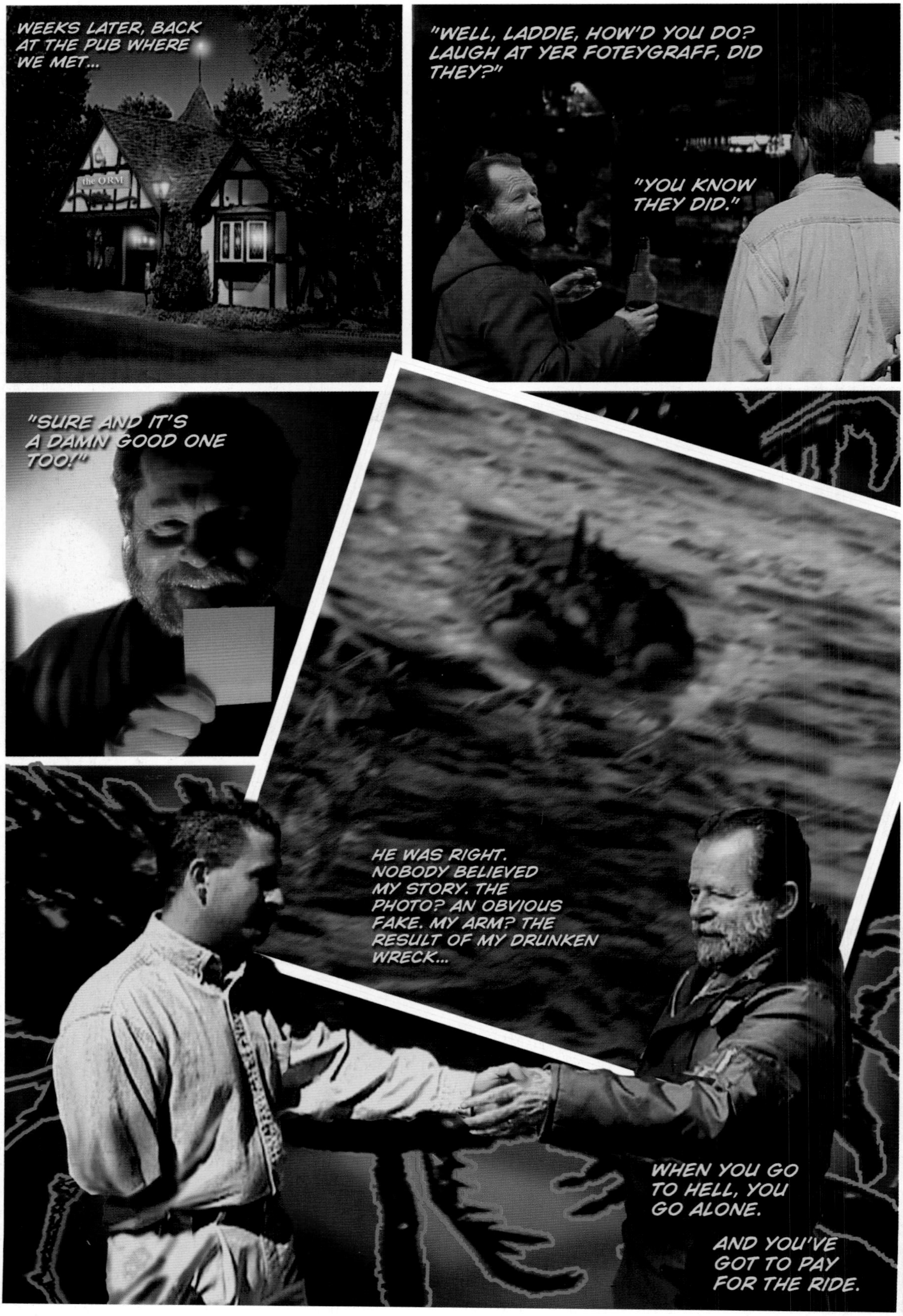
WEEKS LATER, BACK AT THE PUB WHERE WE MET...
the ORM
"WELL, LADDIE, HOW'D YOU DO? LAUGH AT YER FOTEYGRAFF, DID THEY?"
"YOU KNOW THEY DID."
"SURE AND IT'S A DAMN GOOD ONE TOO!"
HE WAS RIGHT. NOBODY BELIEVED MY STORY. THE PHOTO? AN OBVIOUS FAKE. MY ARM? THE RESULT OF MY DRUNKEN WRECK...
WHEN YOU GO TO HELL, YOU GO ALONE.
AND YOU'VE GOT TO PAY FOR THE RIDE.